Praise for
FRIENDS FROM

"An insightful, keenly observant debut about the power and complexities of a lifelong female friendship. Engrossing and wildly relatable."
　　—Carola Lovering, author of *Too Good to Be True*

"*Friends from Home* is a big-hearted story with deep roots in a complicated old friendship. This moving tale of love and life-changing choices had me racing to the final page so I could call my best friend to discuss Jules and Michelle together."
　　—Hannah Orenstein, author of *Head Over Heels*
　　and *Meant to Be Mine*

"Is shared history a solid enough basis for a lifetime of friendship? Set against a backdrop of New York publishing and a very Southern wedding, *Friends from Home* is about deciding who you want to be and who you want along for the ride. This sweet summer read is a thoughtful, relatable tale of female friendship and modern values."
　　—Georgia Clark, author of *It Had to be You*

"We don't talk about friendships fading or changing, but sometimes they do. Lauryn Chamberlain's *Friends from Home* captures the love, sorrow, and continued devotion that comes with reconfiguring the friendships that made you who you are. A perfect book for anyone who's growing up and trying to figure out how their old friends fit in their new lives."
　　—Kayleen Schaefer, author of *Text Me When You Get Home*
　　and *But You're Still So Young*

FRIENDS FROM HOME

A NOVEL

Lauryn Chamberlain

DUTTON

DUTTON
An imprint of Penguin Random House LLC
penguinrandomhouse.com

Previously published as a Dutton hardcover in June 2021
First Dutton trade paperback edition: June 2022

Copyright © 2021 by Lauryn Chamberlain
Penguin supports copyright. Copyright fuels creativity, encourages diverse voices,
promotes free speech, and creates a vibrant culture. Thank you for buying an authorized
edition of this book and for complying with copyright laws by not reproducing, scanning,
or distributing any part of it in any form without permission. You are supporting
writers and allowing Penguin to continue to publish books for every reader.

DUTTON and the D colophon are registered trademarks of
Penguin Random House LLC.

LIBRARY OF CONGRESS CATALOGING-IN-PUBLICATION DATA
has been applied for.

Dutton trade paperback ISBN: 9780593182819

Printed in the United States of America
2   4   6   8   10   9   7   5   3   1

BOOK DESIGN BY ELKE SIGAL

For my parents: all three of them

CHAPTER 1

At first glance, I assumed the Instagram post belonged to a stranger.

I squinted at my phone to see if the face of a distant cousin or an old high school friend of a friend would come into focus, but then it hit me with a jarring *thwack*, like colliding with someone on the street: *Michelle* had gotten engaged.

The caption read, "So #blessed to finally marry my best friend," and the post featured four photos: one of her boyfriend—well, fiancé—Jake, down on one knee in a proposal reenactment; one of the ring, a sizable brilliant-cut surrounded by a sparkling halo of smaller diamonds; and two of Michelle and Jake smiling broadly in identical poses with different sets of family members. Michelle, my Michelle. My childhood best friend was getting married.

In the twenty-nine minutes since it had been posted, the photo had amassed 243 likes. She had more likes than I had unanswered e-mails, which was an honest accomplishment.

I stared, stunned, for another minute, and then I double-tapped a courtesy like to bring the total to 244. *This is supposed to be your best friend,* I reminded myself. *Who cares if she has a cliché engagement post?* The voice in my head shot back, *If she were really still your best friend, would you have had to find out via Instagram?*

I must have sighed audibly as I debated this, because my co-worker Alan poked his head over my cubicle wall to investigate.

"If you blew off that meeting because you were out here Instagram stalking the hot new intern, I swear . . . ," he mock-scolded, crouching behind my desk chair to peek over my shoulder and take a closer look at my screen. Then: "Oh my God, Jules."

"Yeah," I said, as we both stared, transfixed. "Looks like Michelle's engaged?" My voice shot up, making it a question.

After nearly three years at Thomas Miller Publishing, my first job out of college, Alan remained my only close work friend. Sharing a cubicle wall had quickly turned into sharing a daily three P.M. coffee break, and our constant proximity had fostered a work-spouse intimacy between us. Alan knew the entire story of my seventeen-year friendship with Michelle, and so although he had never met her or visited our tiny Alabama hometown, he had some idea of what the news meant to me.

"If I ever announce my engagement by saying 'so blessed to finally marry my best friend,' just kill me," I added, because it felt like I should say something else. "Not that I'm really the engagement-photos type. Same goes for you."

"I would *never.*" Alan put his hand to his heart in faux shock.

"You wouldn't, but only because Marcus would never let you."

"More evidence that he's my soul mate." Alan stood up to head back to his cubicle. "Anyway, uh, wow. Congratulate Michelle for me."

"I will if she ever bothers to call and tell me the news herself."

"Wait," Alan said. "She hasn't actually told you yet?"

As I considered the question, I wondered if I really felt as bitter as I sounded. The last time Michelle had called me, a few weeks before, I had looked at her name, saved in my phone as "Michelle— your BFF," and it struck me that the title seemed like more of a respectful nod to our shared history than a day-to-day fact. Some-how, though, it still stung that I wasn't the very first person she'd think to call with news of her engagement. *Or maybe she cared more about gloating on social media than actually talking to the people closest to her.*

I waved a hand dismissively. "I'm sure she'll call. Whatever, I don't care."

"If you really don't care, then why are you acting so huffy at her engagement post?" He raised an eyebrow at me in a "caught ya!" expression.

"I'm not *huffy*," I said, annoyed. "And you're the only person I know who would use that word," I added, softening. "How am I huffy?"

"You were aggressively sighing. I heard you."

"I was aggressively sighing because I accidentally bought a soggy sandwich for lunch again."

"Stop going to that cheap deli." Alan rolled his eyes. "Go to Pret. There, solved."

"And also because I'm still reading that shitty manuscript."

He pushed up his horn-rimmed glasses, the Warby Parker frames that every guy in the office under thirty-five seemed to be wearing, moving them higher on his nose. "Well, the last manuscript to come across my desk was about a postapocalypse zombie-hunter love triangle, so I don't even want to hear about it. Pass. What about me screams 'dystopian-teen-romance editor'?" He snorted out a laugh. "Actually, don't answer."

"Sounds hot?"

"It's not. What do they think it is, 2008? *Hunger Games* has been over for a decade!" he half shouted.

"Shh," I hissed.

"Anyway, back to the matter at hand. Yeah, I get it. The social media post is eye-roll-worthy, not the marriage. Right?"

"Exactly," I said, but I kept turning the word *marriage* over and over in my mind, trying to make it fit, trying to apply it to someone my own age. I smoothed my hair behind my ears and held my hands there, cradling my head as if the very idea of what it might mean to be someone's wife exhausted me.

But Michelle had been trying on the word *wife* for years, I knew, the way some women try on earrings. She had practiced and dreamed of wearing the word herself. When we were younger, I think most of us assumed we would graduate college and get married the same year. In our town, it was far from uncommon. I didn't particularly think I *wanted* to be married, but it was what our older cousins and sisters did, and I didn't give it much thought, assuming that husbands were given out right after diplomas. But I moved to Ithaca for college, and then to New York City, and I realized there were plenty of things I could want instead. A completed first draft of an essay collection, or an apartment all to myself. Getting engaged at twenty-five somehow seemed like borderline child marriage in New York, even though I knew it verged on old-maid status in our little corner of the South.

Alan patted my shoulder and said, "She should have called. You're right. But let it go, okay? Now, for real, back to work." And he walked back to his desk.

I pursed my lips and nodded.

But I couldn't let it go. I spent the remaining hours of my workday only half-focused on the manuscript pages.

I stared at the shoddily affixed wall of my cubicle. In between my calendar and color-coded rows of Post-it notes, I had this photo of Michelle and me pinned up. I had quite a few photos—the rest predominantly featured Dana and Ritchie, my closest friends in New York—but that one with Michelle had always been my favorite. It was a staged shot from our high school yearbook, taken when we had beaten out a dozen romantic couples to be named our high school's "dynamic duo." In it, we're sitting in the classically cool teal convertible she drove in high school, and we're totally decked out in stylish sunglasses and colorful headscarves, doing our best Thelma and Louise impression. Our cheeks are pressed together, and we're smiling like we have a secret.

Michelle was Geena Davis, by the way. But that goes without saying.

It had been her idea to use *Thelma & Louise* as the artistic inspiration for the photo. She was the one who always got us in and out of everything. It'd be her idea to skip class, but when we got caught she'd talk her way out of trouble just by hiding behind her pearly smile and "who, me?" southern demeanor. I, on the other hand, had hair that frizzed in the humidity, a smile that probably would have benefited from braces, and I had never successfully charmed my way out of anything.

"It'll be perfect," she had said when she pitched me the photo-shoot idea. "Think about it: Thelma and Louise, Michelle and Julie. Off on the big adventure of the whole rest of our lives."

"As long as our adventure doesn't end in the Grand Canyon."

"Right. Less death, more Brad Pitt," she agreed.

Thinking about that day always made me nostalgic, and I knew I should call and congratulate her on the engagement. That's what a friend, a *best* friend, would do. I should shrug off the fact that she hadn't called me, realize that she was busy, that engagements and wedding planning seemed to make even the most sensible people lose their heads—and calling Michelle "the *most* sensible of people" might have been a charitable description. But it certainly didn't *seem* like Michelle had been very busy recently.

Michelle and I called each other often enough to catch up, as we always had since high school. But for the past year or so, we had started talking at cross-purposes. I'd ask her about her travel plans or her family, and she'd inevitably turn the conversation to her re-lationship with Jake. And then I'd be guilty of it, too: She'd ask me about my boyfriend, Mark, and I'd talk about my work. Appar-ently, my interest in gossiping about guys had peaked in high school, and now it felt like we were losing common ground. We'd recently had our most bizarre exchange when she called me in the middle of the day on my work number. I picked up, assuming that anything that would make her call my office line had to be important. "Is it Marcia? Jonah?" I asked, terrified that something had happened to her mom or brother.

Nothing had. She needed to know if it was ridiculous to have a new tote bag embroidered with her existing monogram, considering that, "if everything went according to plan," she might have new initials soon enough. It was the first time in our friendship that I felt like I had nothing to say to her.

"Aren't you at work right now?" I asked, not caring enough to respond to her "emergency" question.

"Yes," she said, as if she couldn't imagine why I would be confused. Michelle worked as a social media specialist for a Birmingham jewelry boutique. Maybe online shopping was just par for the course there, and what did I know? "Anyway, I just don't want to have to change anything to Jake's last name in a year or whenever."

I hadn't told anyone that I felt like we were out of sync. It seemed like saying it out loud would make it true. But our *Thelma & Louise* days felt very far away.

My phone started to buzz, pulling me back to the present. Sure enough, the lock screen flashed: "Michelle—your BFF." She must have gotten the notification that I had liked her post.

"Julie! Julie!" she cried out as soon as I answered, her voice higher pitched than her usual even, melodic drawl.

I didn't bother to say hello, either, but tried to match her excitement. "Michelle! I saw—"

"I know, and I know what you're thinking, but it just happened last night, and then Jake surprised me with a party with all our family and friends, and I drank too much champagne, and then

I wanted to get the post up this morning to maximize likes, but you leave so early for work, and I didn't want to bother you. So."

"So." I laughed in spite of myself. "Do you want to tell me officially?"

"Julie, I'm getting married!"

"Congratulations, Miche. I mean it. And I can't believe it!"

"Well, I can. Finally—it took him long enough. Kidding!" She paused, and I didn't know what to say. "But I'm actually calling to ask *you* something. What if I flew up there tomorrow so we could celebrate in person?"

It was easy to forget that Michelle had the means to take $400 flights at the last minute, as well as to book a hotel so she didn't have to share a bathroom with my two roommates. For a split second, I thought about saying no—a full weekend together in New York meant more shopping, more eating out, and more Ubering than I typically preferred, or could afford—but I realized that I did want to see her, and that it meant something that she wanted to see me, too.

"That sounds great, Miche. If you're sure you have the time. I know it's last-minute."

"You were the only person I really wanted there last night, other than my mama, I promise," she said, and I smiled despite myself. "Oops, it's Jake on the other line, I have to go. But I'll book the flight today!"

We said good-bye, and I turned my attention back to the manuscript in front of me. But now I felt even stranger than I had before. I tried to think about what Michelle and I would do in New York together, or if I would be any good at helping to plan a wedding. Michelle had been through the process plenty of times before, whereas I had only been to maybe two weddings ever. She was still close with the people we had gone to high school with, but I had mostly lost touch with our high school group when I left Alabama for college. Many of them were engaged or married. Everyone else we knew from home seemed to have reached this point in life. But Michelle wasn't "everyone else" to me. Everyone else hadn't driven me to school every day in that convertible. Everyone else hadn't been like a part of my family. I used to eat breakfast with Michelle and her mother, Marcia, at their house more mornings than I did with my own mother at ours.

A text came in: "Flight is officially booked! See you tomorrow xx."

"Can't wait!" I shot back, hoping that I really meant it.

CHAPTER 2

The first time Michelle and I talked about her wedding, we were in elementary school. It was actually the week we met—the first week of the third grade.

After my parents split up, my mom and I had moved from Cleveland to Langham, Alabama. At the time, I was a loner of the variety that adults called "artistic" when they were being kind, and other things when they were not. In truth, I was just a late bloomer. It took a while before friends struck me as more comforting than Judy Blume books and silence.

We knew exactly one person in Langham, a small and unfamiliar town forty minutes from Birmingham. Right after my dad left, an old friend of my uncle's offered my mom an administrative job in his company's Birmingham office. So that's where we went. On the first day at my new school, I walked hesitantly into the classroom alone, chewing on the ends of my shoulder-length hair like I used to do when I was nervous. With my eyes cast down, I ran right into her.

"Ow!" she exclaimed, rubbing her arm, and then she looked up at me, her green eyes wide and blinking in the expression of delicate surprise that would become her trademark.

"Sorry," I said quietly, taking her in, all blond ringlets and impertinence. I was mortified that my first move at my new school had been to body-slam the most beautiful girl in the class. Most kids would have left it at that, but not her.

"*How* do you have those Skechers?" she asked in a tone of voice both skeptical and impressed, still not introducing herself. "I wanted white sneakers like that, but my mama says I get everything dirty."

"I'm Julie O'Brien," I blurted.

"Michelle."

I said nothing else, but Michelle, already bubbly and confident, grabbed my elbow and hauled me toward her desk in the front row of the classroom. "We should sit together," she announced loudly for all the class to hear, and I agreed, and pretty much from then on I was *in*. It's funny how kids can be so simple like that, so black-and-white. If someone makes you "cool" on the first day, then you are. I was so grateful to Michelle, even if I was a little uncertain of her. But within the space of about two days, she became the first "real" best friend I ever had. A mutual love for the Backstreet Boys and Chips Ahoy! blossomed into something more. Even at eight years old, we clicked together perfectly. And that's how I ended up at her house—so much bigger than anything I'd seen in Cleveland—on my first weekend in Alabama, planning her wedding to Ashton Kutcher.

Well, not literally Ashton Kutcher. An Ashton Kutcher *cardboard cutout.*

Up through the early 2000s, the local movie theater sold life-size cutouts of teen heartthrob actors. They were overpriced and essentially useless, and so of course Michelle had to have one. On this, the first weekend of our friendship, she decided that she would "marry" her Ashton cutout in a backyard ceremony officiated by me and attended by all her closest friends.

I helped her get dressed in a white ensemble from her antique dress-up chest, which was filled with vintage items cast off by her mother. The long-sleeved lace composition she wore must have been oppressively heavy in the sticky heat of a true southern Indian summer, but Michelle insisted, in spite of a delicate sheen of sweat forming on her forehead. I remember my hands shaking as I quietly did up her buttons, looking around her room at her canopy bed and her bay window seat and wondering in awe how someone like me had been chosen to be a part of her world. I didn't want to do anything to jeopardize the chance I had been given. I wasn't sure how I had won it in the first place. I wondered what I could offer her in exchange for all *this,* for the gift she didn't even seem to notice she had given. I looked down at my hands and saw my jade beaded bracelet, the only piece of jewelry I possessed. It wasn't expensive, but it had been given to me by my father, who brought it home for me after one of his many business trips back when my parents still lived together. Before I could change my mind, I slipped it off and handed it to Michelle.

"Here," I said. "I want you to have this."

"Thanks," she said. I didn't tell her what it meant to me, but as she slid it onto her wrist, I hoped with everything in me that somehow, some way, she knew. The smile she gave me in return told me she did.

After we finished getting dressed, Michelle assembled all her friends on the back side of the antebellum home's wraparound porch, overlooking the sloping hill of her backyard and the river below. She started in on assigning roles to everyone: Ellen Moreland, the smallest and the slightest of the neighborhood girls, would be the flower girl. Rebecca Cassle was tasked with holding Ashton up during the ceremony so that he didn't blow over in the breeze. I was to walk down the aisle as the maid of honor, and then also to perform the ceremony.

"Make sure you say the prayer," Michelle told me, flicking her makeshift veil down over her face. "And then marry us."

"The prayer?" The O'Briens from Cleveland were severely lapsed Catholics. Michelle's family, I soon learned, were every-Sunday Methodists.

"Never mind." She sniffed. "Just say, 'We are gathered here today to witness this marriage,' blah blah blah."

"All right, y'all." Rebecca clapped her hands. "Let's have a wedding."

After the five-minute ceremony (and a gratuitous smooch between Michelle and Ashton's cardboard proxy), we all plopped down in the grass with plastic cups of the Davis family's famous sweet tea. I still didn't know what to say around big groups of girls. My only friends in Cleveland had been Kyle, my next-door neighbor, and his little brother. Most of the afternoon passed in a blur, but I did remember one thing all these years later. As the other girls bickered about whom they might marry, from boys in class to Orlando Bloom, Michelle spoke up.

"I know where my *real* wedding will be. In France, in a castle," she said confidently. "But Ashton might have to wait for me. First I'm going to go to college, and then I'm going to start my own jewelry business. Then we can get married."

I already sensed that this grandiose plan would have been laughed off if any of the other girls had said it, but because it was Michelle, it was taken as gospel. The other girls started to name places they would visit, extravagant things they wanted to do. Then, in a move that surprised me, Michelle threw her arm around my shoulders and pulled me close. Maybe it was a display of genuine friendship; maybe it was a posture to show off that she had become best friends with the "new girl" first. "Julie and I are going to have *lots* of adventures, aren't we?" she asked.

"Yes," I said softly. "We are."

I thought about that day as I got dressed to meet Michelle for our reunion dinner that Friday night. After the Ashton ceremony, Michelle and I never talked about weddings again—not until she got serious with Jake, anyway. Now she wanted to get married close to our hometown, near where she and Jake planned to settle down. So much for a castle in France.

I checked the time on my phone: 5:09, and another message from Michelle confirming that she had gotten a cab at the airport and would meet me at the restaurant in an hour. "But good Lord, this traffic," her text continued. "I don't know how you do it."

"I don't know," I typed back. "I guess you just stop noticing after a while."

CHAPTER 3

An hour later I was walking through the doors at ABC Kitchen, an upscale contemporary restaurant I knew Michelle would like because the food was chic but still "safe"—nothing ethnic or that she would deem too spicy.

I spotted her next to the hostess stand right away, monogrammed suitcase in tow. As I turned the corner, I took in her blond waves, her high cheekbones, the tiny scar on her forehead. She had gotten it falling off the jungle gym in fourth grade and hated it—until I told her I was jealous because it made her just like Harry Potter. Looking at it gave me a weird feeling of being home.

"Julie!" she shrieked as soon as she saw me. I went by Jules now, and had since college, but old habits die hard. "Gosh I missed you!"

"You, too," I told her as she pulled me in for a hug, my face buried in her hair. She smelled like the same floral shampoo she had used since seventh grade, and I realized with relief that I meant it: I had missed her. I was a person who seldom felt absence in a tangible way; it was an afterthought realized only upon reuniting. I handed her the card I had gotten her—the *o* in *Congratulations on Your Engagement* replaced by a diamond ring—and for a moment I felt confident that I meant every gushing word I had written in it.

She tucked the card into her purse to save "for later," and then she grabbed my hands and stepped back to look me up and down. I liked my lived-in New York wardrobe of slouchy T-shirts and dark jeans. It suited me far better than the pastels and cardigans of my Alabama youth, which made me feel like I was perpetually playing dress-up. The contrast against Michelle's sleek pink dress paired with Jack Rogers sandals served as a visual reminder of how different our styles had become. I noticed that we both still had the same habit of tucking our hair behind only one ear—it still worked better with Michelle's smooth waves than with my rapidly frizzing blowout—but that was the only similarity in our outward appearance. I flashed back to years of matching T-shirts and carefully coordinated outfits and felt another wave of nostalgia. When I looked up from her outfit, though, I saw her beaming at me approvingly. "You look gorgeous. And you're almost on time!"

I looked at the clock: 6:05. In retrospect, that explained my ability to get what was usually a coveted reservation at a very "in" restaurant, considering that the only people in New York who eat dinner at six on a Friday are tourists seeing shows on Broadway.

I smiled, though, because that was just Michelle all over. She always had to eat dinner at six, or by seven at the very latest. I once tried to tell her that this was incredibly southern—like her habit of calling it "supper"—but she promptly shut me up with "it's not because I'm southern; it's because I get hungry." I had actually started to find it endearing. It was sort of a relief to have at least one friend who refused to go hungry for the sake of trendiness.

Michelle led the way to our table and I followed, unable to shake the thought of how strange it was to see her there, right in the middle of my ordinary life. I passed ABC Kitchen every day on my way to the office after getting off the L train, and I seldom thought about the fact that I lived and grocery shopped and took the subway in a city that everyone I had grown up with considered a vacation destination. Plus, I hadn't seen Michelle in person in eight months, since my last visit to Alabama to see my mom over Christmas, which was strained, per tradition.

I watched her as she surveyed the wine list, flipping directly to the champagne and then indicating several bottles with a price tag that made me physically recoil. As she waved our waiter over to the table, I found myself oddly nervous about what to say to her, as if she were a blind date rather than my oldest friend. I didn't know why. Conversation had always flowed easily between us even after time apart—and I had seen Michelle around enough shy strangers to know that she could fill up silences like wineglasses, just vessels waiting to contain all her exuberance. Maybe it was that I still needed to learn what to say in the presence of such grand life events. What was there to offer other than platitudes of congratulations? After much more deliberation than should have been necessary, I asked her to tell me the proposal story.

"Oh, Julie." She sighed. "It was *so* perfect."

She detailed every moment for me, from their arrival at one of

Birmingham's best restaurants (he told her it was a client dinner), to the lilies waiting on the table ("Such a surprise!"), to the postmeal engagement party in her parents' spacious backyard, the very one where her first wedding, to Cardboard Ashton, took place.

As she held out her hand for me to examine the ring, which looked even bigger in person than in the photo she had posted, she told me, "Julie, it was exactly like I imagined it. You know, no scavenger hunt or fireworks. Just Jake telling me he loved me and he wanted to spend his life with me. He said he's known it since graduation, and of course I did, too, but now that we're here I guess I am glad that he waited. We're both completely ready for it now."

I couldn't help but remember the three years since Michelle's graduation from the University of Alabama, filled with frantic flip-flopping between proclamations of her happiness with Jake and panic about when, if ever, he would propose. While I had always privately wondered what the rush was about, being the person Michelle discussed all these worries with, however absurd I found them, was evidence that we were still close. Maybe part of my awkwardness in the face of her engagement stemmed not just from my own feelings about marriage, or from confusion about how seriously Michelle took it, but also from the worry that Jake was about to become her true confidant. I would not be replaced, exactly, but relegated to some other space. A break from the drama of all things Michelle could be welcome for a bit—I certainly wasn't eager to weigh in on any more monogram aesthetic choices—but what would it mean for our friendship in months? Or years? I had known Michelle wanted to marry Jake for a while, basically since they had first gone out, but somehow it felt like we were suddenly on the precipice of very real change.

But that all felt ridiculous and, frankly, impossible to voice, so I reached for a supportive engagement cliché: "He's a lucky guy, Miche. As I'm sure he knows."

"Oh, he knows." She laughed her sparkling laugh. If she picked up on any hesitation on my part, she said nothing. "But I'm lucky, too. For having the perfect guy, but also for having the *best* best friend in the world." She beamed at me, green eyes glittering.

Best best friend. That's just the way we had described ourselves when we were kids, introducing fellow classmates to the other on the playground by saying, "This is my *best* best friend." An extra label, a brand-new hierarchy. Just so everyone knew without a doubt where we stood.

"But what about you, babe? How's the job? My book editor in the big city," she cooed.

"Hardly an editor. I'm still an assistant." I paused. "But I love it, I swear. I complain too much."

"Oh, you work so hard, Julie, they'll promote you soon. They just have to."

Not exactly the way it seemed to work in publishing these days, but I hoped she might be right. I remembered a time when anything Michelle said seemed ordained. If she believed it, it happened, and I never once thought to doubt her. I thought about my editor, Imani, who both impressed and intimidated me with her stern but confident demeanor. She seemed to like me, but liking me wasn't the same as entrusting me with a promotion. I wanted to ask

Michelle about that, to see if she had ever felt that same uncertainty at work, but then:

"So, is it too soon to start talking wedding details?" she asked.

"I see the appetizers are here, so no. Actually, I'm impressed you made it this long. I'm shocked I even got the proposal story before you broke out centerpiece diagrams or something."

She swatted at me playfully. "So, I'm between something local, like the country club, or going farther and doing something in Atlanta, near his family. Jake is fine with either, though I'm sure his top choice would be to just elope in Vegas or something. Men." She shook her head.

"Men," I agreed, forcing a small conspiratorial chuckle, but I felt like the proverbial kid at the grown-up table, knowing nothing about men and maybe not much more about myself.

"But we have to decide soon." She grinned. "I used to think I'd want a summer wedding, but now I'm thinking March or April. I want it warm enough to be outside; I just don't want to wait so long to tie the knot."

I couldn't believe it would be so soon. I did the mental calculations. March was only seven months away. If anyone could pull together a Pinterest-ready wedding on short notice, it would be Michelle and her mother. But that fast? It occurred to me that she might be rushing to have the wedding before her birthday, in May, when she would turn twenty-six. I took a big sip of champagne. "A spring wedding! Perfect," I remembered to say.

"And now the news I really wanted to talk to you about. You'll be maid of honor, of course!" Seeing my shocked expression, she quickly added, "Oh! I mean. I didn't ask. We've talked about it, but

I should ask. Julie," she said grandly, "I know we don't get to see each other nearly as often as I'd like, but you're still my oldest friend. My *best* best friend," she added with a wink. "Will you do me the honor of being my maid of honor?"

"I— Yes!" I blurted quickly, not really thinking about it. "I guess we kind of decided when we were eight, didn't we?" She grinned at me, and I grinned back, her enthusiasm rubbing off on me.

Then I realized that I didn't have a clue what I had just agreed to do. I had never been a maid of anything before. Actually, I had only ever attended two weddings, and one barely counted. I had been to only my friend Dana's older sister's ceremony in the Hamptons and a "dinner party" reception for an older cousin's elopement.

Michelle reached across the table to hold my hand, even though she had to wedge her arm in between our champagne glasses and around the bread plates. "And Mark will be able to get time to fly out, too, I hope," she added, referencing my boyfriend. "How are things with you two?"

"Good. Mark is good," I said, suddenly monosyllabic. For the past year, Mark and I had been happily involved in what seemed to be a very New York sort of relationship. We usually spent the week separately, as Mark traveled three or four days at a time for his consulting job at McKinsey. From Monday to Thursday I met Dana and Ritchie for happy hour, or explored my neighborhood, or buried myself in bed alone under piles of manuscripts. And then Friday would come around and Mark and I would see a movie or go out to a bar with friends. In any case, it seemed to be going well. He made me laugh, and he didn't seem to want me to overhaul my life to fit his.

Michelle had recently asked if Mark and I might move in together—though she herself "preferred to save that for marriage, of course." But it made sense why she would feel that way. Her parents had purchased her a two-bedroom "temporary" condo in Birmingham, and when I visited her I stayed in the sprawling guest bedroom and had my own set of floral towels in my own bathroom. I enjoyed time away from my roommates when I stayed with Mark on weekends, and his apartment was much nicer than mine, certainly, but any move of that magnitude seemed like a vague notion of the distant future, the relationship equivalent to the advent of flying cars. None of my friends in New York were in truly serious relationships. We were "seeing someone" or else were "thinking about getting back on Hinge," but at twenty-five, "the one" was more likely to refer to a rent-stabilized apartment, not a husband. Even those of us who were certain they wanted to get married eventually, like Ritchie, were taking their time.

"Well, y'all are such a great couple," Michelle crowed. "I bet you'll be calling me one of these days to say you're engaged, too. It can happen when you least expect it. Even to you." She winked, while I downed several sips of champagne without taking a breath.

I finally came up for air. "Maybe." *Absolutely not.* "Anyway," I made up for the brief silence, "Mark is actually gone on business until Monday, so it's just the two of us this weekend. Like old times."

"A sleepover at my hotel? Does it feel like 2005 in here, or is it just me? Sounds good, and you can show me around tomorrow."

My enthusiasm for playing tour guide had died down somewhere around the end of my first year in New York, but I decided we could do a little shopping and go to some restaurants in the neighborhood. And Michelle would be gone again in only a couple of days. I felt a mixed sense of sadness and relief thinking about her departure, the way I often felt seeing her since we had graduated from college. It always seemed to bring about the same paradox: I missed her, and I missed the world we had once lived in together, but these sporadic reunions also required a certain degree of reminiscing that felt more like playing at friendship than the thing itself.

"To old times." I raised my glass.

"And to all the new ones, too," she said as we clinked champagne flutes, her voice bright and hopeful above the din.

When the check arrived, I saw that the bottle of champagne Michelle had ordered cost $150, making the dinner twice as expensive as I'd planned. I swallowed and reached for my card without saying anything. Michelle had paid for her flight and for us to stay in a hotel, and she had been picking up the tab at our dinners for years, slipping her card to the waiter discreetly and assuring me I could "get the next one." She looked up from her phone as I replaced the check folder on the table, and for a second, I thought she might ask if I was sure or offer to split. I winced when she simply smiled and said, "Thanks, babe," but I *had* made the reservation and offered to take her to dinner, I reminded myself. I wanted to treat her to something. Next time I would be more careful about the restaurant's wine list. In the meantime, maybe I could pick up some more work; I had been freelance editing for a professor at Columbia on the side, to make extra money. I picked up my champagne glass and chugged the rest of it, determined to get buzzed enough to dull the sting of the price tag, before we called an Uber downtown to BINY Karaoke, a place we had been to twice in one weekend when Michelle visited me in New York during my intern summer. Michelle loved karaoke.

After climbing the grimy stairs to BINY's attic-like space, we settled on a private room for the two of us while we "warmed up" and a pitcher of some kind of vodka-based punch to distract us from my off-pitch Whitney Houston stylings.

"Start with Kelly Clarkson?" I asked as Michelle flipped through the songbook delicately, touching the sticky laminated pages as little as possible with her middle finger. "Since U Been Gone" was a middle school, singing-into-the-hairbrush favorite, but Michelle one-upped it.

"No way." She raised her eyebrows. "Divinyls."

"Noooo!" I howled, and then she doubled over in drunken laughter, pressing her face against the disgusting songbook in her lap, not caring thanks to the drinks, or the moment, or probably both. "You know I'm still not over that. I'll never be over that."

"I love myself, I want you to love me . . . ," she warbled, and I covered my ears.

"Oh my God, I hate you!"

"Was it Mike LeMore who made fun of you?"

"It was all of those guys."

Some memories will always hold visceral embarrassment, even far beyond the awkward years of adolescence. The Divinyls were one such trigger for me. At a sleepover at Darcy Palmer's in ninth grade, we had taken turns belting out our favorite songs on one of those personal karaoke machines, a Christmas gift from her parents. This was the mid-2000s, so most of the girls chose the standard sleepover fare of the time—"London Bridge," "(You Drive Me) Crazy"—but I decided to be different. I saw "I Touch Myself" on the track list, and since my mom was a huge fan of eighties and nineties throwback radio, I knew every word.

As usual, my social skills were just a half step off. I thought everyone would be impressed by my "offbeat" taste, but no one knew the song. No one except Darcy, that is, and she knew one crucial fact about it that had somehow slipped by me: It was about masturbation.

I know, I know. Who could possibly be surprised that "I Touch Myself" was about, you know, touching yourself? But my mother, open as she often was about her many brief relationships, hadn't given me much in the way of practical sex education. I had always thought of the song in abstract terms. It also has to be said that the experience of growing up in Langham was largely a sheltered one, with sex viewed as a taboo subject, a cardinal sin tucked somewhere between intravenous drug use and not following SEC football.

Anyway, by Monday morning, when Darcy had told the entire freshman class about my "favorite song" and what it said about me, public opinion was not entirely kind. Girls were "blessing my heart" up and down the hallway. I ignored it until I opened my locker and found a note dropped through the slats, reading only a single word: "Slut." I shrank, looking into the darkness of my locker and wishing I could climb right into it, when Mike LeMore and his football buddies sidled up next to me.

"Why don't you give my hands a try, huh?" he said, his friends snickering behind him. "I could do it better."

Then they all disappeared, ribbing each other and laughing as they walked away.

Michelle had heard what was happening by the time I shyly confided in her at lunch. I hoped for sympathy but expected her to do nothing. Making a scene wasn't her style, and to force a confrontation would risk alienating Darcy and her crew by calling her out in front of a crowd. I knew Michelle wouldn't stick her neck out like that. It turns out I was right—she had something else in mind.

She pulled my hand and dragged me to stand next to Darcy's lunch table, far enough away that it looked like we were having a casual conversation, but close enough that everyone could hear.

"Bless their hearts," Michelle said loudly, overenunciating. "You only like that song because your daddy *produced* the Divinyls album. How silly."

At last, the fact that no one knew my estranged father or much about him played to my advantage. Now he was absent only because he was a successful music producer in LA—no, in London; no, in Sydney. Rumors swirled for days and then died down. Was the story absurd? Of course. But if the most beautiful girl in school said it and sided with me, then it had to be true. Michelle had that kind of power over people. To save me, and to make both of us look better at the same time. It's why I worshipped her. She had even gone so far as to say that my father sometimes sent us demos from his label, but, no, we wouldn't be sharing them with anyone else.

Remembering this, combined with the serious onset of drunkenness, made me warm with feeling. I grinned at Michelle as I grabbed the karaoke songbook.

"Come on, do it—your daddy produced that song, after all," Michelle goaded, and we howled with laughter again.

"Only if you sing it with me. And I need to finish this drink first."

"Well then, bottoms up."

We clinked plastic glasses, chugged the overly sweetened drink, and queued up the song.

We sang for an hour in our private room and then we took the show on the road, moving into the public space and performing more Kelly Clarkson and then older Shania Twain hits for everyone from the makeshift wooden stage. Michelle danced around me, flipping a pink feather boa around her shoulders and stealing the show like she always did, in spite of the occasional off-pitch note. But she had worn heels that were appropriate for ABC Kitchen and thus wildly unsuited to BINY's beer-soaked floor, so when I saw her starting to wobble I grabbed her arm, guided her downstairs, and hailed us a cab on Canal Street.

"Where are Ritchie and Dana?" she asked as I slurred the address to the cab driver. "I thought y'all were always out together."

"We used to be." I laughed, somewhat surprised that she actually remembered my Cornell friends by name. "But Dana is a first-year law associate and Ritchie is at Goldman Sachs, so things are crazy. We only go out all together like once or twice a month."

"You don't have an accent anymore." Michelle looked at me wide-eyed, as if it was the first moment she had noticed. "I swear

I even heard you say 'you guys' earlier tonight," she said, feigning disapproval.

"It went away after a couple of years in Ithaca." But the real truth was, I had never really had an accent. I lived the first seven years of my life in Cleveland, after all, but over time I had shaped my inflection to be more like that of Michelle's and Marcia's, loving their soothing drawl and finding that it helped me to fit in better at school, too. In contrast, at Cornell, fast-talking and New York accented seemed like the way to be. I found that I could shape my voice in that direction as easily as I had once picked up Michelle's *y'alls*. Ritchie taught me to stop calling all soft drinks *Coke* and start saying *soda*. Adaptability was a side effect of being an eternal transplant.

"Well, y'all still probably go out more than I do. It's more for special occasions now, you know?" Michelle leaned her head on my shoulder, drowsy affection a betraying sign of her drunkenness.

"This from the girl who once went out sixteen nights in a row freshman year at 'Bama? I think that was some kind of record. Like, what is there to do on Sunday nights in Tuscaloosa?"

She laughed tiredly and laced her fingers with mine as the cab sped up Bowery, and the simple gesture gave me that "I'm home" feeling again. "Well, things change."

"You're getting married, Miche." The truth of it struck me suddenly.

"I am," she half whispered, sounding reverent. Amazed.

"You know married women can still go out, right?"

She sniffed. "*You're* the one who once said marriage is a death sentence."

"No, I didn't," I contradicted. "Or if I did, it was probably back when I still thought boys had cooties."

We both laughed, but I felt a false bottom under my words, like a trapdoor that might give out. Marriage didn't feel like a death sentence, no, but something about it did feel like isolation, like Michelle might be exiled to a country I couldn't or didn't want to visit. But in that moment, I wanted her to be happy far more than I wanted to defend myself. "For you, it's going to be wonderful, Miche."

"I know it will."

I smoothed her hair as we pulled up in front of the hotel, wondering if I would ever feel so certain about anything in my life.

CHAPTER 4

The first writer I ever fell in love with was Joan Didion.

It was her essay "Goodbye to All That" that did it—a cliché choice, but it was mine—and I fell for her and publishing and the idea of New York at the same time. We read the essay collection in AP English my senior year of high school, and the second I finished it I spun in my desk chair toward Michelle and told her I had to move to New York City. "But it's about *leaving* New York," she said, laughing at me, and she had a point: Didion's seminal essay is not an endorsement for the city at all. The sense of ennui she describes is real, and I felt it myself sometimes, but it didn't matter. I fell more in love with New York all the time, in spite of everything there is to hate.

Now, years later, when I crossed the threshold of my tiny walk-up apartment, full of dust from the crumbling moldings of the ceiling and the mice that scratch inside the walls, I still sometimes thought about her words. "To those of us who came from places where . . . Wall Street and Fifth Avenue . . . were not places at all but abstractions . . . , New York was no mere city. . . . To think of 'living' there was to reduce the miraculous to the mundane."

I had done exactly that, I thought, heaving two heavy grocery bags onto the counter after climbing four flights up. I had reduced the miraculous to the mundane. Wall Street was a subway stop on my commute, and Times Square a tourist trap to be avoided at all costs. Even still, I couldn't imagine ever leaving the city, and I did actually feel relieved to be home after the posh weekend in the hotel. Parts of being with Michelle—belting out our old favorite songs, walking arm in arm down Orchard Street—felt as natural as breathing. I could be a version of myself with her that no one else would ever see. Yet, other parts, like when she dragged me through Central Park and three different Kate Spade stores only to ask how I could live in a city that was "so tiring," were less welcome. As I watched her get into an Uber bound for JFK, a mix of nostalgia, sadness, and excitement washed over me. Every time we said good-bye now reminded me of the last day of summer break before we had gone away to college. It felt like I was stepping between lives.

I surveyed the apartment as I unpacked my Trader Joe's bags, finding it mercifully quiet, and contentment settled in as my shoulders unclenched from carrying the heavy bags. Both of my roommates were out. They kept odd hours, one working as a freelance makeup artist for celebrities and the other a production assistant on several New York–based TV shows. These were the kinds of jobs no one had back in Alabama. Growing up, becoming an astronaut would have seemed more likely, because at least I knew astronauts existed. There were whole industries, whole careers, that seemed to exist only on the island of Manhattan. Terry and Demi were quiet, and we coexisted well—as well as any three people could in four hundred square feet—but the reason we lived together had nothing to do with friendship and everything to do with broker fees.

No one warns you about the broker fees. When I had first moved to the city three years earlier, I got off a Delta Connection shuttle at LaGuardia with my diploma, a promise of a publishing job, and $1,645 painstakingly saved from a series of odd jobs in Ithaca. (There are people who remember the exact figures in their bank account when they first came to New York, and people who do not. I assume the ones who don't had a few more numerals to keep track of than I did.) I thought this would be enough money to cover my first month of rent, and that my job could get me a lease, even if I had to have roommates. My publishing salary was tiny, but I was sure I could make it work. I hadn't grown up with much.

As it turned out, those who were new to the city like me were typically subject to broker fees in addition to rent and security deposits, forced to fork over up to fifteen percent of an apartment's annual rent in exchange for the privilege of signing a lease on 150 square feet of the New York dream. If it sounds like extortion, that's because it basically is. That might have been the end of everything, but thankfully, Dana, who had grown up in the city and moved back the very same week I did, offered to spot me a screened-off corner of her living room for the month it took me to find a lease I could jump onto. Since then, I had lived in a series of apartments, some nicer than others, before finally landing six months ago with

Terry and Demi on the border of East Williamsburg and Bushwick, a more recently gentrified neighborhood that wore its "trendy" label in a relaxed, almost disheveled way, like a sweater slipped off one shoulder. In between old industrial buildings and the canal of standing water off the sound, new cocktail bars and back-room restaurants cultivated a sophisticated air that aimed to say, "What, this old thing?" This attitude put the rent at the upper edge of what I could afford, even though I lived a full thirty-five minutes away from my Manhattan office. But I found myself liking it enough to stay.

The apartment buzzer blared like a fire alarm as I finished unloading the groceries. "Who is it?" I barked into the intercom, annoyed, balancing a bag of apples in my free hand.

"Uh, Mark?" my boyfriend called back, a note of hurt in his voice audible through the intercom static. Between the good-byes to Michelle and the after-work errands, I had completely forgotten I had invited him over as soon as he landed at the airport.

"Right! Sorry!" I apologized. "Come up, I have beer."

A few minutes later, Mark rounded the turn of the fourth staircase, suitcase and garment bag in hand. His blond hair looked a little disheveled, and he still wore his traveling outfit of sweatpants and scuffed sneakers, but catching a glimpse of him before he spied me in the doorway, I saw him as I had the first time I noticed him across a crowded bar. His slightly clenched jaw, his smile when he finally looked up and saw me. A growing familiarity sometimes dulled the edges of his attractiveness, but these moments when my awareness of it rushed back heightened all my senses. I wondered if anyone ever saw me anew in that way. Patting the back of my frizzed hair, I decided probably not.

But Mark grinned at me anyway. "Hello, gorgeous." He bent down to kiss me. "Missed you. How was the weekend with Michelle?"

"Missed you, too. And it was . . . good," I told him as I walked toward the fridge to get the six-pack of beer. I grabbed a bottle for each of us, opening them immediately, and then took a swig and hoisted myself up to sit on the counter. "It was just a lot of catching up."

"Come on, give me more than that," he said, sidling up to the counter to stand between my legs. "I'm sure you guys got up to some stuff."

"Well, the biggest news is that I agreed to be her maid of honor."

Mark set his beer down and regarded me with a look of surprise. "Well, that's . . . great? Did you expect it?"

"I thought bridesmaid," I admitted. "But it makes sense. She did make me swear to take the job back when we were, I don't know, eight?"

Mark had been the best man in his older brother's wedding a year ago—I hadn't attended; we had met only a couple of months before—but that was the extent of our mutual experience. I shrugged and told him I assumed I'd find out more details soon.

"Anyway, after she popped the question at dinner Friday, we just did some karaoke at BINY. Your rendition of 'Total Eclipse of the Heart' was sorely missed."

"It's not eighties night without me," he quipped. "So, I bet she's mostly just psyched that Jake finally proposed, right?"

"Of course, you know Michelle." I paused to take a swig of my beer. "But why does everyone keep saying 'finally'? Michelle. Her mom. I mean, it's not like they've been together a decade, and it's not like she's forty years old."

Mark shrugged. "Well, I guess when it's right, some people just know. Seems like they're the kind of people who have known for a while."

Silence hung in the air between us for a moment before he launched back into chatter.

"Anyway, my trip was good, too. The great metropolis of Omaha isn't the most exciting place I've ever been, but we're still doing good business with some insurance companies out there. I think I made some major progress this weekend, and my boss was there to notice, which was great."

"Sounds productive." I carried our beers over to the couch and collapsed, still a little sweaty from the humidity and the four-story climb to the apartment. "So, Netflix and chill tonight?" I asked in a flirty voice. "But with some actual Netflix involved?"

Mark raked a hand through his hair. "Uh, sure. But football actually starts tonight. I was thinking maybe we could go over to Josh's apartment and hang out with some of the guys later?"

"The guys" meant Mark's friends from Penn, who had all grown up in the tristate area and moved back the second they had their diplomas in hand. They had always been nice enough to me and I liked them fine, though I didn't see us becoming best friends; more than a few of them read the Goldman Sachs Elevator Twitter account unironically. They tolerated me in about the same way I tolerated them, gamely asking a question or two about the books I was working on, but only until they turned their attention to the sporting event of the moment on TV. They correctly assumed I wouldn't mind.

"Yeah, sure," I acquiesced as I sipped the dregs of my beer. Mark still spent a lot of time with his college friends, whereas I tended to be more and more interested in spending time under a blanket reading. But that was part of why our arrangement worked. When I needed time by myself, he seemed perfectly happy to go out with his friends and then pick up right where we left off once we'd had a weekend apart.

This time, though, I actually wanted a break from being inside my own head. "You know, after this weekend, I could definitely use some time off from thinking about weddings. Let's go," I told him. "Bring on the dudes and the wings."

The next morning, I woke up at seven with Mark still snoring next to me. He and Josh had drunk five beers to my two while we watched the Giants beat the Panthers in a meaningless preseason game. I rolled over slowly and quietly crept out to the living room on my tiptoes. After grabbing my book off the coffee table, I lay down on the couch to read and drink coffee until I had to get ready for work, stretching out to take advantage of the full three cushions. The worn-in sectional sofa dominated the space nearly from wall to wall, but the room didn't feel claustrophobic; like many of the old warehouse-style buildings in East Williamsburg, it had a high-ceilinged, airy quality that reminded me of Michelle's parents' house back in Alabama, despite being about a hundredth of the size.

I splayed open the book on my lap and positioned myself perfectly under a beam of morning sunlight, happy that neither Mark nor Terry and Demi had stirred yet. Ever since the discovery of "Goodbye to All That" in high school, reading true stories about someone else's life—biographies, essays, didn't matter—had always been my favorite way to spend a lazy morning. It was the only time I ever felt all my other thoughts quiet themselves at once. But before I even flipped the first page, my phone buzzed on the coffee table beside me.

The message came from Darcy Palmer, but it had been sent in a group text to all Michelle's newly named bridesmaids. It contained a link to one of those BuzzFeed listicles, entitled "You Know You're from the South When . . ."

Almost immediately, my phone started to vibrate with responses from Rebecca and Ellen, all of which were some variation on "so true, y'all." Suddenly, my empty apartment felt very crowded. I hadn't stayed close with anyone from our high school group of friends other than Michelle, but my relationship with her meant they were still fixtures in my life, acquaintances I saw once a year but still never seemed to know how to connect with.

"Love my 'Bama girls!" Michelle chimed in with a heart.

I clicked the link and was decidedly unsurprised to see I didn't relate to the list at all. I wasn't from Alabama originally, and I didn't have any southern family. In college at Cornell I had never dressed up for a road trip to the Carolina Cup or—thankfully—gone to an Old South fraternity formal. I hadn't seen a band in Nashville for years, and, as Michelle had pointed out, apparently I had stopped saying "y'all" without noticing. And I didn't care.

But I realized that Michelle thinking I had left *her* behind—or vice versa—did still bother me. I sent back two laughing emojis in a small sign of solidarity, and then I sent my own group text to Ritchie and Dana.

"Drinks tonight? I know you're both busy and important but plz plz plz."

They responded immediately, just like I knew they would. Then my phone buzzed a third time, but it wasn't Ritchie or Dana, or even Michelle. It was my mom.

I put my phone on do not disturb and picked my book back up.

Before Alabama, my mom and I had been incredibly close.

I slept in her bed on the first night in Langham, in our new, tiny, unfamiliar house, and, if I remember correctly, for several nights after that, too. Hundreds of miles away from the only home I'd known in Cleveland, she'd pull us close together under the comforter and say, "Well, aren't we just two peas in a pod?" I felt both deeply loved and paralyzed with fear, because "two" felt like a very small number against the world. It also meant that our third wasn't coming back.

It wouldn't be accurate to say that I had ever really known my father well, or that I could miss him in any kind of specific way I could attribute to his individual characteristics rather than the general "dadness" he represented. In Cleveland, he had been in and out of our house regularly. He worked in sales, and he traveled for days or sometimes weeks at a time. I learned later that some of these trips had been for work and some had not. Of course, I had no idea at the time how disruptive it all was. At age four or five, I assumed that all fathers disappeared for long periods and then reappeared at random, popping through our front door like a jack-in-the-box and offering presents or fantastical stories before disappearing into the bedroom to "sleep off the jet lag."

He was a regional salesman, another thing I learned later. There were no time differences.

The truth is, when he finally left us for good, I didn't even notice at first. I assumed he had taken off on another long trip, and my mom didn't correct me, at least not right away. It was May, so I remember waiting for school to end and playing tag with my neighbor Kyle, mostly. As May turned to June, my mom spent more time in her room, or in the bathroom on the cordless phone with the door locked. This wasn't completely unusual—my mom had cycled through what we referred to back then as "her moods" ever since I could remember. But still, I must have known something was more wrong than usual, because I remember being afraid to knock on her door and ask her for a dollar for the ice-cream truck on a sweltering day at the beginning of summer vacation.

Then one day my dad walked in the door, and I thought I had been silly to worry. But as it turns out, he was back just for a day. They wanted to tell me together that they were splitting up. We would have to give up the house, they explained, but it would be okay. As if it were that simple.

"We'll be getting a brand-new house!" my mom exclaimed, too much desperation in her enthusiasm for it to be convincing. "Won't that be fun? Daddy can't come right now because of work. He has to travel. But it'll be an adventure for just you and me, Julie."

I didn't cry when they told me, I am sure of that, but not of much else. I don't remember what that moment felt like, not in the way that I can access so many other parts of my emotional life as easily as I can flip to a page in a book, and so I can only assume that I didn't fully understand what was happening. My father stayed the day, just a few hours past that conversation, and then he was gone. At the end of the month, I was shocked to find out that we were moving to Alabama, where Mom had found a job through the old friend I'd never heard of. Just the two of us, peas in a pod. Dad would probably call soon, my mom said, as I struggled to fall asleep in her bed that first night in Langham. It was just that he was so busy.

I was afraid to ask any more questions and afraid to start school, but I tried to believe that things would work out. My mom would take care of things; my dad would call. Maybe he would even come back. I could survive until then.

Then two things happened at once: I met Michelle, and my mom met a man.

Daniel. Close-cropped hair, tailored jacket, hulking frame. She met him at work, I think. He was the first, as it turned out, of many. There were so many short-lived relationships in the intervening years that it was hard to remember specifics about any of them. My main mental picture of him is of his suit buttons. They were what fell at eye level for me. My mom started to drop me off at Michelle's house, grateful I had made a friend so quickly, for the free babysitting if for nothing else. I didn't mind her dating. It was the irregularity that bothered me. I would beg for a sleepover at Michelle's, and my mom would tell me no, that she'd be back to pick me up later that same night. Then, inevitably, she would call the Davis house to extend her date into the next morning, and Marcia would come into Michelle's room to rumple my hair and say, "Guess what, pudding? Looks like you can stay the night after all." Once or twice I caught her muttering something under her breath after she delivered this news, but Michelle and I would just grin at each other and rush to pull out the trundle from under her ornate canopy bed. I was in awe of Michelle's dollhouse-style furniture. Marcia and Rich, Michelle's dad, would both come into her room to watch us perform a dance or host a talent show, clapping at our antics as fervently as if they were at a Broadway performance.

I wanted to be someone's "pudding." I wanted the trundle bed. I wanted that family. And when I was with Michelle, I got to pretend I had those things.

But I missed my own family, too, sometimes. Finally, I asked to call my dad. It had been months since he'd left.

"Julie." My mom looked past me, staring over my shoulder out our kitchen window. "The number he gave me isn't in service. But don't worry, I'm sure he'll call us when he has time."

"Let me try the number."

"No." She walked past me into the living room, uncharacteristically brusque. I followed her.

"Mom, come on. If it's really out of service, then why can't I try it?"

Silence.

"Where is he?"

She either didn't know or wouldn't tell me.

"It's not fair!" I yelled, storming around the corner into my

FRIENDS FROM HOME   [45]

room and flopping down on the thin quilt covering my twin bed.
I wanted a plush comforter like Michelle's. Envy mixed with fear.
I felt something unspooling inside me, the threads that had held my
life together coming loose. "You can't keep me from talking to him
just 'cause you're mad! What if he doesn't even know we're here?
You're lying about *something*!"

"Julie, don't you think if I knew exactly where *he* was I'd go
there? There are things I need from him, too, you know!"

I believed this at first. We had been a family once, eating
Sunday-night dinners around our old, cramped kitchen table in
Cleveland and picnicking in the park on my dad's odd days off. My
mom must have missed him, too. When I thought of it that way, I
blamed my dad. But then I thought of Daniel, my mom's frequent
disappearances, how hasty our move had been. Maybe I couldn't
trust her. But for the time being, I just said, "Okay, I know," and
buried my face in my pillow until she left my room. Something
changed between us then. I now know that, in her own way, she was
trying to protect me. But I wonder if she'd been honest with me
then, we might have had a different relationship now.

And so David O'Brien, whose name I bore even as it caused
confusion and whispers around Langham about my family, remained a mystery for almost ten years. My mom continued dating;
I continued my twice-weekly sleepovers with Michelle. My father
receded into the background. That is, until one day in the Langham
High School library in the middle of my sophomore year, when a
Google search finally turned something up. A David O'Brien, of
the proper age and profession, was living in Chattanooga, Tennessee, just north of the state line. Maybe he had been there the whole

time. I told this to Michelle in the hallway outside our English class, watched her eyes widen. I leaned against the lockers, arms crossed, trying to posture like I didn't really care. It was just interesting information, I said.

But Michelle saw through this immediately. She grabbed my hand. "Julie," she said in a breathy voice. "When I get my driver's license next month . . ."

She didn't have to finish the sentence; I knew. "And it's only a two-hour drive," I answered her.

CHAPTER 5

———

Dana met me outside my office on Twenty-First Street that night after work. We hugged hello, and she led the way down Broadway toward Union Square, dodging traffic while still typing furiously on her work phone.

"Ritchie said she's already at the bar," I told Dana. Or, more accurately, I told her shoulder; she had three inches on me in flats, so she really towered over me in her workplace heels. Even wearing them, she outpaced me with her long stride, barreling down the street as I loped half a beat behind.

"Well then, come on," she said. "I don't want to miss the one-dollar oysters. Happy hour ends at seven." I kept pace as we crossed Nineteenth Street, and I looked over at her as we passed under the shadow of the multistory Equinox that stood at the intersection.

With her glossy hair and Saint Laurent bag, it was easy to see her as a million "New York woman" clichés come to life.

She had intimidated me the first few times I saw her on our freshman floor at Cornell, walking around in silk camisole pajama sets and a towel tied expertly around her head. Then I ran into her at an off-campus kegger and she hugged me like we were old friends, asked why we hadn't hung out yet, and then gamely grabbed my legs to lift me into a keg stand. As it turned out, she was easy to be around—fast-talking, brash, loudly opinionated, and different in so many ways from most of the girls I had grown up with. It's probably why I liked her so much.

Even though she no longer intimidated me, her ambition was still cutting. She had signed on at Davis Polk immediately after graduating from NYU Law, and her first months of billable hours marked as much time as I had probably worked all year. It reminded me of something she'd said about New York when I had first moved there: "Everyone here is hungry for something," she told me. "Ambition is the only thing we all have in common."

"They're out for blood, is what it really is," I responded, and she snorted. But the reality was that I wanted to be one of them. I wanted to build a real life in this city, a life greater than the one I had arrived with. I just needed to figure out how to do it.

"Fuck this fucking phone," Dana said, dropping the device into her bag as we walked up to the bar entrance. It was the first thing she had said aloud in ten blocks.

"So it was a good day, huh?" I joked, pulling the door open for her.

"Actually, I've had worse. This is the first time I've even tried to go anywhere before nine o'clock in a month."

"At least my version of overtime is reading in bed."

Ritchie waved at us from a high-top table next to the bar, having reserved us the last available spot in the place. She had her thick black hair pulled back in a sleek chignon, and she wore her recently purchased red-framed glasses—a trend she shamelessly admitted she had copied from Ali Wong, who happened to be both Chinese and Vietnamese like her. They looked chic paired with her artistic but serious wardrobe of sharp-cut suits and asymmetrical dresses. She held up her glass in a "cheers" gesture, and I could see that she was already halfway through her first bourbon.

"You know a good way to get guys to stop hitting on you?" she said by way of hello as we sat down.

"What?" I asked.

"Telling them you work at Goldman." When I met Ritchie in a humanities distribution requirement our freshman year at Cornell, she had been a graphic design major. She had the best eye for design of anyone I knew—her East Village apartment looked straight out of *Architectural Digest*—but by our sophomore year she had pivoted to economics with design as a minor. She signed on at Goldman right after her intern summer, with a plan to save up money for a few years and then strike out on her own to start a design firm. If anyone could do it, it would be her.

"Wait, what happened?" Dana asked.

Ritchie tilted her head subtly in the direction of the bar. "See that tall guy at the bar? He was over here hitting on me, asking what bourbon I'm drinking, whatever. And then he asks what I do. I tell him, and suddenly he remembers he was 'meeting a friend at the bar' and cuts me off midsentence."

"Maybe he was meeting a friend at the bar."

Ritchie snorted. "Is his 'friend' that twenty-year-old blond girl he's chatting up now?"

"Round of drinks says she's a PR assistant," Dana said. "I'll ask."

"Nah, who gives a shit. Having a good job weeds out the weak. If they can't handle it, then bye," Ritchie said, as Dana waved her arm to try to flag down a waitress. "There's nothing wrong with the PR girl. But there *is* something wrong with the guys who can't date a woman who works more or makes more than they do."

"Hear! Hear!" Dana said. "But there are worse problems than complaining that we make too much money," she added, shooting Ritchie a look as I gave a halfhearted smile. "Let's get drinks."

Ritchie refilled her bourbon, Dana ordered a martini, and I, the perpetual lightweight of the group, got a glass of white wine. We caught up about work and traded stories about mutual friends from Cornell. But when Ritchie brought up a couple from the year ahead of us who had just gotten engaged, Dana told me it was time to spill the details about Michelle's wedding.

"So, maid of honor, huh?" Dana asked. "Good luck. I did it for my sister last year and it was . . . a lot. Remember?"

After weeks of stress leading up to the wedding, Dana's sister, Jane, had gotten so drunk at the rehearsal dinner that she had spilled a glass of champagne on her future mother-in-law and thrown up all over the front porch of the upscale bed-and-breakfast. Dana had stayed up the rest of the night doing damage control with the venue, and then we spent the next morning plying Jane with Pedialyte so that she wouldn't be too hungover to make it through the outdoor summer ceremony.

"Don't listen to her." Ritchie waved a hand. "It's exciting. Anyway, you never told us what you think about her fiancé. Didn't she meet him at, like, a frat party?"

Ritchie and Dana had met Michelle when she visited me at Cornell, and it hadn't gone particularly well. Michelle had brought up sorority rush and how important it was that the potential new members they recruited get along with her preferred fraternities, and Dana rolled her eyes hard enough to make me worry she had detached a retina. Ritchie asked Michelle a question or two about rush at the big southern schools—she was familiar only with "recruitment" in the sense of summer associate positions at investment banks, and she was genuinely curious.

"So, how do you get to join? How do they make the invitations after rush is over?" Ritchie had asked.

"Well, as long as you make it to pref night, and you maximize your options, then you'll get an invitation on bid night," Michelle answered, oblivious to the fact that none of us understood a word of the jargon that had become second nature to her.

"'Maximize your options'? Sounds like when you're talking about equity."

"What?"

"Stock options?"

"Okay, who wants a drink?" Dana stretched out her arm, inserting an open bottle of vodka directly in between them. I knew she'd have a joke or two to make at Michelle's expense later, while

Michelle would probably hint to me that Ritchie seemed "nice but clueless."

I simply felt anxious and conflicted. I had grown up hearing Marcia's stories about her beloved Tri-Delt sisters—who really had become her lifelong friends—and I knew that if I had stayed in the South I probably would have followed Michelle into rush, too. Did Ritchie and Dana know that about me?

I could have gone either way, but I chose Cornell. In the end, I had known I wanted a new path for myself. Langham wasn't my place, not really, not in the same way it belonged to the Davis family. But I still felt conflicted every time Dana made a joke about Michelle's attitude toward Greek life and university as a whole—which she still did on occasion.

"So, is she marrying him because he was in the *best* fraternity?" Dana mocked, right on cue.

He had been, but I ignored her. "Jake is . . . tall. Brown hair, blue eyes. Uh, successful. He's a lawyer," I told them. "The thing is, after meeting him one time, I knew the names of all five of his uncles, where his summer house was, and what law firm he wanted to work at. And he forgot my name. Seriously, he called me June like three times. He apologized later, but still." I took a long sip of my wine. "Hey, she loves him."

"So . . . it's that you think he's an asshole? Or that he's not good enough for her?" Ritchie asked.

"Is anyone ever good enough for your best friend?" I joked. "Also, she actually said 'can't wait to finally marry my best friend' in the Instagram announcement, so I might have lost that title."

"Oof." Ritchie laughed. "Whenever I get married, I promise my husband will be—at best—my third-best friend after you two. What is with this needing one person to be everything to you? It just sets you—and them—up for failure."

"Can you even imagine getting married now, though?" Dana fake-shuddered. "Hideous. I still feel like a child." No one I knew in New York under the age of thirty seemed to be able to imagine getting married.

"A child that will probably make partner in her firm at thirty." I rolled my eyes at her, but I felt the exact same way. "Anyway, let's talk about something else."

I listened as Ritchie started to talk about the drama surrounding a new exhibit at the Whitney. I wanted to be present in the moment, to just be with Dana and Ritchie and stop worrying so much. I told myself to shut up and stop thinking about marriage, and I ordered another glass of sauvignon blanc. But half an hour later, the second round of drinks turned into a third, and I turned the conversation back to Michelle.

"You know, I want to be happy for her. I *am* happy for her," I insisted loudly, trying to talk over the group of young associates who had wedged themselves up next to our high-top table with their cans of Narragansett Lager. "But getting engaged, buying a house near our hometown, letting Jake decide everything—y'all should hear the way he can talk over her—" I slammed my wineglass down for emphasis, and it sloshed over the rim onto my hand.

"Whoa, bitch." Dana laughed. "That's your last one, I think."

"I literally haven't heard you say 'y'all' since freshman year," Ritchie said.

My head felt fuzzy. "Okay, I'll stop," I promised. "It's just—she's been so obsessed with the idea of getting married that I feel like she'd marry any guy with a good job if she'd been dating him for a couple years. It never used to be like that. I don't know when she got so obsessed with marriage. College? Her sorority sisters, some of them used to joke about getting 'MRS degrees,' but I don't actually think they were kidding. Isn't that crazy?" I knew this wasn't my business, not really. I just had to voice it to someone so I didn't accidentally let it slip, horrifyingly, to Michelle.

"Maybe." Ritchie shrugged. "But you know you can't ever say anything either way."

"Or maybe life is all about timing," Dana said, coolly sipping her martini. "Maybe we all just marry the person we happen to be dating at the time we decide we're 'ready to get married,' and that's the way the game is played. Is that really so bad?"

"Maybe not." I shook my head. Anyway, what did I hope to accomplish? I didn't even dislike Jake, not really, not nearly as much as I had made it sound. What I didn't like was when Michelle's life made her feel like a stranger to me. "Anyway," I said, "cheers to Michelle, and also cheers to none of us getting married at twenty-five."

"I'll drink to that." Dana raised her glass.

"To doing our own thing," Ritchie echoed, draining the rest of her bourbon.

Dana and Ritchie felt like home, too.

CHAPTER 6

I woke the next morning sweating, twisted up in the Egyptian cotton sheets. The bedding set had been a Christmas gift from Michelle. Left to my own devices, I always bought the cheapest thing at Bed Bath & Beyond. I kicked them off furiously, waking Mark in the process. In my barely awake, hungover state, I had forgotten I had tipsily invited him over.

"Okay, I know I'm a heavy sleeper, but there are more humane ways to get me up," he groaned, rolling onto his side to face me.

"Sorry," I said, giving him an apologetic kiss. "Give me a few glasses of wine and I literally can't tell if you're here."

"Ouch." He laughed, pulling a mock-hurt face and shoving me playfully. "Kidding. You feeling okay this morning?"

I rolled onto my side to face him and threw an arm across his bare chest. "I'm okay. Just a headache. And I had a weird dream."

"Oh yeah? Tell me."

Mark could be impatient about a whole host of things, from traffic to clients to the unreliable radiator in his apartment, but he had a strange patience for listening to me ramble, which I appreciated. In the dream, Michelle and I were driving through our hometown in her car, the teal convertible that she had in high school. Neither of us said a word, but when we reached the corner of Mount Olive Road, she paused for the stop sign, opened the car door, and then shoved me out. I tumbled down the hill for what felt like hours.

"Anyway," I asked Mark, "isn't this pathetic? Michelle gets engaged and my subconscious thinks she's trying to get rid of me or something." *And even if she was—would that be such a bad thing?*

"Maybe you feel like she's leaving you behind. That's normal, I guess," he offered, smoothing part of my disheveled hair behind my ear. "But there's nothing to worry about. You're her maid of honor, right? You've known each other your whole lives."

That much was true, at least. For seventeen years, our names had been said in the same breath. A friend of Michelle's mom once believed that she had one daughter named "Michelle Angel," a perversion of MichelleandJule, since every story she could possibly have told about Michelle would have had me in it. "I'd better get home to MichelleandJule," she'd say.

"I don't think she's leaving me behind," I countered, sounding a bit more stung than I'd meant to. "I'm the one that left; I know that. I'm just worried we don't have that much in common anymore. And maybe it's just going to keep getting harder."

I thought about this. It seemed different for Mark. He grew up in Connecticut, and he kept up with almost all his high school friends. If one or two drifted away along the way, so what? People grow up in different directions.

That's the strangest part of adulthood, the part that no one had warned me about. Everything significant that happens in life starts to happen to *only* you. Whether you get a promotion, move to another country, get married—your friends can support you, but they can't come along with you. All of a sudden, everyone is on a separate timeline. It was different when we were young. Growing up, Michelle and I had started every grade together, coordinating matching outfits for every first day of elementary school. We had gotten our driver's licenses together at sixteen, graduated from high school and celebrated our college acceptances at eighteen, and even had our "first" legal drinks together at twenty-one. Our biggest milestones were all shared. It was scary to think that had ended and something else would have to take its place.

Mark stretched and sat up, and I looked at the clock, knowing that he was already running late. "Go get ready," I told him, rolling over lazily to grab my phone. He had a flight back to Omaha to spend the rest of the week on his project there, and he preferred to arrive exactly seventy-five minutes early to the airport.

I started skimming through my e-mails. I didn't need to be at work for another two hours, but I liked to get a preview of what the day would look like. I scrolled past the daily news update from theSkimm, flagged a request from a colleague to "sync up" on a project, and then I stopped at a subject line reading, "Urgent!" My heart beat faster until I glanced at the sender's address.

Sure enough, Michelle.Davis17@gmail.com.

I clicked the "to" field and scanned the list of Michelle's brides-maids: Rebecca, Ellen, and Darcy—all from our high school—as well as Sylvie and Jen, two of her Tri-Delt sisters.

"Hey, y'all," it began. I scrolled down the page.

> Couldn't be more excited to have the best bunch of bridesmaids in the world! Now, I know Jake and I just got engaged (can't believe I've already been a fiancée for a week!), but it's never too early to start on our most important order of business: dress shopping! Not just for my gown, but for bridesmaid dresses, too. Okay, seriously, I know that the shopping process can get a little crazy (looking at you, Jen!), but I promise I won't be one of those bridezillas who makes you wear something hideous and then swears that you'll "totally wear it again." You may not wear it again, but I have a vision, and I promise it won't be awful, and y'all will look gorgeous!
>
> To sweeten the deal, how about a brunch and bridal shopping day on Saturday, September 25th, at Loveliest Bridal? RSVP to me and mark those calendars! Love, your favorite bride.

I started the travel math right away. September 25 was less than four weeks away. That meant nothing to the five other bridesmaids, who all lived reasonably within driving distance, but a trip back to Alabama would cost me far more than an afternoon. I could stay with Michelle, but I mentally tabulated $250 for a flight, another

$30 at least for brunch, and then the cost of a bridesmaid dress it-self. I already knew I had to fly back for the wedding, and hadn't Michelle mentioned a fall bridal shower on the cab ride between ABC Kitchen and the karaoke bar? Or was that something else wedding related? (Mental note: Drink less.)

I rolled over, groaning as I turned facedown into my pillow. I heard Mark call, "Bye, Jules," as he let the door fall closed behind him.

I wanted to be there for Michelle, and I didn't want to fail on my first assignment as her maid of honor. And yet, the prospect of spending an extra weekend with "our" high school friends was less than appealing. I had become friends with Darcy, Rebecca, and Ellen because of our shared affiliation with Michelle, but we weren't friends with *one another,* just with her. The fact that I generally kept my distance from Alabama certainly hadn't made us any closer. Darcy seemed to outright resent me.

Still, I knew how important dress shopping was. And I told myself that I would have been there in a minute if I could afford it, but the security deposit for my apartment had all but cleaned out my savings, and living paycheck to paycheck reminded me too much of my broke early college days and filled me with a constrict-ing kind of dread. I decided to text Michelle and let her know as soon as possible that between the shower, my annual Christmas visit home to see my mom, and the wedding, I couldn't manage another trip.

"Just got your e-mail," I typed before my resolve weakened and I booked a flight I couldn't pay off on a credit card. "Would LOVE to be there for dress shopping, but I have to save $$ for the shower and wedding so I won't be able to make it this time—send a million pics and let me know what dress to order from NYC. Call me later if you want." I added an *XO* and hit send, hoping that Michelle was already getting ready for work and we could talk later.

Fewer than thirty seconds later, my phone started to buzz. I didn't need to check the caller ID; I knew.

"Hey, Miche, I'm so sorry I can't make it," I said as soon as I answered, attempting to cut her off at the pass. This was something decades of friendship had taught me. I could tell when Michelle was about to begin building a case for what she wanted like she was still on the Langham High debate team. "It's just really short notice for flying in and I can't swing it right now."

She paused. "Okay . . . but hear me out. I'll pick you up from the airport, and I'm paying for brunch and everything, I swear."

"That's so sweet," I told her, and it was. It also lined up perfectly with Michelle's sensibilities. She wanted to treat her friends while simultaneously remaining ignorant of the fact that a free brunch and a glass of champagne at the bridal shop couldn't come close to covering the cost of a flight or a dress. "But it's just too expensive right now. So I'll see you for the shower? If you haven't found your dress yet we can go shopping then?"

"I'd *really* love to have you there, Jule. I mean, you're the maid of honor! Maybe you could work something out with your mama to come in September. I know she'd want to see you more." Did she mean that as a kind suggestion? I wondered. Or did it hold a subtle accusation about my strained relationship with my mother? I had known Michelle long enough to understand that it could be both.

"She probably would," I conceded. "But we're already planning on Christmas, and don't forget she has to work weekends a lot."

I left "unlike your mother" off the end, but I imagined we both heard it. If Michelle could play passive-aggressive, so could I.

"Well, maybe you could—"

"Plus," I jumped in, closing my eyes and rubbing my temples with my free hand, already feeling like the world's worst maid of honor. My hangover headache intensified. "Mark has been gone so much. These weekends are pretty much the only time I get to see him."

I knew that would get her to relent, and it did. "Aw, okay." She paused. "I understand. I guess I'll see you for the shower and at Christmas, right?"

"Yeah. I mean, of course. I'll be there."

"Can we talk about bridal styles, though? I'm thinking that I want something classic but still with pizzazz, you know? Maybe trumpet shape?"

"That can't mean shaped like an actual trumpet."

"No, like, tight on top and flared at the bottom. Maybe a mermaid style!"

"That would look good on you. Hey, Miche, I have to—"

"Is A-line too boring?"

I looked at the clock on my nightstand: 8:34. "Michelle. I have to be at work in less than an hour now. Don't you?"

"I took a half day to get started on some planning. But okay." She sighed. "Go, we'll talk later. I'm just bummed you won't be there on the day."

"Me, too."

"You are the one who dressed everybody for my third-grade wedding, remember?"

"How could I forget?"

"Ellen would have worn her dress backward otherwise."

"And wouldn't that have been tragic? But I'm sure she's learned to dress herself since then." I thought about Ellen for a minute: sweet, dainty, and prone to speaking to me in the same overenunciated voice she used to address her kindergarten class. "Well, probably."

Michelle snorted a laugh, and she sounded like my best friend rather than the bride threatening to overtake her. "All right, I'll let you go. You can order your dress on your own, but keep your phone on you on the twenty-fifth—I want you weighing in on every little choice via FaceTime."

"Virtually, I will totally be there," I told her. "Promise."

Everything had worked out, but as I got ready for work, I still felt strangely on edge. On my subway commute that morning, I noticed more collisions than usual: A man in a pinstripe suit bumped my hip with his briefcase as he slid past me to grab the last open seat. Two teenage girls leaned against each other shoulder to shoulder, their heads bumping as they both tried to close their eyes for a few more minutes of sleep before school. A woman ran into me while I climbed up the steps at Fourteenth Street, knocking me backward into the crowd behind me, and my frustration surged as I fought my way forward again.

It was exactly what I had moved to New York for, ironically: the intense proximity to other people, to what I thought of as the diversity of the human experience itself. I did still feel the familiar jolt of energy as I turned north on Broadway and walked toward my office, but a strange sense of displacement flowed through me, too.

Virtually, I will totally be there, I had said to Michelle. But really, our friendship had been almost entirely virtual for years, sustained through phone calls, texts, and likes on her frequently updated Facebook statuses and carefully filtered Instagram photos. Sometimes it all seemed like barely a shadow of what we used to be. I didn't want that to be the case. I shook off the thought as I got settled at my desk, quickly making a separate e-mail folder for all things wedding related, promising myself that I would be as present as possible, and then moving back to sort through the rest of my perennially overwhelmed inbox.

I had only made it through the first third before I felt a single tap on my shoulder. I knew it had to be my boss, Imani.

"Jules," she said in an even tone, no lift in her voice to suggest a question. "Come into my office."

I had one-on-one meetings with Imani once a week when she gave me all my assignments, but she had rarely called me into her office without scheduling it first. As I followed her across the room, I caught a glimpse of Alan discreetly making the sign of the cross for my benefit.

You're not getting fired, I reassured myself, while still mentally tabulating my year's total of sick days (four) and vacation days (only two so far: the Fourth of July long weekend at Ritchie's parents' lake house in New Jersey). I stayed standing until Imani made a sweeping gesture with a manicured hand, indicating that I should sit.

Imani took the seat across from me behind her modern faux-marble desk, smoothing her lavender sheath dress. "I'll tell you straight off," she said, dispensing with pleasantries completely. Imani always had a straight-to-the-point, confident demeanor. Publishing was a difficult field for anyone, but it could be notoriously unwelcoming to women of color. Imani had fought her way into a very senior position. For this, and so many other reasons, I admired her. Because of that, I was also incredibly afraid to let her down.

Imani laced her fingers together. "Jules. As you know, it's crucial to Thomas Miller that we build the absolute best team."

I nodded.

"And not just in terms of talent, but in terms of dedication. We've taken note of the extra work you've put in over the past several months, as well as your commitment to the company over the past several years as an editorial assistant, and we'd like to offer you a promotion. Assistant editor, effective immediately."

I let out the breath I hadn't realized I'd been holding. I couldn't believe this was finally happening. I'd held the editorial assistant title for nearly two years longer than I'd originally expected. Now, here in one fleeting moment, was the manifestation of what I had hoped for so long ago. Long enough that I had had to stop thinking it would happen soon, or else every day that I woke up without it happening would have been depressing.

"Ohhh my God." *Get it together, Jules. Be professional.* "What I mean to say is, thank you, Imani. I absolutely accept."

She proffered me a piece of paper with the company's official letterhead, detailing the promotion and signed by Howard, her boss. I felt relieved that we weren't having the negative conversation I feared, but I noticed no compensation increase listed.

I hadn't negotiated properly when I took the job out of college. I sensed it at the time—and publishing was notorious for low salaries, after all—but then Alan had plainly told me as much. Feeling grateful to have made it to New York, and blessed to have a job that could help me make my loan payments at all, kept me from asking for my due. But now, as Imani rose to stand in front of me, a steely expression on her beautiful face in spite of the allegedly good news, I thought about the frustration with my life I had felt so acutely up until she called me into her office. I thought of every time in my past that I hadn't spoken up.

"Before I leave, I'd like to discuss a compensation increase commensurate with the way my role has evolved over my time here."

Imani raised her eyebrows. "You do know how it works. Salary reviews happen at the end of the year. We can look at making an adjustment then."

I took a deep breath. "But I didn't get a raise last year. It's September. In accordance with me accepting the position, I'd like to be evaluated now. I'd be happy to talk to Howard myself."

Imani raised her eyebrows. "Well, we absolutely consider you to be an asset to the company. I can speak to him, and I believe we can have your salary review moved to October."

"Thank you," I said, trying to keep my voice steady as we both stood up. I reached across the desk to shake her hand.

"Thank you, Jules," she said coolly, but I detected just the hint of a smile playing around her lips as I turned to leave, and I couldn't help feeling as though she was just the tiniest bit impressed.

Alan took me out for a drink after work at my favorite neighborhood spot. With $4 drafts and a friendly crowd of fiftysomething regulars, I always felt right at home. It wasn't really Alan's type of place—he would likely run a finger along the sticky bar, asking if I thought it had been wiped down since the Bush administration—but it was a convenient and cheap place to throw back a celebratory shot or two.

"Congratulations, Jules." Alan raised his beer in a toast. "If there is anyone who deserves to excel in the fucked-up world we call the publishing industry, it is you."

"Thanks." I took a big sip. "I think I'm actually even more excited about the fact that I tried to negotiate a raise than I am about getting the promotion."

"Well, it's about fucking time. On both counts."

Alan and I drank in silence for a minute. I had taken a job in publishing after Cornell because I had dreamed since second grade that there might be a career that would let me read for a living. But it was more than that. I wanted a life that stretched beyond working in Birmingham, watching my mom frantically trying to find another man, and going on "blind" dates with acquaintances from high school. I had moved away from home, graduated from college, landed the job. What would there be in the world beyond that, and why had it so far eluded me? The promotion had made a start, certainly, a significant one. But now that I had it, I could tell it wasn't the thing itself.

I said this out loud to Alan.

"What's next, you mean? I, uh, think a lot of people get married as a way out of answering that question." He laughed. "But, no, seriously. I ask myself that all the time."

"I know it's corny. Everyone thinks they're meant for something bigger. But still."

"We'll let it slide. So, what *are* you most passionate about?"

"Reading?"

"Well, hence the publishing career. Duh," Alan scoffed. "But I'm serious."

"Me, too."

"Helpful. No, what do you wish you did more of? What do you wish you could do that you don't do now? And do not say adopting a dog."

"Okay, fine. Writing," I said. I thought about how it had always felt like me making the best of myself, the only time I felt like I was truly in charge of a narrative and a life, even though I had only ever done it for fun. "But I've never felt like I can re-create what I like to read. The essays, the memoirs, I don't know—taking the truth and elevating it to an art form. That's what I want to do."

"That's . . . poetic." I couldn't tell if he was being earnest or sarcastic.

"Shut up."

I closed my eyes for a minute, feeling a tingle spread through my body that let me know I was already buzzed. "So what about you? Any secret passions?"

He ran a hand over his jawline, stroking his stubble in a parody of serious thought. "Well, I know I've told you about creating an app."

"Tell me the latest idea again?" Alan went to Stanford, and while he had majored in English, a couple of guys from his freshman dorm followed the stereotypical Silicon Valley dream of developing an app, making connections, getting rich, and dropping out. With that experience in mind, Alan had been pitching me app ideas on and off since we had become friends. Not that I had any idea about how to start one; I was just a very engaged audience.

"An app that lets you book specific tables or bar seats in a restaurant. Like how you book a seat on planes and some cost more. I swear, it'll be a hit." He gestured to the bartender for another beer. "I could already be a famous founder, you know. Evan Spiegel stole Snapchat from me."

"Oh my God, we've been over this. Evan Spiegel did not *steal* Snapchat from you."

"Naked texting app! I thought of that years ago!"

"Not the same as stealing it. I keep telling you that." I laughed and knocked my forehead against his shoulder.

"No, really, though. It's not about Snapchat," he said, slinging an arm around my shoulders. "It's about figuring out 'the thing.' You know, what am I *really* supposed to be doing with my life? Something bigger that I could point to and say, 'That was me. I made that.'"

"God, we sound annoying." I laughed. "A 'search for a greater purpose'? Seriously?"

"Hey, everyone has always wanted a purpose. I think we're just the first generation to demand it this obnoxiously. But seriously, I have to get started on the restaurant app. If I had just moved on those other ideas, then *I* would be the tech billionaire married to Miranda Kerr. Or, you know, whoever the male version of Miranda Kerr is."

"Marcus is honestly sort of the male version of Miranda Kerr. But if Miranda Kerr were an accountant?" I hadn't spent too much time with Alan's boyfriend, but I approved of him completely. He seemed warm, empathetic, attentive—all the things you would want in someone dating your friend. It didn't hurt that he really was model attractive, either.

"You and Miranda Kerr actually have the same lips," Alan said, evaluating me with a slightly drunken gaze. Then he winked. "But you'll be much more successful."

"Thanks." I grabbed for the new beers that had been dropped off for us. "You know, Michelle is the one who actually looks like a model. I think in high school I was hoping that it might somehow rub off on me."

Alan raised his eyebrows. "And I hoped I'd grow up to look like Jared Leto. But seriously, Jules. You have to start seeing your life on your own terms."

Maybe it was the alcohol, maybe it was the pleasant exhaustion settling over me after a long day, but I wanted to tell Alan a million things right then. Mostly that I didn't know where the rest of my life might lead, or what it might even mean to be "good enough," but that having friends like him made the prospect less frightening. Instead I just said, "You're a really good friend, you know?"

"You, too." He smiled. "But I have to tell you, if you ever ask me to be *your* maid of honor, I'm going to say no."

CHAPTER 7

I quickly discovered that my promotion didn't merely symbolize a move up the ladder after three years of loyalty. It meant continuing my job while also taking on the work of a recently departed editor. I should have known, honestly. But at least it was a move up.

I found myself still photocopying contracts in between assisting a senior editor with several newly assigned manuscripts. It was a lot of work on top of the freelancing I sometimes did on nights or weekends to supplement my publishing salary, but I told myself I didn't mind, even when the workload meant coming into the office that Saturday while Dana and Ritchie took the jitney to the Hamptons for one last September weekend trip.

But this particular Saturday was different. *This* Saturday was Michelle's bridal-shopping day.

I had never imagined picking out my wedding dress, or even

what shopping for wedding dresses might be like. Michelle had a bridal magazine that we flipped through around the time that we staged her wedding to Ashton Kutcher—probably *Martha Stewart Weddings*, knowing Marcia's subscription tastes—and I asked Michelle if you ordered them from the catalog like I had seen my mom do from Delia's. "No." She rolled her eyes at me. "You go to a special store and try them all on." As if everyone knew.

Now I was about to watch Michelle do exactly that. The plan specified that I should tune in to the shopping trip on FaceTime from my cubicle. And sure enough, at twelve thirty, my phone started buzzing, spinning like a beetle on its back as it vibrated loudly on my desk.

"Hi from the bridal shop!" Michelle chirped as soon as I swiped to answer. She squinted at me. "Are you in an office? Why are you in an office?"

"Well, I wanted to tell you in person, but this sort of counts. You were right—I finally got promoted! So right now I have more work. But it's great."

"Julie! Congratulations! I'm so proud. I knew it." She grinned, and I felt her energy light me up inside. Michelle still had that effect on me, as if her sprinkled compliments were magic dust. "I want to hear everything later. But right now: dresses."

"Right. Dresses."

"Sylvie is going to hold the phone," Michelle said. She gestured to three dresses hanging next to her in a fleur-de-lis-wallpapered fitting room, each looking puffier and more meringue-like than the last. "I'm going to try on these first, and you can tell me what you think."

"Sounds good."

Sylvie took possession of the phone. "Hi, Julie," she said flatly. While Michelle had "totally bonded" with Sylvie during their first week in the Tri-Delt house sophomore year, the same easy rapport had never developed between us, even though I had visited Michelle often during her four years at 'Bama. She spun the phone to show me a blurred view of the room, and I saw Ellen waving before she set the device down on the fitting-area couch, and I was left staring at the vaulted ceiling until Michelle emerged in the first dress.

She was stunning. Even as Michelle and I had seen each other less often over the years, her face still remained almost as familiar to me as my own. But every once in a while, I would catch a glimpse of her in which she looked wholly unfamiliar. I saw her as a stranger might, and it knocked me out every time. Her hair fell in perfect waves, framing the sides of her heart-shaped face even though she claimed she "looked gross" and "hadn't even showered." Even the ugliest of the three dresses flattered her as I watched her twirl in front of the three-way mirror, dazzling even through the grainy quality of the stream. I thought I had no particular feelings about weddings at all, but my heart leapt up inside my chest as I imagined Michelle actually walking down the aisle.

"You look absolutely beautiful," I told her when she retrieved the phone from Sylvie.

"Thanks. But I don't know, that last one . . ."

"Yeah, that last dress, not so much."

"Agreed. I don't know if I'm going to find what I want here; this definitely isn't my style," she said in a hushed voice, ever polite.

"We're going to start looking for bridesmaid dresses instead. I'll call you back with choices."

I worked absentmindedly for what might have been an hour, and I decided I was ready to quit when the phone finally buzzed again.

"I wondered if you had been smothered to death by a pile of taffeta," I joked. "Find anything?"

"We did," she squealed. "Julie, I think we found the bridesmaid dresses!"

Already? "Show me," I said with as much enthusiasm as possible. I braced for the worst; after all, I hadn't seen any contenders, and weren't bridal horror stories always centered on having to wear something like a magenta taffeta bridesmaid dress? But I told myself I would even wear a burlap sack, as happy as Michelle sounded.

"They're perfect!" She held up a pale peach dress with a sweetheart neckline, gauzy, nearly floor-length. It wasn't exactly my style, but it really did look lovely.

I smiled. "Beautiful and elegant, Miche."

She said something to one of the other women offscreen, then turned her face back to the screen. "All right, hon, I have to go," she said. "All the girls are going to buy theirs, and I'm going to send the ordering info to your e-mail right now!"

After we hung up, I finished one final page markup and decided to call it a day. I refreshed my e-mail once more before packing up my laptop, and I saw that Michelle had already sent the link to the dress. I clicked on it, prepared to get out my credit card, but when I reached the landing page I felt myself catch my breath.

The dress cost $395.

Finances had been a point of awkward tension between Michelle and me for as long as we had known each other. It was inevitable from the first time I went to dinner at her family's country club and I remarked out loud at the china, telling her that my mom and I didn't usually eat off "the hard dishes." Marcia had blanched. In my younger years, my mom had relied largely on paper plates and affordable microwavable cuisine.

Somehow, though, this felt different. It was one thing when the financial divide existed only between our parents, with Michelle and me aware of money only in a theoretical way, like gravity. We knew it existed and it was important, but it had very little to do with our day-to-day thoughts. As adults, it occupied a different place between us, one that was much more awkward to discuss. And so we pretended that it didn't exist as much as we possibly could. The wedding was going to force my hand.

But it wasn't just about a $400 dress to wear for only one night, I thought, unable to quell my frustration. It was the idea that Michelle actually believed that her wedding merited her six closest friends dropping a combined thousands of dollars at the bridal shop alone. I worked through a range of emotions as I walked out of my office and then descended into the subway at Union Square. It stung in a strange way every time Michelle seemed to be oblivious about money, but perhaps part of the fault was mine; we had had this fight once before.

For Michelle's twenty-first birthday, she had planned a trip to New Orleans with her sorority sisters and invited me along. The invite came in an e-mail with a list of costs, including three dinners out and a five-star hotel. I begged off with a finals-related excuse, not telling her until much later that the issue was money. I thought she had been oblivious and presumptuous. But when I finally brought it up she argued that if I had told her the price tag was the only problem, she could have helped me or worked out something else, suggesting that I had been evasive and hurt her feelings.

I started off indignant, then softened. Considering how generous her family had always been with me, I knew she was telling the truth, and they would have helped. Even if I thought she had approached the subject the wrong way, she had a point: The Davises had taken me to their country club, paid for me to take gymnastics lessons with Michelle, given me dresses to wear to high school dances. Was I making the same mistake again now? I could appeal to Michelle, or even Marcia, for help with the dress cost.

But I didn't want to feel like a charity case anymore. I didn't want to have to be sponsored, I told myself. I wanted to make my own way.

And yet, I suspected the hidden underbelly of my resistance was something else. I had learned that accepting money from someone grants them a certain degree of influence and power in your life. When Marcia paid for my gymnastics classes, I started wearing the more modest leotards she deemed appropriate. When we went to the country club, it was suggested that I needed etiquette classes. I had no doubt that Michelle and her family had given to me purely because they loved me, and I loved them in return. But I didn't know how to reconcile love and independence, the girl I had been in Langham under the Davises' roof with the woman I wanted to be on my own, a person whose life they might not understand. It was better to pay for the dress myself, I decided, than to invite the complications of financial dependence back into my life. But I still felt uneasy. Roiling somewhere deep in my stomach, anger felt so much like embarrassment, and embarrassment felt so much like guilt.

I texted Dana after I got off the train at Grand Street. "Bridesmaid dresses for Michelle's wedding cost $395. Is this normal?"

"No," she wrote back. "Protest. Show up in your underwear."

"Haha. I guess I'm ordering it, but no more oysters until next year."

Dana could more than afford a $395 outfit and routinely argued her cases in sheath dresses and power suits that cost three times that amount. *That never bothers me,* I reasoned. *It's the fact that Michelle didn't even ask.*

My phone buzzed again, but it wasn't Dana. It was Michelle.

"Sooo glad we found the dresses today!" the text read. "You're going to look better than everyone—but don't tell them I said so."

"And you'll be the most beautiful bride," I shot back. Over text, I couldn't seem to make myself say anything else.

I swallowed the uncomfortable thought that maybe Michelle *had* known I would balk at the price, and that's why she had picked the dress and sent everyone else to the register before showing it to me. Surely that wasn't true, I told myself. But I knew there would be plenty more unexpected expenses I'd face over the next six months.

March couldn't come soon enough.

CHAPTER 8

If I had been waiting for a financial reprieve after the bridesmaid dress debacle, it quickly became clear that I wasn't going to get it. The floodgates had opened, and the invitation to Michelle's bridal shower arrived from Marcia only a week later, enclosed in an over-size lilac envelope with extra postage. I opened it carefully on my way up the stairs to my apartment, and with its floral appliqués and engraved script it looked like a wedding invitation itself. Marcia requested the pleasure of my company in four weeks' time.

I dialed Michelle as I opened the door to my apartment. This time, she picked up right away.

"Just got your shower invite, Miche," I said, sandwiching the phone between my ear and my shoulder to continue examining it with both hands. "*Very* classy. Should I come into town for the whole weekend?"

"Well, yes, of course," she said, a tone of warning high in her voice, as subtle and yet crisp as the top notes of her expensive perfume. "And don't feel *too* bad about not helping to plan the shower. All my friends are around here anyway, and it was just so much easier for Mama to do it."

I recognized the slight dig for what it was, but I registered it as fair. All the other bridesmaids would be bringing baked goods and coordinating party favors with Marcia—and more than one of them likely had complete Pinterest boards dedicated to the occasion.

"Let me know what else I can bring. I can pick up flowers, or anything you need day of, too. It'll be great to see everyone." *Except Darcy,* I omitted. "By the way, I need some advice about something, too," I said, thinking about the group of interns I had started to manage. "Since the promotion, I'm overseeing this intern group. I'm just not sure how to give them the best advice; I don't know if they relate to me."

As I started to tell her about their latest project, their endless questions, and the fact that I didn't understand how I could simultaneously feel so young and yet so *old* in the presence of nineteen-year-olds, I realized I didn't want to stop talking to her. It reminded me of when I would call her on my mom's old home phone back in elementary school, lying on my bed and talking for hours even though we had been at school together all day. I couldn't remember what we had talked about then, what thoughts and problems an eight-year-old could possibly have had to express, but I knew the feeling of never wanting to hang up had been much like the one I was experiencing now.

"I think you should see it as a compliment that they're giving you more to do," Michelle said, and I smiled. "Remember when they made you head of the mentor program in high school? You can totally handle it. Listen, we'll have a glass of wine and talk about it more after the shower if you want. I'll take you to this great place, Jacques'."

"That sounds—"

"Actually," she said, raising her voice a bit, "it's where Jake wants to have the rehearsal dinner, so we need to see it anyway. It's not cliché to have it at a French bistro, is it?"

"No. I don't . . . think so?" I listened as she launched back into her latest wedding plans, and I felt a strange sort of sadness inside me. The call lasted only another minute, Michelle breaking off mid-sentence to take a call from her florist.

I wasn't looking forward to making awkward small talk with Michelle's sorority sisters at the shower, but the bigger issue with the trip to Alabama was that it meant seeing my mom. Family drama in my tiny family of two suddenly seemed inevitable.

Marcia had sent Judy a shower invitation, Michelle warned me before we got off the phone. She hadn't exactly sent it out of friendship; the last time the four of us had tried to have lunch together, my mom had interrupted Marcia in the middle of a conversation, then actually patted her head before launching into a long rant about picking up something "strange" in her aura. Michelle looked like she wanted to crawl under the table, but Marcia remained stiffly polite. Still, I overheard Marcia in the bathroom later, complaining that she had just set her hair and now it was flattened. I wanted to apologize for my mom's frequently tone-deaf outbursts, but I wasn't thrilled with Marcia at the moment, either—couldn't she have just laughed it off? That was the week before I moved to New York.

Even if Marcia might have been baffled by Judy, she treated me as an entity apart, as if I had more to do with her and her family than the northern transplant single mother who had brought me to Langham in the first place. Still, she had invited my mom to the shower as a courtesy. She was the mother of the maid of honor, after all. This meant that my mom and I would be seeing each other, whether she ended up actually attending the shower or not. A phone call was definitely in order.

The frequency with which my mother and I talked on the phone depended on whether she had a boyfriend at the time. It went in cycles: When she hadn't been dating anyone, calls came semifrequently. When she was in a more serious relationship, they all but disappeared. But when she was going on casual dates with someone new, she would sometimes call multiple times in a week, gushing about a potential future with the latest Match.com bachelor, peppering me with questions and prodding me to analyze his behavior and whether or not it was problematic that their astrological signs foreshadowed potential conflict. I couldn't tell if she intended for me to respond like a daughter, a friend, a therapist, or a fortuneteller. And so I always answered *that* question in the same way: "Your sign *was* compatible with Dad's, and look how that turned out. It doesn't mean anything."

Mom was a Cancer, Dad a Scorpio. This had been repeated to me many times throughout my childhood, at first as if it were a prescription for happiness, and then as if something in the universe were at fault for the relationship's ultimate failure. Dad hadn't believed in her "mumbo jumbo," as he once called it. But she had certainly been correct in predicting that *something* about their relationship was off.

When I got up to my apartment, I slapped the shower invitation on the fridge with a takeout magnet, walked into the bedroom with my phone, and closed the door behind me, even though Terry and Demi weren't home.

Calling my mom in Alabama felt somehow like time travel. Or maybe it was more like dialing into another dimension. Either way, it was an act that required solitude. I sometimes dissolved into an earlier version of myself when I spoke to her, and I felt acutely the dissonance between the person I had been when I lived at home with her eight years ago and the person I had started to become. Being here, alone in a New York apartment that she had never seen and probably never would see, jarred me every time. She had never met Dana or Ritchie or Alan; she had no concept of the people or places that comprised my New York life. I didn't know if that made me feel independent and hopeful, or sad. Maybe both.

I sat down on the edge of the bed, facing toward the exposed brick wall. She picked up on the third ring, which I expected. If I was remembering correctly, we were currently between boyfriends.

"Jule, hi," she exclaimed. Cheery this time, a pleasant surprise. "I'm glad you called. I wanted to tell you, I just finished a shift and I was thinking of starting back up on that adult coloring book! Maybe you could help me get it published. You know, the one I started sketching a few months ago after I saw that gardening coloring book at the bookstore, which really wasn't all that well done, so I thought that if a *gardener* can do it . . ."

In one of her energetic moods, my mom never declaratively finished her sentences, so it was usually necessary to just jump in. "Yeah, I remember. Sounds like fun. Anyway, I was just calling to see if you got Marcia's invite to Michelle's bridal shower. I'll be in town Friday and Saturday, since the shower is Saturday morning."

I could hear her teakettle whistling in the background, unattended, and then her crashing across the small living room to turn off the stove. "Oh good. Do you want to stay here?"

She had turned the smaller of the ranch home's two bedrooms into an "office"—a graveyard for her unfinished personal projects, like the adult coloring book and her attempt at a romance novel—after I left for college. That meant I spent the annual Christmas visit on the living room futon. Given the size of the living room, part of the futon was actually positioned underneath the Christmas tree while it was up, and I would wake up every morning covered in fallen needles from the ankles down. I would not be staying there.

"No, I'm going to stay in Michelle's guest room," I told her. "But let's get dinner after I come in on Friday?" Michelle would be busy with party preparations out at the Davis house anyway, I assumed. "I land at around two thirty."

"Okay, that's probably good. I might have a date later that night anyway. Did I tell you I've found all kinds of new matches lately? You know, I thought I had burned through all the divorcés in Birmingham, but it turns out they were all camping out on eharmony! You'll have to help me look when you're here. I always thought eharmony was for old people, but, well, I'm you-know-how-many years now, so I guess I can consider the occasional sixty-year-old. Don't tell anyone."

"I won't. So, uh, everything's good?" It was a delicate balance, checking in on her enough during our catch-up calls but not inviting a full-on gossip session about, say, the sex lives of her friends Mindy and Eleanor, who made beeswax candles and sold them at the local farmers' market. My mom had once told me about some tantric uses for that candle wax that I would probably never be able to unvisualize.

"Good enough? Oh, I guess." I heard her sigh. "But work is still less than ideal. And the water heater went out last month, and the bill on that thing, well. That's a struggle."

This was always hard for me to hear. In the right mood, it made me sympathetic, and I ached to tell her that I could help, even though I barely made enough money to cover my own expenses. Other times, it simply frustrated me; I didn't want her finances to be my responsibility. I hadn't asked her for money since I was a teenager, and I resented the frequent inclusion in her financial affairs. I swallowed. "I'm sorry to hear that. Anything I can do?" *Please say no.*

"Oh no, of course not," she said, sounding upbeat again, and so I merely felt guilty. She just wanted me to empathize, and instead I had leapt to thinking about myself. *For good reason,* the voice in my mind hissed. I scrambled for something else to say.

"Okay, well, Mark is coming over soon," I told her. "Sorry, I have to go. But I'll see you soon."

"Okay," she said. "Tell Mark hi from me! Bye-bye." And the line went dead.

Mom was absolutely infatuated with the idea of Mark, even though they had never met in person. At the very least, this had given us more fodder for phone conversations than we had had for several years. My mom was by no means a traditional homemaker of the Marcia variety, but twenty years of the single life had clearly worn her down on the concept, and I knew she not so privately held the belief that it would be comforting if I eventually "settled down" with someone.

I tossed the phone across the bed onto my pillow. The conversation had ostensibly gone well, and I would see her in person soon. But my body felt heavy with discontent as I sat there on the edge of the bed, staring at the wall, wondering what it might be like to have a mother whose counsel encouraged me or gave me energy, rather than draining it. Before I could move to get up, I heard Mark rapping on the door.

"Jules? You here?"

"How'd you get in?" I called back.

"Door was open."

"I'm in the bedroom."

He opened the door slowly. He had figured out that the living room was my preferred spot when none of my roommates were home, and apart from at night, I closed myself in the bedroom only if something was wrong.

"Are you okay?" I could hear him trying to subtly determine the degree of upset.

"Yes." I swallowed. "I was just talking to my mom about going home for Michelle's shower. She says hi, by the way."

"Tell her hi, too." He sat down beside me. "Are you worried about going back home?"

I didn't answer Mark's unspoken question—was I worried

about seeing my mom—because I honestly wasn't sure how I felt, and I didn't want to have to explain it. Things were different for him. He loved taking the Metro-North up to Connecticut one Sunday a month, passing lazy days with his parents and his brothers when they were around. Instead, I laid my head in his lap, sprawling across the bed, and I asked a random question. "I need a subject change. What did you want to be when you grew up? Like, when you were a little kid. Sorry if I've asked you before and I don't remember."

He thought for a minute. "No, I don't think we've talked about it." Mark had a reliably encyclopedic memory, so I trusted him on this. My memory was a sieve, he liked to say. Probably true. I remembered intense moments of emotion, expressions on people's faces, snippets of conversation—little tidbits coming into focus like a Polaroid—but day-to-day details weren't my strong point. I was always plotting my next move, he said. I rarely remembered my last one.

"I wanted to be a research zoologist. Like a Jane Goodall type," I told him. "To travel the world on my own."

"Hence the publishing job?" he teased.

I was surprised that it stung a little bit, but I knew he meant it to be funny. "Shut up. Okay, now you."

He shrugged. "This, I guess."

"Bullshit. No one under the age of eighteen knows what McKinsey is."

"Hey!"

"Well, it's true. It's something you find out about the second you get to college. Ivy League colleges, that is. They stand in those little booths at the career fair, telling you about this great field called 'consulting' that you can do if you're suddenly panicking about having an English degree . . ."

Now it was his turn to tell me to shut up. "No, I mean, I wanted to be in the business world. Eventually get my MBA." He paused and then pulled me into a sitting position. "Actually, that's something I wanted to talk about. When I was flying back from Omaha this week, just bored as hell, I realized I think I'm ready for a change. I'm really going to start studying for the GMAT and take it in a few months. I think it's time."

Mark had been talking about the GMAT since the summer we first met. He had already been at McKinsey for a year at that time, and, like many consultants, he was intent on working his way up by working long hours for a few years and then cashing in on a free ride to business school.

I told him that if he wanted to stay in consulting, it seemed like a smart idea to me.

"It depends on my score, but if I can do well, my top choice would be Penn. Keep it in the family." Mark's mom and dad had met at Wharton, so *that* wasn't intimidating at all. Then, after a pause, he added, "So, let's say I did get in."

"Okay," I said. Being both a double legacy and an alum had to count for something. "And you probably will. So? That's great. Right?"

"I mean," he said, "would you ever consider moving to Philly?"

The night I met Mark, I told him two things as we sat side by side in a sticky booth at BBar, intermittently making out: The first was a lie, that he was the first person I had made out with at BBar, and the second was the truth, that I didn't think I would ever leave New York. I had come too far, worked too long, wanted it too much. That was still true.

"I think I would want to stay in New York either way. For work. This is where publishing is," I reminded him gently. "But Philly is only an hour and a half away." It would be an easy commute, if we were still dating when any of this ever became more than theoretical. I felt a flash of sadness at the idea of Mark leaving, the sting sharper than I expected. But I knew I would put my career ahead of any relationship at this point, and it made sense that he would want to do the same. As Dana was prone to saying, there was still "a lot of life to live" before settling down.

"Well, I mean, I could also stay in the city. Columbia or NYU, maybe," he said, a little too quickly.

"No, I want you to go." I couldn't believe that he wouldn't go to the best school possible—what if he got into Harvard? "No matter what, you should do what you've always wanted. I mean, obviously."

Mark opened his mouth like he was going to say something, then paused, his jaw slack.

"What?"

He leaned down to kiss my forehead, a gesture simultaneously sweet and somehow patronizing in a way I couldn't quite put a finger on. "Nothing. Well, I definitely don't have to decide anything just yet," he said. "I have to get a decent score first."

CHAPTER 9

When I stepped out onto the curb at the Birmingham airport the weekend of Michelle's shower, the humidity hit me full force. I had forgotten that an Alabama October still sizzled like full-fledged summer. Feeling my waves frizz up as the stickiness enveloped me, I remembered why I had always been so jealous of Michelle's fine, silky hair.

I hauled my suitcase into the trunk of a cab and gave the driver Michelle's address. She would probably already be out at her parents' place decorating for the shower, but I knew how to find the key hidden in a special sleeve under her doormat.

"So, in town for business or pleasure?" The taxi driver looked at me in the rearview mirror, clearly eager to strike up a conversation. From the flight attendants to the cab line, I had forgotten how chatty the South could be. I thought about the complicit silence of New York Uber drivers, which never felt rude but instead like a tacit admission that we would both rather focus on our own thoughts than force small talk. I already couldn't wait to get back to the city.

"Pleasure, I guess." I tried to smile politely while keeping my answer short. *It feels more like business,* I thought. I looked out the window and trained my eyes on the emerging city skyline. There wasn't much to see, but I remembered the days when it had looked so impressive and foreboding from my comparatively rural vantage point. When Michelle and I were in middle school, Marcia would drive us into the city on occasional Saturdays for a shopping trip at the Riverchase Galleria mall, and I always thought of it as a trip to the big city.

My suitcase rattled in the trunk as the cab bumped over I-20. It contained a pair of pajamas, athleisure shorts and tanks for running around the city, and a secondhand Lilly Pulitzer dress left over from high school that I knew would find approval from Marcia, even though it had been relegated to the back of my closet in New York for three years. I also had four necklaces, because I still didn't trust myself to pick the right ones to match the shower dress without Michelle's counsel. Packing had presented a challenge. I had skirts and cardigans for work, black sheath dresses for book parties— selected with advice from Dana—and ripped jeans for nights out dancing in Bushwick. I used to be all pastels, but now I had nothing to wear for a garden party bridal shower. Eventually, I had grabbed my phone and done a quick Google search, actually typing in "what to wear to your best friend's bridal shower when you are the maid of honor." Ridiculous, I decided. But then I remembered the one floral dress in the very back of my closet and breathed a sigh of relief: All hail Lilly Pulitzer, the patron saint of preppy prints.

I shouldn't have been worried. But it didn't help that most of the guests were old acquaintances of mine, and they were the real reason I usually dreaded going back to our hometown. Around those people, I could feel myself fading back into a person I wasn't even sure that I liked. Old friends, like Michelle, could allow you to be the relaxed, lived-in version of your former self. The paradox is that sometimes they *require* you to be that person, as though they can't understand you any other way. I could feel a gap between us when I referenced an inside joke she couldn't find funny, or a memory she hadn't been a part of, and I wondered if she felt the same about me.

As the cab driver finally turned off at the exit, I realized that I had forgotten to text both my mom and Michelle that I had arrived. I thought about it for a minute and then sent the same message to both of them: "Sorry, forgot to text—I landed in Birmingham. See you soon x."

"Ma'am," the cab driver said. "We're here."

Ma'am instead of *miss*—yikes. I brushed it off and looked up: Michelle's building, named Parkside Condos, loomed over us, casting a shadow across the street. The first time I had visited Michelle there at the end of our first postgrad year, the building's modern facade, all new brick and sleek glass, amazed me. I told her that living in a building with a name was a big deal in New York; she pulled a face and told me she couldn't wait until she and Jake could get an actual house somewhere quieter, ideally in Mountain Brook or some other nice Birmingham neighborhood closer to her parents out in Langham. The vast, often Tudor-style homes in Mountain Brook struck me as eerily quiet and depressingly cut off from any sort of excitement—especially for the cost, which could reach into the millions—and I had been surprised Michelle found it so appealing. Though to be fair, she probably felt similarly confused about my desire to live in an overpriced shoebox with roommates from Craigslist.

I thanked the driver, paid, and headed inside, past Michelle's suited doorman, who mercifully remembered me. I found the key under the mat where I expected, and I spotted fresh flowers and a note on the foyer table as I stepped inside. And, thank God, she had left the air-conditioning on.

"Julie!" the note read. "I'm already out at my parents'—major crisis with the food for tomorrow. If you're seeing your mama, know that y'all are welcome for dinner at ours. Otherwise, see you tomorrow at 10. Sharp! Haha. XO."

As much as I wanted to drink a glass of wine on the Davises' sprawling veranda while Marcia fussed in the kitchen—nothing took me back to simpler times like hearing her clink pans and call, "Y'all better get in here and help"—the idea of spending time with Michelle, her family, and my mother all at the same time seemed more than I could handle. Instead, I would meet my mom at a restaurant. That would make it easy enough for her to join me for an early dinner at six before her drinks date at eight. In the meantime, I could just barely squeeze in a nap. I hauled my suitcase into Michelle's guest room, threw back the floral duvet, and fell asleep.

That evening, I called an Uber to the restaurant. Forgetting that I didn't need to account for New York traffic, I got there ten minutes early. My mom arrived fifteen minutes late.

"Julie!" she called loudly as she flung open the door. I didn't flinch, not at her shouting and not at her use of my old nickname. I was used to it. "Am I late? Damned traffic."

"Hi, Mom. It's fine," I told her, gesturing to the hostess that we were ready to sit down. As we walked toward the table, my mom began to unwind the first of two wispy scarves draped around her neck. It appeared that the scarf phase, which had been preceded by the giant-necklace phase, continued to endure.

She smiled at me over her shoulder as we followed the hostess. I saw myself in its quick flash: the broad spread across her face, the subtle dimple near the left corner, the warmth in her brown eyes. Then she turned away and folded the second scarf over her shoulder, painted with a rendering of a Monet, which I recognized as a gift from a boyfriend who had been at Christmas dinner during my freshman year of college. She had kicked him out before New Year's.

I stared at her for another moment, awash with the strange sensation of seeing so much and yet so little of yourself in the person who made you.

We turned our attention to the menus and studied them for a few moments in silence. "So," she finally said, setting her menu down on the table with a declarative *thwack*. "How are you, really?"

"Fine. I like my apartment; roommates are nice enough. Work is good. Mark is—"

"Mark! How is he? It's been so long. Maybe it's about time I meet him."

I ignored her second statement. "Mark's doing well. He's still traveling back and forth to Omaha for the project he's consulting on, so we're both really busy. I did get a promotion, though, so—"

"Omaha, well. That's a long way from NYC. Hey, maybe he could get a project down here, huh?"

I sighed. "Yeah. Maybe one day."

She held up her hands. "But I know, I know, you love New York."

I half smiled. Well, at least one thing I had said to her over the past few years had gotten through. "I do. You know, you should come up and visit." We both knew that this was unlikely to happen—and most likely impossible unless I let her stay in my room so she didn't have to pay for a hotel. Our relationship did seem to function best with a thousand miles between us, but it might be nice to have her come up once or twice. To see the life I was making there before it was made.

"Well, of course, you know I'd love to. Hey, maybe I'll even be able to bring Jeff!"

Jeff: the guy she was going on a second date with after we finished dinner.

This statement evoked a pattern that had repeated itself throughout my childhood. My mom had been endlessly enthusiastic about planning things for us to do. She chased me around the playground, whooping as she followed me down the tunnel slide. She planned daylong antiquing trips to nearby towns, picking out knickknacks to match her latest décor vision and letting me touch and play with everything, to the shopkeepers' chagrin. She had a spirit, an indomitable energy, unmatched by almost anyone else I had ever known. And when she was in a good mood, when her sun shined in my direction, nothing was warmer. But these outings followed another pattern, too. Mom would inevitably invite some guy she had been on a date or two with to join us, always hopeful from the first day that this one was "the one." Sometimes he would come and we'd play at being a family, but more often than not he'd balk at the prospect of a full-day date with her daughter and she'd spend the first quarter of the day inconsolably upset. Then she would recover and we would have fun, but she'd still do the exact same thing the next time. I hoped it would work out between her and Jeff, but past experience taught me not to count on it.

Still, if her flightiness grated on me, I had to remember that she was also the woman who had volunteered to chaperone field trips every time she could get off work, and had come into my elementary school classroom for arts and crafts even in what seemed like the deepest haze of her depression after she and Daniel had broken up. Our relationship had never been straightforward. She hadn't been someone I could feel effortlessly close to, someone I could trust implicitly—at least not in a way that seemed at all similar to the bond between Marcia and Michelle. But I found that I couldn't let our relationship go, either. I didn't feel like I wanted to break away from her as much as I wanted to rewrite things, to change so much of how we had related to each other when I was growing up.

"Jeff would be welcome to come if he wants to," I told her.

"Good. Now, let's order some food. I'm starved!"

The rest of dinner was uneventful. She regaled me with tales of Mindy and Eleanor and the homemade candles, plus a few dating stories sprinkled in for good measure. At the end, I even got to tell her about my promotion and share that I had decided to try my hand at writing some essays in my spare time, even if she couldn't pretend to be quite as interested in that as she was in hearing about my love life.

"I think I'm going to skip the shower tomorrow," she told me as we walked out the door. She pulled an envelope out of her purse. "I have a card to send with you, but I thought I'd just let it be Michelle's day. And yours. Look, we both know old Marcia isn't exactly crazy about me." She chuckled, unbothered.

I suspected that she was canceling partially out of a preemptive hope that the "date" with Jeff would stretch into the next day, but there was no point in trying to probe that theory. Or it was possible that she had been more perceptive about the nature of Marcia's courtesy invite than I'd thought. Either way, she meant well—and in the end, I was relieved. "Michelle will appreciate the card," I told her. "Really. I'll tell her you say hi."

"Thanks, baby. Have a good time."

"You, too, Mom." She wound her scarves around her neck and twirled away in a flourish, wiggling her fingers back at me as she started down the block.

"Bye," I called after her, and then I looked down at my phone to call an Uber back to Michelle's, my mind already far away.

CHAPTER 10

I don't know exactly what I hoped to find on that morning ten years ago when Michelle and I set out for Chattanooga in her convertible to look for my father.

Maybe I wanted to confirm the story that I had been turning over in my mind ever since my mom stopped me from calling him years earlier, to prove that she had been the only thing keeping us apart. Or maybe, instead, I wanted it to be his fault. Maybe I wanted him to hang his head sheepishly, to hear him apologize. There were so many things I wanted, and so many things I was afraid of, so when Michelle asked me if I really wanted to go, I couldn't think of anything to say but, "I think so?"

"Then, let's get this show on the road," she said, turning her head toward me in the passenger seat as she idled the car at the end of her parents' drive. The click of her turn signal sounded like a ticking bomb. *Did* I really want to do this? My breath caught and she saw my panic rising. "Julie, I know how big of a deal this is. We don't have to do it today if you don't want to."

I breathed in deeply. "No, I want to."

"Well then, here we go. If we're not back by sundown, you know my mama is going to start snooping around." Our cover story for the day was that we were working on party preparations with the spring fling dance committee at Rebecca's house. It wasn't completely a lie—Michelle really had signed us both up for the planning committee, without asking me, of course.

"I think the better question is, are *you* ready? Like, you know you don't need your turn signal for the driveway, right?" I teased.

"Shut up," she said, reaching across to squeeze my hand. "I'm a natural."

The drive calmed me down. Michelle and I blasted our favorite songs, from old-school *NSYNC throwbacks to that 3OH!3 hit that was all over the radio that year. Michelle screamed the first time a semitruck squeezed past us on the highway, making us both jump, but other than that, it was perfect. Just the two of us off on a road trip, the convertible's top down, wind whipping our hair, on one of the first hot days of summer. It was a quintessential teenage moment, one that felt right out of a movie montage. Now that Michelle had her license, we could finally experience the unique freedom of just being able to take off somewhere alone, to go miles from home with no one watching us. Was this what the rest of my life could be like? I wondered. It was so much fun I almost forgot where we were going.

We pulled up to the ranch home on Mountain Creek Road at a crawl, squinting at the address on the mailbox to make sure it matched the one listed on our printed MapQuest directions. Suddenly I felt incredibly hot. I wished I could put the roof up and turn the air-conditioning on full blast. *What if he doesn't even remember me?* I wondered. *No, that's impossible. You can't forget your daughter. Or can you?*

I crossed my arms in front of my chest, my heart thumping hard.

"What if the info online was wrong?" I asked. Why hadn't I thought of this before? "What if he doesn't even live here?"

"Then we'll go right back home."

"What if he's not there? This is creepy, right? Creepy. I should have tried calling first."

"So you could just freak out and hang up? No way."

I turned my head and stared. I looked at the red front door with its brightly polished brass knocker. I sized up the yard, which was nothing special but did boast well-tended shrubs and flowers along the sidewalk to the front door. Everything looked midsize, middle-class; these people had more money than my mom, that much was clear, but with none of the intimidating, capital-S Success of the Davis family. Why did I want to walk into the boring-looking home of some stranger?

I said this to Michelle.

"Well, if your daddy really does live here," she countered, "then it's not some stranger."

She was wrong, though. He was a stranger. I didn't expect Michelle to understand why it suddenly felt that way. But I realized that it had been almost ten years since I had seen him, and I felt the weight of every one of them as I sat there in front of the house, afraid to move.

She clicked the button to unlock the car and threw open her door. I knew she would walk up the path to the front door and ring the bell, with or without me. So I swallowed my fear, got out of the car, and followed her.

In my fantasy, he answered the door himself, but of course he didn't. Instead, the door swung open to reveal a woman of slight stature, with a close-cropped blond bob and pink lipstick. She looked to be in about her late twenties, and I felt my heart unclench a little bit. We had the wrong house. She regarded us with a furrowed brow and a confused expression as a miniature poodle trotted across the hall behind her, yapping.

"Can I help y'all?" the woman asked, propping the door with a manicured hand, flashing long acrylic nails that looked like talons.

"Um, sorry to bother you. I think . . . ," I said.

"We're looking for David O'Brien," Michelle jumped in.

The woman sniffed but then turned to look over her shoulder. "David, honey," she yelled loudly. Blood rushed to my head. "Some . . . girls are here to see you. Now, what is this about?"

"We were just . . ."

"This is Julie O'Brien," Michelle said. "His daughter."

The woman immediately backed away from the doorway, blurring into the background of the entryway like a film dissolve. A man appeared in her place, his bulk filling the doorframe. He looked heavier and shorter than I remembered him, but there he was, with his same coarse, wiry eyebrows and broad shoulders. My father.

He crossed his arms in front of his body and spoke before I could find my words. "Well, this is a surprise. Did Judy send you out here?"

No greeting, no smile, no surprise. Nothing. Like I was a solicitor he wanted to dispatch as quickly as possible, instead of his daughter.

"No. I found out you lived here and I . . . wanted to see you?" I didn't mean for it to come out like a question, but it did, just the way it always had when I was scared. I hated my stupid, scared voice. When he didn't respond, I thought maybe I hated him, too.

"Mr. . . . O'Brien, sir," Michelle began, polite but insistent. "Julie and I drove a long way to see you."

"Julie, maybe your friend can wait in the car while we talk? It's been a long time." He stretched out the word *long,* and I couldn't tell if it was for emphasis or if he had developed a drawl in the decade I hadn't seen him.

Michelle stayed put. I couldn't tell if I wanted her to never leave my side or to evaporate immediately.

"Maybe we could get together another time," I offered. "I know it's a surprise, us just showing up. Is that your . . . is the woman your . . ."

"She's my girlfriend." He slumped against the doorframe, and for a moment it looked like he had fallen and caught himself. I wondered if he could be drunk. "Look, Julie, I'm sorry. This is a surprise. I . . . it *is* good to see you. You're almost all grown up."

A pause.

"But I decided—we decided, Judy and me—a long time ago that, uh, I wasn't cut out for the parent thing. Not then."

I took a step back, shrinking away.

"And I don't know about now, either. I'm just being honest. Don't want to make more problems than I already have." He sighed. "But look, here's what. You could give me your number, and maybe I could try to call? Let you know the next time I'm down the Birmingham way? We could have lunch."

He didn't pull out a cell phone, so I reached into my bag to search for a pen, my heart beating all the way up in my throat.

And then I realized: Birmingham. Michelle hadn't said where we had driven from, but he knew. *He knew.* My cheeks burned, humiliation and anger coursing through me as swiftly as my own blood.

"You knew I was in Birmingham? The whole time?"

"Well, Judy—your mom—"

"No, you know what, you can't have my number," I spat. *He could have come to see me anytime. He doesn't care. He never cared.* "And we're leaving."

I heard him say my name, "Julie," in weak protest, but Michelle and I were already barreling toward the car. We ran right through the flower bed, her hand in mine, and we didn't look back.

We pulled into my driveway at dusk. The sun hung low in the sky, sagging slowly behind our roof. Michelle and I hadn't talked much on our drive home. I issued a matter-of-fact "Fuck him" when we got in the car, a declarative statement meant to sound more confident than I felt. Michelle said it back like an echo, "Fuck him," even though she never swore, and then we let the radio take over.

"Thanks for going anyway," I told Michelle as I unbuckled my seat belt. "You're the *best* best friend." I had never meant it more.

"You, too."

"Get home before your mom calls Rebecca's entire family."

"And the police." Michelle laughed. "But you know what? I'm staying, if that's okay. I'll just call and say I wanted to go over to your place for a while." This was unusual: I could count the number of times Michelle had hung out at my house on one hand. I always stayed at hers.

I looked at her, and she stared back at me. Her expression solemn, she just nodded. *I'm staying.* She knew when I needed her, in a way no one else in my life had ever seemed to.

We walked up to the faded blue door together, me full of a mix of feelings toward my mom that I hadn't felt before: sadness, but remorse, too. When she had kept me from calling my father, when she had stalled or lied about his visits, she wasn't keeping him away from me because she was angry. She had been protecting me from him. From the fact that he couldn't or didn't want to be the kind of father I needed. She let me be angry with her instead.

I kicked off my shoes quickly on the frayed mat next to the door, and I called out for her. She had said she'd be waiting for me for dinner after I got back from Rebecca's.

"Mom?" I called in the direction of her bedroom. "Michelle's here." There were only six rooms in our ranch house, so she must have heard me. Had she gone out? Then I walked into the kitchen and saw it. Scrawled on the whiteboard affixed to our refrigerator, a message: "Out with Hank. Left money for pizza. XO."

My desire to apologize to her melted away faster than an ice cream in an Alabama summer. She couldn't have known that this, tonight, was the moment I most needed to see her, but I blamed her for it anyway. I opened the refrigerator door just to slam it shut. If everyone in my family could disappear at any moment, then fine. So could I.

Michelle didn't try to tell me this was okay. "I'm sorry," she said quietly.

"I was going to apologize to her. Tell her I knew why she didn't want me to see him."

"You still can," Michelle offered. "You can talk to her tomorrow. But you also don't have to."

I made a noise that was somewhere between clearing my throat and a laugh, and I knew she recognized it to mean "as if."

"Let's just go back to my place, then." I started to follow her out the door, and she paused for a minute. "I'm not going to say this is all okay, because it's not. But you have us, Julie. You've always had us."

I nodded, but the thought didn't comfort me, not really. Right then, I didn't care about whom I had, only whom I didn't. *My own mother, my own father.*

That night at Michelle's, I did what I always did: I helped Marcia braise the chicken; I laughed at Rich's stories about impossible clients. Michelle said nothing about our trip, she didn't bring up my dad again, but she also didn't leave my side all night. It was true, I thought to myself, I did have the *best* best friend in the world. But as much as I wanted her family to truly be mine, they weren't. I could sit on their veranda, sleep over in Michelle's canopy bed, study Marcia's movements as she expertly prepared dinner for the whole family—complete with a homemade pie. But it wouldn't erase looking at my dad in that doorway, knowing that he didn't really care if he ever saw me again. I hadn't seen him since.

There wasn't anything for me in Alabama, not really. I started researching out-of-state colleges the very next day.

CHAPTER 11

The day of the bridal shower, I called an Uber to Michelle's parents' house.

We drove through town, passing the Langham outpost of Jack's burger chain, my old high school with hydrangeas blooming at the foot of a letter-board sign that saluted the football team with a GO MUSTANGS!, and the local library where I had once checked out musty Baby-Sitters Club paperbacks. When I finally wound my way up the hundred-foot drive to Michelle's parents' house, it felt like I had traveled back in time.

The walk to the front door reminded me of dozens of times I had been dropped off there, a gift in my hand on my way to one of Michelle's elaborate birthday parties. Marcia would meet me on the porch between the azalea planters and usher me inside, and

I would feel equal parts happy and welcome, but also guilty that I wanted to be a part of their family so much more than I wanted to be a part of my own.

Marcia opened the door this time, like always. Because I still pictured her in my mind at thirty-five, I was always surprised to notice that she had aged, but she had done so gracefully. Her porcelain skin seemed thinner, a bit stretched, but her foundation was immaculate—a look I could never achieve—and her green eyes still held their signature balance of sparkling warmth and subtle iciness. Another feature, clearly unchanged, that she was still taking seriously: the classic southern maxim "the higher the hair, the closer to God."

She pulled me in to kiss my cheek right away.

"Darlin'! We're just so happy to see you. It's been so long since you've been here," she added, a remark that could have been either an observation or a judgment. "Michelle is in the living room. Go on in."

"Yes, ma'am." She looked down at my feet commandingly, one eyebrow raised, and I slipped off my sandals—no shoes in the Davis house, even during parties—and I smiled sheepishly in return, ending our wordless exchange in which she both reprimanded me as a daughter and then forgave me with a look. When I moved to New York, I learned that many people characterized the South by its "belles," painting them with one brush as soft southern flowers, but this depiction rarely left room for the quiet strength and authority of its women. Marcia wasn't a flower; she was an oak, unchangeable over the course of decades, like centuries of southern women before her.

"The prodigal daughter returns," she called out from the foyer as I made my way to where Michelle sat in the formal living room, flanked by the two earliest arrivals, her college sorority sisters Jen and Sylvie.

"Hi, Julie," they chorused together.

I crossed the room hesitantly with my gift, as though I had disturbed a sisterhood that I didn't belong to. I shrugged off the thought; I had known Michelle for longer than any of them. I also chided myself mentally for acting like a teenager back in the high school cafeteria, thinking of people as divided up into cliques. I smoothed the bottom of my dress as I sat down on the plush sofa across from Michelle, Jen, and Sylvie.

"How are you?" Michelle asked, reaching across for a hug. "Tell me everything. Flight was good?"

"I think I forgot how much strangers talk to you down here. I've been in New York too long. But, yes, everything's good. Mark says hi."

"Mark is her boyfriend," Michelle clarified to the others. "They've been together for a while. Over a year now!"

Jen flashed me a knowing "you're next" smile, displaying what seemed like a hundred perfect teeth, as Sylvie said, "How sweet!"

I didn't have a reply, and I was grateful when the doorbell rang, announcing the arrival of the next three shower guests.

"We'll talk more later," Michelle mouthed at me.

The shower consisted of the usual guessing games and storytelling about the bride and groom, mostly led by Michelle's college cohort, who had known both Michelle and Jake from the beginning of their relationship.

I watched as Michelle delicately folded colorful sheets of tissue paper pulled from gift bags to save for future use, a carbon copy of Marcia at our childhood birthday parties. She had always done the exact same thing, shadowing Michelle as she opened presents to ensure that nothing got torn and there was never a mess. I snapped photos as Michelle had instructed, while Sylvie sat next to me writing notes in a Lilly Pulitzer planner, matching each gift to its giver for future thank-you notes. Michelle detailed how she might use each thing, talking about desserts while she examined a KitchenAid mixer, and cooing as Jen praised a cobbler recipe as "totally perfect" for a summer picnic.

I had no interest in talking to Michelle about any of these things. And still I felt excluded.

Even though I made a show of rolling my eyes at Dana when Michelle posted floral arrangements on Instagram, and even though I spent hours at brunch complaining about the drama over the bridesmaid dresses, I was still somehow jealous of the intimacy. Of what I thought maybe we had lost. I hadn't even known what to get Michelle for a shower gift. In September, I had seen a bauble necklace in the window of a boutique in Williamsburg that looked like something she would wear, and I bought it excitedly. Then I told Dana and Ritchie, and Dana informed me that bridal shower gifts were "like, houseware stuff," and her sister had received mostly kitchen supplies. I couldn't believe we were supposed to buy whisks and tea towels for our friends, but I put the necklace away for Christmas and bought a set of colorful, overpriced spatulas at

Williams Sonoma. Looking at all the other gifts Michelle had opened, I was glad I had listened.

Discreetly, I turned my phone faceup on the sofa next to me and typed a text.

"Do you know how to make cherry cobbler?" I fired off to Dana.

"Wtf?" she responded only a minute later. "Why would you ask me that?"

After the last of the shower guests finally filed out three hours later, Marcia slipped into the kitchen to rinse plates, and I found myself in a rare moment alone with Michelle. I grabbed her hand and pulled her along with me toward the sofa, and when we sat down, I crossed my legs under me and faced her like we did when we were kids. She had launched back into discussion of wedding centerpieces when I surprised myself by blurting, "Michelle, how did you know?"

"Know I wanted peonies? Well, it wasn't going to be roses, was it?" She sniffed.

"I meant . . . wait, what's wrong with roses at a wedding?"

"You're not serious."

"What? Never mind. No, I mean, how did you know you wanted to marry Jake? You've been talking about it since college, but when did you *really know*?" Spending the day with her at the shower had finally made everything feel real: Michelle was really going to get married, and I was really going to stand up beside her. I wanted to understand what made her feel ready to bind her life to someone else's, while meanwhile I didn't even feel ready to commit to a commercial-free Hulu subscription. "And don't give me any of that 'I just know' bullshit."

She laughed. "But it sort of is the kind of thing you just know, Julie. You feel it. We can't all be as analytical as you."

"Okay, fine, so you always knew. When did you *decide?*"

"Well." She paused. "Maybe first right before we graduated, when he promised to do law school here because I wanted to stay near home. He was planning his future, see, and I knew I was in it. And then when Jen and Sylvie got married, and we went to their weddings together, I knew I wanted that for myself, too. For Jake and me, I mean."

I remembered that. Jake's decision to stay in Alabama for law school because of Michelle made me realize for the first time that their relationship was truly serious.

"I actually think Mark might be getting serious about us staying together, and I don't know how I feel about it," I told her, volunteering more than I had about our relationship in a long time. I hoped the admission would make it so that conversation could flow easily between us again, that we would finally feel as though we were standing on common ground. "He asked if I would move to Philadelphia if he goes to Penn for an MBA. I don't know if it's that I'm not sure about him, or if it's just that I don't see why things can't stay the way they are. But what if I try to move and then I change my mind about him—or he changes his mind about me? There's a lot of life left, Miche."

Michelle cocked her head quizzically. "Hon, you love Mark. Don't you?"

"I . . . yes?" Could it all be that simple? "He's a big part of my life."

"Then maybe you're overthinking it," Michelle said, appearing satisfied. "Y'all are a wonderful couple. And when it's the right time, I think you'll know."

"But what if there's never a right time?" Waiting for the "right time" was useful only to people who thought such a thing existed. I had never seen a reason to believe that any kind of fortune existed in life other than the luck you made for yourself.

She shrugged. "I just mean that someday you'll know. You know, that there's just more to life than, I don't know, trying new restaurants or making more money. Eventually you just want to be with the person—the family—who really loves you."

"Well, I think there's already more to my life than—" Michelle looked at me, brow arched in a manner that was hard to read but that looked more like a warning than an invitation. I steadied myself. "Never mind, I get it."

"You worry too much."

"No, it's just, I don't know. It's just weird being back home. Forget it." I rearranged my face into an expression that I hoped looked bright and unbothered, the one I used in photos. "Tell me more about those centerpieces."

"Are you sure?" Michelle asked in a moment of awareness. "I feel like I've bored you enough with those for one day. Want to do something else? Get a pedicure? I'll pay."

"You don't have to pay," I said, knowing at the same time that if she insisted at the register, I wouldn't fight her. Money meant different things in our lives, as much as I tried to pretend otherwise.

"But, yes, let's go. And you can talk to me about the flowers during. It's fine, I swear."

Michelle found my hand and squeezed it. "You're the *best* best friend in the world," she said.

Michelle spent the first ten minutes of the pedicure in a passive-aggressive text-message fight with Marcia over the font on the wedding invitations. When she was confident that she had won, she dropped her phone into her monogrammed Michael Kors tote and turned to face me with an expression that bordered on apologetic.

"Well, I won at least." She shrugged. "It's Darcy who's doing the invitations, anyway, so I didn't want her caught in between me and Mama. She's a calligrapher, you know," Michelle added, and I wasn't sure if I was supposed to be impressed.

"It's nice that she's doing it."

"Look, I know you think Darcy is a little over-the-top sometimes." Michelle looked at me levelly. "But when you're around her more often, she's a great friend, I swear."

That wasn't the way I remembered it from school—Darcy's contribution to the group mostly seemed to be starting gossip, like in the case of the "I Touch Myself" drama—but I didn't say anything. Michelle smiled at me expectantly, wondering if she had convinced me of Darcy's loyalty.

I smiled back, almost giggling, but it was really because the technician had started to pumice my feet. I had gotten a couple of pedicures in high school as part of my mom's well-meaning effort to have us bond through a girls' spa day, a strategy we abandoned after a few attempts. I didn't mind doing it with Michelle once in a while, but I had never liked them. I couldn't stop being ticklish any more than I could get used to someone else touching my feet. When Ritchie and Dana went I usually sat next to them in an unoccupied chair and sipped a coffee, saying I didn't want to spend the money. Which was partially true.

"You literally have the world's most ticklish feet," Michelle said when she heard me laugh. "I don't get how you don't like this."

"I don't get how you don't like *Westworld,* but here we are." I had tried to convince Michelle to stay home for a marathon of the HBO show, which I had already seen, but I would never give up trying to get her into it.

"It's just . . . too graphic."

"We'll always have *Gilmore Girls.*" Michelle and I had watched the entire series together, and we loved it down to the last sappy detail.

"True. Anyway"—she leaned toward me conspiratorially, resting both her forearms on the left armrest of her chair—"I do have something to tell you that's not about the wedding."

"Wait, let me guess. You've ordered that blender thing that Sylvie wouldn't stop talking about at the shower. A Vitamix."

"I already have one."

"Should've known. Hmm, you've finally decided to change your condo color scheme from coral accents to mint green?"

"You're just the worst," she said, laughing.

"I am. But seriously, you know I'm just jealous that you know how to pick a color scheme at all."

I had never cared much about interior design, but this envy was actually rooted in truth. After we moved to Alabama, my mom redecorated our house every few months on a whim. *Redecorating* is a loose term; she bought yards of cheap fabric at wholesale to fashion into "curtains"—bright electric yellow when she needed cheering up, near black when, inexplicably, she decided that too much light was getting in. The secondhand floral sofa always stayed, but new knickknacks were invited in every so often to deck the coffee table and the mantel over the faux fireplace. I had liked the safari phase (I kept the ceramic elephants, purchased at a garage sale and each missing part of its trunk), but I was sorely against her fifties revival effort. Fiestaware is heinous enough; knockoff Fiestaware is something else entirely.

Marcia redecorated somewhat differently. The Davis house changed every five or six years in keeping with the trends of the time, but the furniture was always a variation on cream—it had to feel "clean," Marcia said. A professional decorator was always consulted. And now, whether learned or inherited, Michelle had her mother's eye.

"Well, you always have me for décor advice," Michelle said. "Even if you never take my suggestions."

"Okay, really, tell me: What's the big nonwedding news?"

"I'm thinking about quitting my job. For real."

This didn't shock me. Michelle had been at the jewelry boutique for two years, and while it seemed like an ideal fit for her interests, I had always seen her working somewhere bigger. Her degree was in social media marketing—a modification, as she had started out at 'Bama declaring business until she backpedaled during her sophomore year, but it made sense; she was better with people than I could ever hope to be, and she could sell anyone on anything.

"Wow, Miche. If you're happy, that's great. What are you thinking about doing now?"

She looked at me, confused. "What do you mean?"

"I mean, do you have a new job lined up for when you leave? Or are you going to start looking?"

"No, Julie, I'm not—I'm not looking for another job. I'm going to focus on my Instagram and really getting a style blog going. What good is a social media degree if I can't use it on myself, right? Plus, we'll be so busy with the wedding, and then moving to the new house, and then who knows . . ."

"Oh," I said. "Oh."

I told myself to ask more questions. To be understanding. But anger bubbled up inside me, and I felt like I had to clench my teeth together to keep it from erupting out of me. To keep myself from lashing out with something I'd regret. *Must be nice not to have to work. Must be nice to have always had everything given to you.*

While that was my first childish thought, my bigger worry was that Michelle would regret this. She could do anything, couldn't she? She had been the only student to get a 5 on the AP calculus test our senior year. She'd been surprisingly fearless in science class, dissecting our frog when the stench of formaldehyde had made me nauseated. That didn't mean she had to be a surgeon or a mathematician or even anything at all, but could this possibly be the life she really wanted? Decorating the new house, issuing style tips on her fledgling blog, waiting for Jake to come home?

"Julie, say something." I hadn't realized I'd gone silent.

"Sorry, you surprised me." I swallowed. "Um, this is what you want?" I thought about things Michelle had said she wanted when we were growing up. The jewelry business, a big backyard for catching fireflies, to move to France. To have great adventures.

"It is. Look, it's nice getting a discount on bangles at the store, but I'm not doing anything so important there." Then she looked at me pointedly. "I know you might not understand because all y'all in New York define yourselves by your jobs or whatever"—she said *jobs* as though it was in quotation marks, like she doubted what we actually did all day—"but it keeps you so busy all the time we can hardly talk. So, for me, I'd much rather focus on seeing if I can work for myself, and taking care of the move, and I can always go back to something if I want to."

I was still irked by her comment about "jobs." "I'm *busy* because I'm working *two* jobs right now," I pointed out, resisting the opportunity to add that most of the money from the freelancing went directly toward traveling for her wedding events. "But I love working in publishing. Like, it's not just a hobby."

"Well, you shouldn't have to work a second job because your first one doesn't pay you enough to survive," she said matter-of-factly, flicking the page of a magazine.

This was actually a very good point. "Well, you're right about that, anyway."

"Hey, actually, have you ever thought about going to law school? Way better money. A lot of Jake's friends actually started out as English majors. There's a lot of reading in law!"

That stung. I knew Michelle was a little oblivious to what my work meant to me, but I hadn't expected her to say something like *that*. I would never go to law school. Still, I didn't want to fight with her about why, so I turned the conversation back to her news.

"Anyway, so, you're . . . happy?" I finally asked. "Taking the time off, I mean?"

"It's always been my plan at some point."

"Some point" had meant when she had kids, a realization that seemed to creep slowly up the back of my neck like a vine, making me shiver. I shook off the thought; I wasn't even close to ready to contemplate that. "But at this point?"

She nodded slowly, staring just past me, a faraway but contented look in her eyes. The shift was nearly imperceptible, but as a smile curled at the edge of her lips I could tell that she had dropped out of her default mode. She no longer seemed to be trying to sell the idea to me, and, paradoxically, it made me more willing to listen. "I *am* happy."

"Well then. I'm happy for you. I am. And I can't wait to see how the blog turns out."

"Hey, maybe you could feature on it," she said, cheerful and animated again. "I'm thinking more of a southern vibe, tailgate style and everything, but you could be our trendy New York guest!"

My hometown friends seemed to think that fashion sense was something you were gifted upon booking a one-way ticket to New York, like they handed it out along with luggage tags at JFK. "Oh, definitely. 'Ten Ways to Style Black Leggings with Black T-Shirts.'"

"Always stealing the spotlight," she teased, her voice warm and honeyed with affection, though I imagined we both silently knew that I never had.

I looked down at my toes, now glossed with a dark red. Michelle's were bright pink. "Your toes look good."

"Yours, too. Anyway, about the job—I just wanted to tell you. My schedule will be different. I'll be doing a lot with Mama, too, volunteering and starting Junior League. But I'll probably have more time to visit you."

"That'll be nice," I said automatically. Would it? Now that we were seeing each other more often for wedding planning, a part of me missed the relative peace of our annual Christmas visit and biweekly phone calls. I remembered a time many years ago when it had been easiest to be with Michelle alone; outsiders were intruders, breaking the spell that existed between us. Resentment—anger, even—would coil tightly in my stomach like a snake when someone walked into a room where the two of us sat alone in rapt conversation. *Leave,* I would practically hiss. *Leave us alone.*

Now I was desperate for someone else to walk in and break the silence.

"So. Random question game—go," I said, a desperate bid for a new subject.

Michelle and I had always played this game growing up. The premise was simple: Ask the first question that came into your head, and the other person had to answer as fast as possible. The question could be silly—"Do you eat mac 'n' cheese with a spoon or a fork?"—or deep, like "What's your biggest fear in life?" In the past, it had prompted some of the biggest laughs Michelle and I had ever shared, and also some of the most serious talks. Whatever the questions, it made me feel like we were on the same wavelength. I didn't know how else to grasp that now.

"Okay, um. Johnny Depp or Brad Pitt?" she asked.

"Depp, obviously."

"No way, Brad. Your turn."

"Day at the beach or day in the mountains?"

"Are you seriously asking if I would go hiking? Pass."

I started laughing. "So . . . beach?"

"The random question game is boring if the answer is obvious, hon."

"Okay, fine. Your turn."

"Top three things you'd take to a desert island."

"Duh," I said. "Sunscreen, water, and a book. A bag of books, if that counts."

"Always too practical." She shook her head. "It's supposed to be fun. Assume the necessities are there."

"Come on, what would you take?" I kicked off the salon flip-flops and got ready to stand up.

"A cooler of wine and Skinnygirl margaritas, a phone with unlimited battery." She paused. "And you."

CHAPTER 12

After landing at JFK on Saturday night—Michelle had protested my leaving a night early, but it cost $150 more to fly back on Sunday—I headed directly to Mark's apartment. I found him exactly where I expected: on the couch watching *SportsCenter* and drinking a glass of scotch. Somewhere around our unofficial one-year anniversary, I started finding myself able to intuit his movements, his reactions, his text-message responses. On good days, I found this to be a sign of intimacy, something that I had never truly captured with anyone other than Michelle. Sometimes it seemed like I had the ability to *hear* a thought enter his head, as clearly as a door squeaking open at the hinges. Other times, I worried it was a sign of boredom.

I dropped my suitcase by the door and walked over to join Mark on the couch, kissing him on the cheek before grabbing a glass for myself and then curling up on his chest under the blanket.

"So," he asked, turning down the volume on the TV. "How was it?"

I raised my eyebrows at him and sipped my scotch silently. I wrinkled my nose; too bitter.

"That bad, huh?"

"The scotch? Yes. The shower? It was beautiful, except when I felt like a total outcast. Also, Michelle is quitting her job. Permanently, apparently."

"Well, good for her if that's what she wants to do?" Mark had a habit of framing his opinions as questions when he wasn't sure I would agree with him.

I shook my head. "I just don't understand how she's so *sure* it's the right thing to do. That's a huge decision."

That was something I had never found the right words to explain. What Michelle wanted no longer made sense to me the way it had when we were younger, but at least I could see she knew exactly what it was she wanted. I would have given anything for the certainty I had heard in her voice when she turned to me at the nail salon and said, "I *am* happy." I had so much *want*, I sometimes felt, and I needed a receptacle to place it in. Something big enough to hold it. I had no trouble seeing what was in the negative space. I didn't want to get married at twenty-five. I didn't want to quit my job. I definitely didn't want to move back to Langham. But I still couldn't see my bigger picture.

"Anyway, I have to go back home again pretty soon, for Christmas," I reminded Mark. By Michelle's wedding, I would have spent more time in Alabama than I had in any year since graduating high school.

"You're sure it's cool that I don't come with?" Mark looked forward to his hometown Christmas traditions—high school reunion night at the local bar on December 23, church on Christmas Eve, bundling up for a long walk through the snow after presents had been opened on Christmas—but he had charitably offered to spend a couple of days in Alabama this year so long as he could be back with his family before Christmas morning. But his being there wouldn't make it any better, and I didn't need to ruin both our Christmases.

"Yeah, it's fine. I'll manage."

"Hey, I have an idea," Mark said, putting his hand on my knee. "Let's go out. I've been studying for the GMAT all day."

I didn't want to talk the Michelle situation to death any more than he wanted to keep thinking about the GMAT. "That's actually a great idea," I agreed.

I had taken Mark's suggestion to go out to mean that he wanted the two of us to go to dinner or out to a bar. What he actually meant was that he wanted to assemble "the guys" and get bottle service at a club.

He was on the phone with someone he kept calling "J-Dog" when I came out of the bathroom. He held his hand over the receiver and whispered that I should invite Dana and Ritchie.

Screw it, then, I thought. *We're all going out.*

At the risk of sounding boring, I had never loved the bottle service club scene. Not when Ritchie and Dana surprised me with a trip into the city for my twenty-first birthday, and not when we had the one wild, illegal-substance-fueled night after Dana took the bar exam. (Okay, fine, I liked it a little bit that time.) But clubs mostly seemed like they were designed for the Michelles and Danas of the world: those who looked model-attractive enough in spandex dresses to make people fake-laugh at their inaudible jokes over the sound of the DJ's throbbing bass. I preferred a quieter dive bar with a separate back room for dancing to nineties throwbacks. After a weekend of contemplating cobbler recipes and ogling silicone kitchenware, though, I decided I could make an exception.

Once we had pulled together a big enough group, everyone met up at Josh's West Village studio, cramming into the all-stainless-steel kitchen to take their turn at shots from an ice-covered Belvedere bottle. Like college, but with sleeker appliances and pricier spirits.

"So, your friend Ritchie . . . what's her deal?" Mark's friend Dan whispered in my ear as we drank, fiddling with the top of his pastel-colored button-down with one hand and pointing tipsily at Ritchie with the other.

"Ask her yourself," I responded, resisting the urge to roll my eyes. I didn't actively dislike any of Mark's friends, but in groups they always came off to me as juvenile—financiers who would drop excessive amounts of money on bottle service and still not be able to work up the nerve to hold an in-depth conversation with a woman until they were wasted. Dan held up his hands and backed away, a "who pissed her off?" expression on his face.

Ritchie and Dana and I moved into the living room to finish a last drink before the two-block walk to the club on Fourteenth Street.

"Mark's friends are idiots," Dana said in a matter-of-fact tone. "But, damn it, Josh is hot."

"Go for it, then. We're only young once."

"Does Mark have *any* friends who aren't . . . I don't know, frat dudes?" Ritchie asked, wrinkling her nose as Dan walked into the room and shotgunned a beer in our sightline, clearly for her benefit.

I wondered what Michelle and Jake did with their "couple friends" on Saturday nights. She once mentioned that they had game nights with Sylvie and her husband—a fate that seemed even less appealing than going to a nightclub filled with underage Instagram models. Surely there had to be a middle ground between playing Scrabble in your pajamas and dancing on tables to Diplo.

"He has a few older friends he's close with who are married, actually," I told her. "They just never go out anymore."

I hated the stereotype that couples got seriously involved or got married and just stopped seeing their friends; existing in that bubble struck me as both boring and exhausting. Part of that must have been what Mark and I were subconsciously fighting against.

"Lame," Dana yelled. "Unless they also work a hundred hours a week, and then they're forgiven. Wait, I think I'm drunk."

"Then I think it's time to go." I pulled her to her feet.

The club had the same energy as the apartment preparty, but with both the volume and the temperature completely amped up. The dark room throbbed not just with the bass, but with a tangible humidity seemingly made up of the stickiness of spilled drinks, fragmented drunken conversations, sweat, and the pungent Drakkar Noir cologne of the man at the neighboring table. It hung so heavy in the air I thought I could taste it. Dana, Ritchie, and I stuck to the far side of the table, where things smelled marginally better, attempting to dance standing on the banquette seat until our heels got the better of us. Mark and friends mixed drinks and passed their bottles around, until Dan finally got up the nerve to come over and talk to Ritchie again.

"So," he yelled over the pounding electric beat. "What do you do?"

Ritchie drunkenly held a finger up to his mouth, shushing him. Then she threw her arms over his shoulders. He grinned and they started to dance. Dana and I exchanged a look, and she shook her head, laughing. Seeing that Ritchie and Dan had paired off, Mark swapped places with Josh and slid his arm around my waist. It was a nice gesture, but the club remained too sweaty for it to actually feel pleasant.

"Hey, hot stuff." He kissed my ear.

"Hey yourself. Having fun?"

"Hell yeah. Just not as much as those two." He jabbed a finger in the direction of Ritchie and Dan, who were now making out.

"Classic." I checked my phone—1:52 A.M. I had been ready to leave for a full hour. "You okay with getting out of here kind of soon?"

Disappointment flashed over Mark's face for an instant, but then he squeezed me tighter. "Actually, yeah. I can think of something I'd rather do than drink more with these fools." He winked at me.

I had something I would rather do than drink more, too: sleep. I wanted to sleep off the weekend and bury my conversation with Michelle somewhere in the past that would make me stop thinking about it. I also wanted to take a shower, but I forced myself to smile back at Mark because I did want him, too. "Then let's get out of here." I grabbed his hand.

When we got home, I ran up the stairs barefoot with my heels in my hand. Inside the apartment, we collapsed on the bed. Mark pressed his nose and forehead drunkenly against mine.

"I missed you this weekend. And I missed this . . . ," he trailed off, pulling away to lift my shirt over my head. My bra followed, and I felt the cool air on my skin more strongly than his lips kissing down my chest. I had missed him. But after the long night at the club, my body was stubbornly refusing to respond, and I stared across the room at the dresser and then the mirror above it, watching us.

My thoughts drifted in the space of the few moments that Mark was kissing me in a teasing way, attempting to whip me into a state of frenzy to match his own. Sometimes I loved this, and sometimes I very definitely did not.

The first time we slept together was that first drunken night at BBar, when the successive strawberry margaritas tipped me over the edge and had me ripping apart his button-down and climbing on top of him with an enthusiasm that surprised me. It didn't surprise me because the experience was new to me—far from it—but because I hadn't felt any passion for him at all prior to that moment.

Not earlier in the night at the bar, and not even when we arrived back at his apartment. He was very attractive, but I was not attracted *to* him, that crucial and elusive distinction. But there, in the blurred darkness of his apartment, so grown up contrasted with my own sublet with roommates, I felt an intensity I couldn't have predicted. Some of it had to do with him, the night of dancing, his whispers in my ear that made me wonder if maybe he could be right for me after all. But a lot of it, if I am honest, was about a feeling that I had something to prove.

What was it exactly? A need to show myself that I was over the men (boys, really) who came before him? The desire to prove that I could build a life far from who I had been, far from college, even farther from the tiny town that had once known everything about me? Was there something about him in particular that would help me on the journey to who I wanted to become? Or maybe he was just a vehicle for asserting myself, attractive because he had been the person interested in me at that crucial moment. It may have been any of those reasons or all of them, but once the (quite good) sex had finished, I felt such an unusual sense of *accomplishment.* But then, because things are always complicated, he leaned over and nuzzled my ear as he had earlier in the night, so clearly happy, and I felt that first small tinge of something else, too. Real feeling.

Sex still felt like it was about something to prove, I realized, though that something had drastically changed shape over time. Nowadays, it seemed like it was one part for pleasure and one part to show myself (ourselves?) that everything was still fun, light, exciting, that nothing was missing. It was that way from time to time with all longer-term couples, wasn't it? Yes, I decided. However miraculous or ordinary a relationship's beginnings, we all seem to end up in about the same place. A regression to the mean, of sorts, I told myself, though it bears noting that I barely passed statistics freshman year.

"Babe? You with me? You okay?" Mark paused and looked up.

I was not. "Mm-hm. Sorry, I'm a little drunk. Just in my head, that's all." I felt lost in my head a lot lately.

He nodded. "Is this about seeing your mom?"

"Sort of."

"Michelle?"

"I'm done talking about all of that right now," I said, but in that moment the fact that he cared at all made the difference. "Do-over? Start again?"

"Yes," he said, kissing me again. "And no talking necessary."

I kissed him back and relaxed into the promise.

CHAPTER 13

I hadn't been behind the wheel of a car in years, I realized, watching the trees fly past as we sped up the Merritt Parkway. It seemed strange now that half of my adolescence had taken place in cars, Michelle whipping her convertible around the sharp edges of winding back roads with me riding shotgun, or me making out with Trent Worthington in his pickup truck out by the dead end of his street. Now, if I got in a car at all, it was to send e-mails from the back seat of an Uber on the way to a meeting or to sit beside Mark on the way to visit his family, like now. Mark had rented a car and we were on our way up to his parents' house in Connecticut.

Mark's family had been the easy choice for Thanksgiving, even though I wondered about what signal I was sending by spending the holidays with him. When he graciously offered, knowing I would be staying in New York anyway, I accepted. I had spent more than enough time and money flying down south already, and my mom had been easily placated when I told her I would see her at Christmas and again at the wedding. Even when I had lived at home, our Thanksgivings had amounted to picking up a rotisserie chicken and watching Hallmark movies on TV until I inevitably went over to Michelle's for a second dinner. We were not a family of many traditions.

As Mark turned off the highway, the roads narrowed and the houses came into view. The now-bare trees stood sentry at the end of every driveway, which were long enough to be streets of their own. When I was growing up, Michelle's Victorian-style house was the biggest I had ever seen, but it wouldn't stand out in Mark's Greenwich neighborhood. We pulled up in front of the white colonial and found three cars in the drive, meaning that Mark's brother and his wife had already arrived.

"Get ready to hear a lot about Boston," Mark warned me as we walked up the steps to the front door. "Chris and Viv have been there for five months now and they have *a lot* of feelings about it."

Mark's brother had defied the Wharton family tradition and ended up at Harvard Business School. It was hard for me to envision this situation causing a family controversy, but apparently it had. Viv had relocated from Philadelphia with him, and apparently Boston had been an adjustment.

"Happy Thanksgiving," the Greenwoods chorused as we swung open the door. I noticed that they were dressed up in the New England hybrid style of holiday and business casual—skirts and cashmere cardigans. The effect looked neither as formal as holidays at Michelle's nor as casual as my mom and me eating turkey sandwiches in our sweats; I was glad I had asked Mark what to wear. My camel-colored crewneck sweater and midi-skirt blended in well. His mom hugged me and led me into the kitchen by the hand right away, warm and friendly, as Mark and Chris fell in behind us and immediately started talking about Chris' Harvard classes.

I sidled up next to his mom at the stove, and she asked me about my work and if any interesting books had come across my desk lately. She told me she had recently read a new book by Jojo Moyes and asked me if I had read it. It had been a popular book club pick for the last year or so, but I hadn't read it. Since my tastes outside work often ran more toward nonfiction, I asked her if she had heard about *Stray*, the last memoir I had finished. She hadn't, which effectively stalled the books conversation, though she didn't seem to mind. Mark's dad came up behind us and broke the silence, playfully aiming to steal a taste of the gravy. Everyone seemed sweet in a Norman Rockwell–esque way, complete with the fireplace and the black Lab sleeping on the floor. I didn't know if I felt quite in step with Mark's family, but I liked them and appreciated their particular brand of familial comfort. Anyway, I was used to being the adopted member of someone else's family.

I watched Mark's mom weave her way around Viv, leaning over her shoulder to add a pinch of pepper to the gravy or stir the green beans, the two of them moving in tandem like dance partners. They had an easy familiarity, the sort of thing that takes years—if not decades—to quietly develop. I wondered if I might ever feel that with anyone new ever again; thinking about the years of confidences, compromises, and adjustments that went into that sort of belonging seemed both enviable and exhausting.

I watched the back of Gloria's head as she continued bustling around the kitchen. Her blond hair was cut into a severe and chic bob, all Anna Wintour, rather than the gravity-defying dos favored by most of the older women I knew in Alabama. But otherwise, from behind, she and Marcia might have been twins: They shared that same stature—and the same gait, which somehow managed to be spritely and authoritative at the same time. These women walked with declarative purpose, even when the only place they had to be was in front of a stove.

My mom wore her hair long and usually loose, and Michelle and Marcia were the ones who taught me how to tease my hair when they realized that I had no idea how to style anything other than a ponytail. I pictured the two of them then in the sprawling country kitchen of the Davis house, where they probably were at that exact moment, preparing their own Thanksgiving dinner. The house would smell like pecan pie, and Michelle's cousins would be playing increasingly rowdy games of touch football on the lawn, and Marcia would holler her classic line, "Y'all better get in here and help," to anyone unlucky or inexperienced enough to wander near the entrance to the kitchen. I preferred pumpkin pie to pecan and I hated being forced into the ritual of touch football, but I still wished for a split second that I could be back in Langham after all. Which home was more mine? Did I belong in either?

I thought that maybe I should step into the other room and call Michelle, or at least send a text, but something stopped me. Instead, I left my phone in my pocket and just went to stand next to Gloria at the stove as the gravy bubbled in front of us.

"Almost ready." She smiled at me. "And, Jules, we're so glad you could make it this year."

"Me, too," I said, and I felt fairly confident that I meant it.

After dinner, we sat in front of the fire, Mark's parents on the sofa, Chris and Viv in the adjoining settee, and Mark and me on the thick Oriental rug that stretched in front of the fireplace, a flannel blanket wrapped around our shoulders. We had one mug of spiked hot chocolate that we kept passing between us, taking too-hot sips and whispering to each other, and for one spark of a moment I forgot all the minutiae of the day, and I just smiled.

"I like being home with you," Mark said quietly.

I turned toward him, accidently knocking his head with mine. "Sorry." I giggled, the schnapps from the hot chocolate suddenly warm in my veins. "I like being here, too."

Mark said something quickly, too quietly for me to understand. "What?"

"I, uh"—he took another quick sip, then looked back at me— "I said, move in with me. Sorry, I meant it as a question. Would you maybe want to move in? With me? When your lease is up."

I inhaled sharply. "Wow," I whispered, shocked. "Wow."

"Good wow or bad wow?"

I didn't know. Move in together? I had no idea Mark thought we were there yet. All I kept at his apartment was a pair of pajama shorts and a toothbrush.

Michelle accused me of lying when I told her I didn't really think about "the future" with Mark after more than a year together, but it was the truth; I wanted things to be the way they were now. Of course I thought about how nice it would be to finally leave the tiny corner of the East Williamsburg apartment, but I wanted to leave it on my own terms, to move into a nicer place because I had gotten a raise, or actually sold a piece of writing. I thought about the magnitude of what he was asking, what it might change for us. If he really did go to business school, would he expect me to move for him like Viv had done for Chris? I tried to imagine Mark making coffee for us every morning, to envision what it would be like to open the door and see him sitting on the sofa when I came home from a long day at work. Could I picture it? I stared into the roaring fire, trying to recapture the way I had felt just moments before, but the spell had been broken.

"Can we talk about it when we get home?" I asked quietly after a long pause. "It's great; it's wonderful. It's just, you know, uh, a lot to process." *Way to be eloquent.*

"Sure," he said, planting a kiss on top of my head. "Don't worry, I was just thinking out loud."

I felt a wave of nausea rising, but I said nothing, just leaned back against his shoulder as the fire started to crackle and collapse in on itself. "I think I'm just tired," I told him. "I'm ready to go to bed whenever you are."

We hadn't said anything more about the idea of moving in together by the time Mark flew back to Omaha on the Sunday after Thanksgiving. I appreciated that he seemed to be giving me time to figure out what I wanted, or maybe it simply meant that his broach of the topic meant a desire, a whim said out loud in the heat of a lovely moment, and not a mandate. That didn't leave me any closer to knowing what I wanted. Why did I suddenly seem to not be in possession of any desires at all?

It wasn't that I *didn't* ever want to live with Mark, necessarily. I just felt a complete absence of any kind of urge to. And believe me, I knew what it felt like to need to do something. When I moved to New York with sixteen hundred dollars, I did it because I felt breathless and compelled, like someone had tied a rope around my neck and pulled me all two-hundred-plus miles from Ithaca. The move wasn't a choice. It was a fact, like something that had always been a part of me and I had somehow misplaced it. When I stumbled across it again, I felt nothing but the purest recognition, and I had been in pursuit of that feeling ever since.

But instead of doing any kind of work to interrogate my relationship, or to think about how I could channel my desire toward my writing or my work, I did what any member of my generation would do: I started scrolling through Instagram.

I watched other people's lives flash in front of me. I saw my freshman-year floormate, Erika Cao, posing on a beach in Thailand on a break from running her successful eco-friendly beauty start-up, and I thought, *Hey, I could go to Thailand! I'll look up cheap flights for next winter!* But then a new thought came less than a second later, metaphorically mowing down the first as my brain yelled, *You'll never run a start-up! And for the record, you're on the verge of getting too old to ever be named one of the* Forbes *30 Under 30, too.*

I sighed and kept scrolling. I flipped quickly past photos of gender-reveal parties and baby photos posted by high school class-mates. I would take a cute picture of a puppy over a newborn photo shoot any day.

Then I came across a picture from Michelle's account. It showed her and Jake posing on the veranda of her parents' house, her left hand stretched out in front of her with the engagement ring clearly in focus. She had captioned it, "Last Thanksgiving until we're husband and wife! I'm so thankful for this man. Four-month countdown 'til #HappilyEverOster!"

If I were really ever going to move in with Mark, I wondered, should that mean I could imagine saying "so thankful for this man" without cringing?

I shook my head. Semantics aside, I needed more time. Instead of making any kind of decision, I begrudgingly liked Michelle's photo, closed out of Instagram, and started searching for a flight back to Birmingham in three weeks' time for Christmas.

CHAPTER 14

The week before I was scheduled to fly back to Alabama, I opened my calendar to slot in drinks with Dana. Helping Michelle stay calm through wedding dress alterations, freelancing, and working on my own writing had dominated my sparse spare time, and I hadn't seen her since the night at the club. She promised "conversation topics that have nothing to do with law, I swear." But as I created a calendar event in between a meeting about a book cover reveal and my Friday flight to Alabama, I noticed something missing.

The calendar date informed me that it was time to "refill BC," meaning birth control. That meant that I should have gotten my period the week before, which I definitely did not. *It's normal to miss a period sometimes,* I reasoned.

You never have before, a different voice argued back.

I shook my head as if that could physically dislodge the thought. No, I would give it another few days, remember to pick up my birth control, and push it out of my mind. Everything was fine. How many times had I watched female friends in college freak out over a period that was a day or two late? They were all false alarms. Our sophomore year, Ritchie had taken a pregnancy test in the dorm bathroom and she hadn't even had sex in the previous month.

You have, though.

I went back to answering e-mails, and I sent a Gchat to Dana confirming that we were still on for drinks. She gave me the thumbs-up, and I dove back into the catalog copy in front of me.

We met up that night at our favorite East Village wine bar. The stools were splintered and uncomfortable, but the happy hour special ran until eight P.M., and the bartender always gave us a glass for free if we lingered long enough. I was already knee-deep in glass number two by the time Dana arrived, and it had still done nothing to quell my nerves. She walked in, took a seat next to me at the bar, and kissed me on the check without hanging up her phone.

"You're getting billed for this, you know. And I'm more expensive than your therapist," I heard her snap before signing off. She dropped her phone in her bag and pivoted toward me. "Jules, hi. I'm sorry. You wouldn't believe this fucking woman. You know what? I'm not going to talk about it. How are you?"

"I'm okay," I began, trying to sound normal. *Stick to normal topics.* "I've been trying to write some more essays, mostly about growing up in Langham. All garbage, obviously—I should stick to line edits for authors who know what they're doing." I took another sip of wine. "Anyway, how was your date last night? Is that the news?"

Dana lived all her life with the same intensity and borderline vicious nature with which she approached her work; dates rarely passed muster.

"Yeah. Well, I shouldn't have gone; he wasn't worth it," she said, waving to the bartender to order a glass of cabernet. "Who has time to do these things anyway? I thought dating in New York would be all *Sex in the* fucking *City*, but I barely even have time to get one drink. By the way, I'm sorry, I have to go back to the office after this." She paused. "Oh, I do have one funny story from the date. He called me Diana."

"That's . . . close?"

"Yeah, but when I corrected him, he could have just said, 'Oh, I'm sorry.' Instead, he actually *tells* me that he had a Tinder date with a Diana last week and that's why he messed up. He legitimately started telling the story of the whole date, what she looked like, the whole thing. And then he noticed I looked pissed, and he tried to recover by—"

"I think I might be pregnant." *Tactful.*

Dana spat her first sip of wine back into her glass. "What the fuck? You think or you know?"

"Just think," I hissed, lowering my voice. The bartender had obviously heard. He was looking down and polishing a glass a little too intensely, flicking his eyes toward us every few seconds. "No, I'm sure I'm not. I don't know what's wrong with me lately. I'm probably just freaking out because Mark asked me to think about moving in together when my lease is up, and I still don't want to talk about it. Maybe this is just, like, a manifestation of my fear of commitment?"

"Mark asked you to move in with him?" She set her glass down hard, the wine sloshing against the rim as I stared at her. "What? When?"

"At Thanksgiving. I don't think it was serious." I conjured the scene in my mind once again, remembering the roaring fire, the haze of a heavy buzz from the schnapps. Mark still hadn't brought up the subject in the last two weeks, either, so maybe it really had been only a drunken whim, something simply said in the moment and then forgotten, as surreal to him as it was to me.

"You guys aren't, like, move-in-together serious, right? Or are you?"

"Well, we were drinking when he said it. Are you freaking out? Don't freak out."

"Well, you don't need to freak out, either. You are obviously not pregnant. You're on birth control. Right?"

"Yes." I didn't tell her I had been frantically scrolling through my mental backlogs, trying to figure out if I had missed a pill. I had been taking them for seven years, and I was generally meticulous, but I thought I recalled a missed day—or was it two?—during an especially hectic week when Mark had been out of town. Was that last month? This month?

"Yeah, you're not pregnant. Remember when Ritchie used to think she was pregnant every single month? Then she'd get her period, like, an hour later."

"I didn't get it this month."

"That happens sometimes? With the pill? Anyway, take a test if you're so nervous."

"Yeah, I will. I'll get one after this. It can't hurt, right? I'll take it soon if I'm still feeling this insane about it."

"Right. Okay, now tell me about the rest of your life," she said, checking her watch. "I have twenty minutes."

After one more hasty glass of wine, we crossed the street to Duane Reade. I felt woozy, balancing on the tightrope between tipsy and drunk. Dana pulled me by the hand to the family-planning section of the store.

"These ones are only twelve ninety-nine." She gestured to a generic-brand pregnancy test.

"I don't know that this is really the time to economize, especially after we just spent forty dollars on wine." I scanned the shelves from the top down, overwhelmed by both the selection and the painful fluorescent lighting. "I had no idea there were this many kinds."

Dana wrinkled her brow. "Haven't you ever taken one before?"

"No. Literally never." I had watched friends deal with pregnancy scares, usually needlessly. As Dana had pointed out, Ritchie honestly did think she was pregnant every time she had so much as a dance-floor make-out. Still, I never thought about it happening to me. I swore a silent oath that I would finally get an IUD, if I could just *not* be pregnant this time.

"Here, take this one." Dana reached for a First Response box and knocked over five others in the process. "Shit."

"Oh my God, I'm drunk in the pregnancy test aisle," I moaned. "This is a mess."

Dana laughed.

"Take this seriously." I glared at her, and she grabbed my hand as we walked to the register.

"Jules," she whispered into my ear, suddenly solemn. "This is going to be fine. No matter what, you know?"

It didn't really make sense, since I could think of about a million ways this could not be fine. But still, as she said it, I somehow knew that it would be.

I avoided taking the test until I was in the bathroom of the Birmingham airport.

At first, my rationale for waiting was to give my period a few more days to show up. I had been sure that it would. When I had no such luck, I decided I couldn't bear to investigate the issue until I had stepped outside the normal sphere of my life. This didn't make any sense, either, obviously, and yet here I was, pulling the First Response pregnancy test box out of my suitcase and opening it furtively in the airport bathroom stall, as coolly removed as if I didn't know myself at all.

When it was over, I laid the stick carefully on the floor between my foot and my suitcase, setting my iPhone alarm to two minutes. One accurate cliché of the pregnancy test experience: It was the longest two minutes of my life. Then the alarm finally went off, and I forced myself to bend my head down to the black-and-white tile to look. This would all amount to nothing, surely.

But then there they were: two unmistakable lines. Parallel, like the path I had wanted my life to take and the road I was now on.

For some reason, in all the happy stories I'd heard of women recounting their pregnancy tests, they had always called the second line "faint." ("It was there, but it was faint, so I didn't want to get my hopes up that I was really pregnant! I took three more tests, can you imagine?") That was my first thought. There was nothing faint about that line. I felt an aching sense of shock that seemed to permeate my bones, yes, but no disbelief. This was real and definite. I placed my hand on my stomach absentmindedly.

My second thought was, *Oh shit*.

I tried to draw in a deep breath, but suddenly I couldn't inhale properly. It felt like getting the wind knocked out of me, but without the blunt-force trauma. I had no idea what to do. Not about the pregnancy, specifically. I knew my options, and they'd been lingering quietly in the back of my mind since the moment I realized I'd missed my period. It was more that I didn't know what to do right that moment. Throw the damn test away, get out of the airport, and call my ob-gyn later? Or should I call someone I really knew? Did I want to tell anyone at all? Calling Mark when he was at home with his family seemed impossible, but I would have to tell him at some point. Wouldn't I? Of course I would. What was wrong with me? My ears buzzed, and the pocket of silence around me in the airport bathroom seemed oppressive. I bent my head down between my knees, trying again in vain to breathe.

I had only ever imagined getting pregnant in one context: as a stupid seventeen-year-old back when I first had sex and had yet to go on the pill. After that, I foolishly thought I was safe. And now here I was, after all those years of birth control taken, and somehow it still had happened. How?

At last, a point of clarity emerged. I had to get out of the bathroom. I wrapped the test in a paper towel before I threw it away, as if I had to hide it from someone, and then I walked out to the curb to grab a cab to my mom's house. I finally opted to call my ob-gyn discreetly from the back seat as the cab bounced and lurched down I-20, and I managed to secure an appointment in a canceled slot for a week later. I could handle this.

I watched as the backdrop to my youth flashed by out the window, feeling a first wave of nausea rising as I caught sight of an old TRUMP/PENCE 2020 sign still on display near the exit ramp. The city of Birmingham itself was politically and racially diverse—I belabored this point to the New Yorkers who made only stereotyped comments—but I knew the deep divide that ran through the city, the beliefs and prejudices that snaked through the surrounding rural communities like tributaries. There was a reason that politics had become an unspoken matter between me and the women I had grown up with.

I remembered Michelle making a comment a few years back, around the time of the controversy over the transgender bathroom bill in North Carolina. She said that she was "all for equality," but that still didn't mean she wanted to see a penis in the bathroom. At the time, I shrugged the comment off.

Now I felt ashamed for that, for my inability to ask questions, for my fear of interrogating our beliefs and finding out how different they really were. Now it seemed all too late. I forced myself to drop the thought, and, hands shaking, I texted Michelle simply that I had landed and that I could "of course" make it to her annual cookie-decorating party on Christmas Eve. I had no idea how I would act once I got there, but trying to maintain a sense of normalcy seemed like the only way I would keep myself from falling apart.

My mom wasn't home when the cab deposited me in her driveway, which meant that I might get at least one small moment of the respite I sorely needed. I found the key hidden in its typical spot and hauled my suitcase inside, hands still trembling. As promised, the Christmas tree was up in the cramped living room, decked with colored lights and crooked tinsel. My mom insisted on buying a real tree every year, a tradition I had always liked more than I let on, even though she almost always forgot to water it. I deposited my suitcase on the side of the futon that wasn't edged up against the branches, and I went to the kitchen to grab a pitcher of water for the dry fir. Still breathing shallowly, I poured a glass for myself, too, and chugged it down.

I found a note on the faux-marble countertop next to the sink. "Julie: Welcome back! Date tonight—Jeff! Probably out late. See you tomorrow?" I set the note down and leaned against the counter, closing my eyes. *'See you tomorrow.'* *Of course.* I wanted to see her immediately and to never see her again, in equal measure.

I looked at the note one more time. "Love you," she had signed it. Maybe she did—I knew she did—but the childish part inside me wondered what it all amounted to. I already knew I wouldn't tell her what I was going through. And anyway, what kind of love did I really have to offer her in return?

It was funny. I remembered that, growing up, Marcia used to tell Michelle and me that loving someone without the hope or prospect that they would ever change was the *only* way to truly love someone. If you didn't love their flaws and shortcomings, then you only loved the person you wanted them to someday become, which was just a way of saying you only loved things and people that served you. Marcia had no patience for that kind of behavior, which she perceived as more selfish than the thoughtless offenses our loved ones often perpetrated. *Loving someone without the hope or promise of change is the only way to love someone.* It was proving harder than ever to love shortcomings, I thought, both in others and in myself.

I lay down on the futon and stretched out, my legs nestled under the branches of the Christmas tree that overlapped the edge. Then again, I thought, Marcia had also always told me that motherhood was the highest calling in life for a woman—the "greatest love in the world," she had said—so maybe she wasn't my best resource right now after all.

I knew it right then, in that moment that saw me as completely exhausted and spent as I had ever been: There was no way I could stay pregnant. There was no way that I could have a baby. Not right now, and not in nine months. I said it out loud to myself, and in hearing my own voice, I knew it was true. It was the climax of what I had begun to realize back in the drugstore with Dana. Even better, I knew that when I told Dana what I had decided, she would comfort me, would assure me that my decision made perfect sense. She would say that, in my place, she would do the exact same thing.

Sometime after that, curled up in the fetal position under an afghan from my childhood and next to the sweet smell of pine, I fell asleep.

CHAPTER 15

The Davis house at the holidays was a sight to behold. Rich decked the trellis with hundreds of petite icicle lights, and inside, Marcia wrapped the banister in a garland from top to bottom, hanging ornaments from the boughs to render it essentially an aesthetic extension of the nearby fourteen-foot tree that presided over the living room. A sprawling nativity scene covered the mantel.

"Sugar," Marcia greeted me first in the foyer, as per tradition. "Merry Christmas. Michelle is in the kitchen."

"I knew she would be." Michelle had been hosting her Christmas Eve cookie-decorating party at her parents' house for nearly two decades, and it always started in the kitchen and then progressed to the glass-enclosed sunroom for drinks and stargazing. I found her hovering over a tray of gingerbread men, with a chef's tube of icing in her hand and Jake standing next to her with a proprietary hand on her back.

"Jake," I said, surprised, as I approached them. "I didn't think you'd be here until tomorrow."

He bent down to give me a dry kiss on the cheek, keeping his hand on Michelle. "Well, my lovely fiancée told me I had avoided this tradition for too many years. I promised to try it out at least once."

Michelle finally set down her tube of icing and turned around. "Next year you can go back to cigars in the library with Dad, I promise. I just wanted to show you off a little. And, Julie, hon, hi," she said, looking a bit sheepish. "I got so wrapped up in frosting that I didn't even hear you come in."

The three of us stood there looking at one another for a moment while no one said anything. I felt the secret I wasn't telling them as though it were physically present in the room with us, hanging in the air like a dense fog. I just stared at Michelle as she delicately smoothed her apron front, and noticed that it was embroidered with her new monogram, the *O* for *Oster* in place of the familiar *D*. The apron lay flat against her stomach, and for a moment I had the irrational thought that I might look pregnant somehow, that Michelle would somehow be able to see it, even though that was impossible. "Nice apron," I said finally.

"Early surprise Christmas present from Jake."

"Nice." I nodded approvingly, while realizing that if a man ever bought me an apron as a Christmas gift, our relationship would be over by New Year's. "Wow, I can't believe we've been doing this since we were eight." These days, when I didn't know what to say to Michelle, our shared past was a haven we could always retreat to.

"Ever since my mama thought we were old enough to be trusted with frosting. Though *some* of us probably still shouldn't be." She shot a flirtatious glance at Jake.

He held up his hands. "Just here to observe. I leave the baking to the ladies."

I tried not to roll my eyes. "Well, Michelle is the only real pastry chef out of all of us."

"I know. That's why I'm marrying her, right?" Jake playfully slapped Michelle on the butt and I looked away immediately. Maybe it was time to start drinking.

I crossed over to Michelle's other side and sidled up next to her at the island. I asked what I could do to help.

"Everyone should be here soon. I don't know what's keeping them," she said, referencing the traditional crew of Rebecca, Ellen, and Darcy with the slightest note of annoyance in her voice. "Let's just move all the cookies off the oven trays and onto platters, so y'all can pick what you'd like to decorate."

I busied myself with the simple task of plating cookies by type, trying not to eavesdrop on the sounds of Michelle and Jake cooing at each other as she worked and he watched. On the one hand, I was happy to see them so content together; after all, even if I thought he was too much a model of old-school masculinity, well, she was the one marrying him, not me. On the other hand, it had me wondering again when we had started wanting such different things out of the men in our lives—and, by extension, out of our lives in the grandest sense.

Now that I was back in her parents' house once again, the place that had been the true home of my childhood, I realized the too-obvious truth that I was the one who had changed the most. I remembered a time when I lit up with the promise of being the Davis family's other perfect daughter. My sophomore year of high school, not long before the disastrous road trip to Chattanooga, Marcia and Rich had pinned my honor roll report card to their refrigerator right next to Michelle's, and it made me happier than making the honor roll itself.

"They're here!" Michelle exclaimed as the doorbell rang. "I'll go take coats, and when we get back, let's talk bachelorette party."

"Great," I said through clenched teeth, and then I accidentally set down a gingerbread man cookie hard enough to crack it.

Once Darcy, Rebecca, and Ellen had joined in, we fell into the usual routine. Decorating cookies with icicle decals hadn't been my idea of a good time since we left middle school, but the mindless rhythm of chatter about the Davises' neighbors refusing to trim their hedgerow or an acquaintance's wedding taking place a week after Michelle's helped to settle me a little. Anything that kept me from thinking about my gynecologist appointment back in New York made for a welcome distraction. For the moment, my biggest worry was trying to figure out Michelle's plans for her bachelorette party and what I needed to do to organize it—and, most important, how expensive it would be.

She waited to raise the topic until we had carried the finished cookies into the next room to share with Marcia, Rich, and their host of guests, as was tradition. Then, while Jake stayed behind for a scotch, Michelle's bridesmaids made our way out into the sunroom to drink champagne out of the crystal flutes that the Davis family saved specially for Christmas Eve and New Year's.

"Another year in the books." Michelle smiled. "And I'm so glad y'all are here. It's these traditions that really make me glad to be where I am."

"Hear! Hear!" I raised my glass from my position on the rattan porch sofa, and Darcy shot me a glare that suggested I had spoken out of turn. I took a sip of champagne and shrugged meaninglessly.

"I'll try to ease off the wedding talk after this, but we do need to discuss the bachelorette party. I have a few ideas."

"Isn't that the maid of honor's job?" Darcy said faux innocently. "Julie?"

"Julie planned the dates for the last weekend in January, of course, but you know me," Michelle said sweetly, but she shot Darcy a withering glance that made her stare down at her lap. I wanted to hug her. "I want a say in everything, so I told Julie we'd make the plans over the holidays. So, thoughts on Cabo?"

My stomach flipped. She wanted to leave the country?

Fortunately, Rebecca spoke up first. "But is it . . . safe? You know, with Zika?" I resisted the urge to roll my eyes at that, but Rebecca had always been the mother hen of the group, sweetly volunteering for safety patrol and passing out hand sanitizer to battle germs. "Whatever you want, Michelle, but there are a lot more safety concerns to Mexico in general. You know."

"Well, we all went to Cabo in high school," Ellen pointed out. "And the resorts are nicer now. I've heard."

Michelle looked around coolly. "Darcy? Jules?"

"The only thing for me, hon, is that Emma is barely six months old." Darcy named her infant daughter. "I'd rather stay closer to home, all things equal. But this should be about our bride, y'all."

I took another sip before I spoke. Clearly, no one really wanted to go to Cabo, but no one wanted to outwardly say no or offer another option. I had never known how much passive-aggressiveness was involved in wedding planning—or maybe it was unique to the women I had grown up with. I suspected the former. Whatever the case, I decided someone had to say something, since in a rare move, Michelle wasn't outright forcing an agenda. "What about Nashville?"

"Nashville?" Ellen parroted.

"That's practically *right here*," Michelle said.

"But we'd make it fun," I added hurriedly. "No one has to fly far," *other than me,* I thought, "and so we can put that money toward hotel suites, fancy meals, anything you want. What do you think?"

"Well, I suppose it would be easy for Emma to stay with Warren or my mama for just a night or two," Darcy offered after a pause, now caught in the difficult position of wanting to celebrate closer to home and not wanting to enthusiastically approve any idea that I had proposed.

It would have been to my advantage to push New York or Atlantic City, but I knew that was all a lost cause. "So, an all-out weekend in Nashville? Michelle, do you have any other ideas?"

"I guess I'd rather Nashville than something tacky in Vegas," Michelle mused. The room waited to read her mood, but in an instant she had plastered a bright smile back on her face. "Okay, let's do it! But I want everything big, ya hear?"

"Promise," I said, opening an iPhone note to start taking down ideas. Nashville would be more manageable, but I still felt faint. Could I possibly pull this off, even in normal circumstances? Michelle started to tick off ideas for activities I could plan, like a burlesque dance class and a themed bar crawl, and I tried to keep up. *Everything will be fine*, I told myself, not believing it.

After Darcy excused herself early to put Emma to bed, everyone else followed suit until it was just Michelle and me left on the rattan sofa in the sunroom. I had stopped after two glasses of champagne for several reasons, but Michelle was on number four or five. Jake came out to check on us after all the other women had said their good-byes, and Michelle had that sleepy, faraway look in her eyes when she told him that she'd be in shortly.

"Just leave us another few minutes, hon," she said, giving him a little wave as he looked at us from his perch against the doorframe. She pulled a chenille blanket up over both of us.

"I know exactly what that means." He looked at Michelle tenderly, and when their eyes met, I almost felt like I should look away. "I love you. Take your time."

"That was sweet," I said as Michelle moved to lean her head against me.

"He is sweet, you know. Most of the time."

"Good." I wanted Michelle to be with someone who wanted *her*, not just a wife. Not just someone to frost the cakes and watch the kids so that he could smoke cigars with his friends. I thought of my father leaving. I thought about Rich. Maybe an instinct for protectiveness made me skeptical, more so than anything Jake had ever done. *He is sweet, you know.*

I looked out the wide sunporch windows at the sloping hills of the yard, illuminated only by the full moon. It was too dark to clearly see the river running below, but I could hear it if we stayed completely still. It was pleasant to listen to, but somehow it sounded more like a distant memory of home than like home itself.

"Maybe I should get going soon, too. I know you have an early Christmas morning tomorrow." The Davis family always attended an early church service and then opened presents, all before Christmas brunch.

"Stay a little. Even with all the wedding planning, I never see you. I'm about worn-out."

"From cookie decorating?" I teased.

She lifted her head from my shoulder to look up at me, eyes wide. "From everything, really. Mama and I have just been doing so much for the holidays, and for the wedding."

"Well, I've heard wedding planning is always stressful," I offered meaninglessly. "But it'll be over in just a few more months, right?"

"But even after we get married," she added tipsily, "I know it'll be more of the same. The same type of work." She sighed and then smoothed her hair behind her ears. I realized that maybe Michelle would have a full-time job after her wedding—albeit an unpaid one. Homemaking wasn't the sort of work I imagine being satisfied by, but it was work all the same.

I looked at her wide-eyed, expectantly, hoping that she would continue. If marriage talk had to dominate most of our conversations, I wanted to hear the reality of her feelings, not platitudes pulled from someone's blog or Pinterest page. "Maybe it doesn't have to be that way if you don't want it to, Miche. Right? Have you and Jake talked about how you'll—"

"Well . . . oh, I don't know what I'm saying. I'm just beat."

"Because if you need my help—with anything, I don't just mean the wedding—you can tell me. I'll—"

"No. You're sweet, but really it all couldn't be going better."

"Seriously? You're sure?"

"I just need a good night's sleep and a pancake breakfast tomorrow." She paused. "You remember the year we tried to surprise my parents by waking up extra early to cook them breakfast in bed? Spilling the batter and ruining everything, though, is all we actually managed to accomplish."

"I remember."

"I just can't wait to see my kids do the same kind of thing." She giggled tipsily. "Think about it, though, a little Michelle and Julie getting into all kinds of trouble like we did? I'm excited for that. Don't tell Jake; I don't think he's ready. But he will be."

I felt a sharp sting in my chest. *I'm not,* I tried to say with my eyes. *I'm sorry.* There were so many things I could have told her right then, but I simply bit my lip and said nothing. I did not tell her about the pregnancy, or about my decision to end it, or even about Mark's asking me to move in with him. I ventured nothing, risked nothing. Fear sat uncomfortably inside me, clenching my chest.

"Never mind all that. I think I might be a little drunk." She laughed again softly. "After all, we have to have a wedding first.

Babies later." She closed her eyes, and I let her rest against me once more even as I stiffened, wanting nothing more in that moment than to be alone.

As her breathing evened out into sleep, I checked my phone. Midnight, and officially Christmas morning. I thought about Rich and Marcia, surely cozy in their pajamas somewhere inside their sprawling house as Marcia finished wrapping a present or two. I thought about Jake, probably reading a brief and waiting for his future wife to climb into bed with him. It all made sense, somehow; everyone knew where they belonged, and someday Michelle's children and her children's children would have their place, too. That didn't mean it came without sacrifice; something was given up, and I sensed that was what Michelle had almost admitted to me when she talked about the work she and Marcia had done, and had always done, to keep the family unit running to perfection. No one among us lives without sacrifice, I reminded myself—another thing Marcia had always repeated. But there were some sacrifices, passed down only from woman to woman as the circle of life endlessly replicated, that I suddenly knew I could not make myself.

That line of thought exhausted me, too. I placed a hand on my still-flat stomach in disbelief, reminded again that it was all more complicated than I ever could have imagined. I turned my head to look at Michelle sleeping peacefully next to me. We hadn't been wholly honest about those complications in a long time, I realized. I could still tell her. I could squeeze her shoulder and wake her up and just tell her.

But then I thought about her putting on a velvet dress for church in the morning, and of all the times she had told me that children were the greatest blessing on earth. I thought about the Bible verse she had posted to Instagram when the Reproductive Health Act passed in New York, the one that read, "Before you were born I set you apart." I had scrolled past it with a lump in my throat, but then I liked the photo below of her and Marcia at their church fund-raiser. I had wanted to do my best to acknowledge the things she cared about. In return, she had liked a photo of me at the Women's March in New York with Dana. I wondered now what that passive approval meant for both of us. Which things about me Michelle really supported, and which ones she, like me, had been silently looking past. It made me angry how consciously I still avoided interrogating this. Was I afraid or simply complacent? And which was worse?

My phone buzzed with a call from Mark. Hands shaking, I swiped to answer.

I heard the indistinct thrum of voices and music in a bar crackling through. "Hello?"

"Jules! Realized I didn't respond to your text when you landed. Hey, Merry Christmas," he slurred slightly.

"Merry Christmas," I said tightly. "Are you out on Christmas Eve?"

"Local bar stayed open for everyone tonight. I'm here with the guys."

"What?"

"The guys. Here with the guys!" he shouted, and I heard a voice, probably one of his high school friends, call out, "Shots!" in the background.

"Well, have fun," I whispered, turning my head to check and

make sure I hadn't woken Michelle. "Enjoy it, enjoy . . . Christmas tomorrow. Let's talk when I'm back."

In his buzzed state, Mark seemed oblivious to the serious implication in that sentence. He simply yelled the same greetings back, told me to have fun, and hung up.

I stared at my phone for a minute in silence. Then, in a gesture that surprised me completely, I scrolled down my contacts and found my mother. "Merry midnight Christmas, Mom," I texted her. "I'm coming home now."

CHAPTER 16

Somehow, that Christmas was the best one my mom and I had ever spent together. She was in one of her good moods. Our quiet moments at home together, drinking tea as we each opened our Christmas present or laughing as we botched a seemingly simple chicken recipe, were a welcome respite from the outside world. It didn't feel like a period of forced confinement away from my real life, as it often had over the years. Of course, our time together was still punctuated by periodic analysis about Jeff or annoyances caused by coexisting in a space scarcely bigger than my New York apartment, but when I left I experienced a strange feeling. As much as being home always reaffirmed how small my life in Langham had once been, this time it was tinged with a bittersweet quality of leaving the only true safe harbor left to me in the world.

But I couldn't hide on the fringes forever, nor did I want to pretend, as everyone at Michelle's Christmas party apparently had, that everything was largely the same as it had been in high school. Instead, I had to decide what I really wanted my life to look like. Within that knowledge came something else I didn't expect: While I still vacillated between shock and anger, a small, quiet corner of my mind was starting to insist that maybe this was going to turn out for the good. *You wanted a reason to change your life,* this voice inside me had started to say. *You wanted to find out exactly what you wanted.* Perhaps I had been bluffing, but the universe had now forced my hand.

On my first day back at the office, I left at three P.M. with the generic excuse of a routine doctor's appointment. Slightly dizzy with nervous anticipation, I made my way to my gynecologist's office. Her practice was close to my office in the Flatiron District, and I walked the five blocks between buildings in a haze. I watched men in suits and with briefcases hustling past Madison Square Park bump into tourists with overfull shopping bags, amazed at the normalcy of it all. I looked for some last sign that this was all a dream. I expected the skyscrapers to change shapes or turn dazzling colors, proving that I wasn't in the real world after all. They remained irritatingly, resolutely gray.

My gynecologist, Dr. Khanna, came into my exam room only ten minutes after I arrived. The scratchy, open-backed gown they had given me made me as physically exposed as I felt emotionally, but she came and stood next to me and put me at ease. She smiled at me in exactly the right way. It came more from her warm brown

eyes than from her lips, which she turned up only slightly at the
corners. The smile seemed to say that she knew I felt awkward and
unnerved but that I didn't have to be. It was compassionate, serious,
light, all in one go. Honestly, that alone was worth my copay.

She glanced at my chart, which I knew contained the results
from the pregnancy test the nurse had run during my preliminary
height-weight-urine-sample exam. "I see here that the test Lita ran
is positive, but the blood she took will be used to confirm that. You
told me that this was not a planned pregnancy, correct?"

"The literal opposite of that."

"Sense of humor intact, I see, Ms. O'Brien. I know this might
be overwhelming, but you're in good hands. We can discuss any
and all options you'd like. This is about taking care of you."

I listened as Dr. Khanna told me that I was probably about five
weeks along based on the date I listed for my last period, and that
the blood test could confirm this as well. I tried to listen, but I heard
a persistent ringing in my ears, growing louder and louder, my face
flushed and hot, until I finally just blurted out what I had really
known all long: "I need to end the pregnancy."

"I absolutely trust that you know what's best for your needs,
Jules," Dr. Khanna said warmly. "We don't perform abortions here,
but there's a clinic I've connected several patients to that's quite
close by. Would you like me to refer you? I can go over the basics
here, and they'll be able to talk to you more about your feelings,
procedure options, and scheduling. You're very early on, so you may
have to wait a week or two, but we can get everything set up now to
give you some peace of mind. Sound okay?"

I nodded, trying to process everything. She made a few notes, and then I found my voice at last. "Thank you. Also, I just feel like I should say that I . . . I don't know if I ever want to have kids."

I didn't know why I told her. Maybe it seemed important because I hadn't been able to admit it concretely before. Somehow, as soon as I heard it come out of my mouth, I knew it was the truest thing I had ever said. And if I was *truly* honest with myself, I had always had an inkling.

As I sat on the stiff, starchy paper on Dr. Khanna's table, I remembered this one particular day. Seventeen years before, right before we had moved to Langham, my youngest aunt had just given birth to her first daughter, Jenna, and my mom drove me and a couple of my cousins over to the neighboring town to meet her. I was sullen on the car ride, wanting nothing to do with them, but I hoped things might look up once we got there.

My cousins went crazy when they saw Jenna. Oohing and aahing over this screaming, red-faced bundle swaddled and wrapped up as tightly as a sprained ankle in an Ace bandage. Her skin looked splotchy, and though that is, of course, normal for a week-old infant, I thought she looked hurt or ill, or both.

The whole scene struck me as painful, loud, and distasteful. I knew I shouldn't feel that way. Babies were supposed to be a blessing, and apparently we were all supposed to be happy, and I didn't know what was wrong with me. I did know, in some naïve and abstract way, that a baby seemed like something that changed life for the worse, something from which its parents might never fully recover. My exhausted aunt Liza, unable to hide her relief at handing the baby over to my mom, stepping into the next room to get a few moments of peace, didn't help the picture.

I wouldn't hold her. I didn't say anything about why, or insinuate that she wasn't cute or perfect or precious. I already knew not to do that, even if I wasn't old enough to understand any of what I was feeling. Ultimately, I think, I found a book and sat in the next room, letting everyone else marvel at the miracle of life.

Liza later looked back on that day as wonderful. Surrounded as she was by her family and her new daughter, the love she felt was enough to make up for her exhaustion ten times over, or so she said.

But I just don't want to have a baby, I thought to myself again. *I never wanted a baby. I don't have to be sorry for that.*

"So that's . . . okay? If I don't?" I finally asked Dr. Khanna. I didn't know what I was asking her for. Forgiveness? A benediction? Something that would counter the times I had been told growing up that women were meant to be mothers? But I knew I was asking her on behalf of both me today and me at eight, my two selves bridged by this unavoidable fact of who I had always been.

"That is absolutely fine, Jules. And when you come in for a follow-up appointment, we can discuss longer-term birth control options for you, like the IUD," she said, offering a kind smile.

I nodded, and then as I stood to leave and gather my things, something remarkable happened. Dr. Khanna placed a hand on my shoulder and stepped toward me. "One more thing," she said softly. "In case no one has ever told you, this is something that is completely up to you. Whatever choice you make for yourself is the right one."

Her words warmed me in a strange way. It started somewhere deep in the core of my body, and then a feeling, one of both peace and certitude, seemed to radiate out from there. But certainty in my decision didn't solve everything. I still had to figure out a way to tell Mark.

When I couldn't fall asleep that night, I distracted myself by attempting to finish up plans for Michelle's Nashville bachelorette extravaganza. The e-mail thread among the bridesmaids, begun in earnest right after Christmas, contained plenty of gems of southern women's diplomacy. To any suggestion I made, there was always a *but*: "But I think that we need balloons that spell out *Mrs. Oster* instead of just regular balloons" or "But I think we'd all prefer Grey Goose over Absolut, right, ladies?" or "I'm fine with anything, but why don't we keep discussing?"

In spite of that, things continued chugging ahead. I had booked a couple of rooms at a downtown hotel even in my haze over Christmas, and everyone had actually cooperated in the end, reimbursing me for their share of the cost by check or Venmo before I had even flown back to New York. Now we were just stuck on whether to book a traditional group exercise class or to actually take a burlesque lesson. The previous e-mail thread responses to this question made this sound like a life-or-death issue. Darcy had responded to a suggestion of neon penis straws with a stern, straight-faced "I cannot and will not be associated with that."

As I checked the thread again, I saw that Michelle had spoken: "Lighten up, y'all," she commanded. "We're doing it." I guessed that meant it was time for me to place a phone call to the burlesque studio.

As I tried to cope with the mental picture of Sylvie straddling a feather boa and Darcy correcting my dance moves, that was the moment I realized it: Given that Dr. Khanna had warned me the clinic would not be able to schedule my appointment until the last week of January, I would have to go to Michelle's bachelorette party pregnant. It seemed like a scene from a B-list comedy, in a context that felt completely unfunny.

Should I even be doing burlesque? I wondered, before realizing that was an idiotic line of thinking. But what if I felt sick? I hadn't had any morning sickness at all, but I couldn't imagine what I would do if it struck on the trip. I made a mental note to look up how common it was and how early in a pregnancy it hit. Deep down, though, I wasn't really afraid of how I was going to feel physically. It was emotional. What would I say? How could I hide this from Michelle?

I had resolutely decided not to tell her about the pregnancy if I wasn't going to go through with it: not now, not ever. I could mentally defend this decision by telling myself that I didn't want to ruin the lead-up to her wedding. Another part of it was the distance growing between us. We had been talking even less than usual except when it came to bachelorette party details, so why should I confide in her anyway? Dana and Ritchie were my best friends in every practical sense, and even they didn't know yet. Thinking about the weeks leading up to Christmas, I couldn't remember the last time Michelle had called me on the phone to discuss anything other than wedding logistics.

But I knew the real reason I didn't want to talk to her ran deeper than that.

Strangely enough, in a roundabout way, I had actually learned about the concept of abortion because of Michelle. We were in elementary school at the time of the 2004 election. Woefully politically uninformed, we only noticed the candidates one afternoon when we mistakenly switched the channel to the local news rather than Nickelodeon. A solemn expression crossed Michelle's face as Kerry crossed the stage, and she leaned over to whisper in my ear, "My mama says he says it's okay to kill babies. Isn't that horrible? That's why we can't vote for him."

Aghast, I ran home that evening to tell *my* mother what I'd heard. She was measured and diplomatic for once in her life: I remembered her response as she told me that, no, he wasn't out murdering children. She explained the concept of abortion in very general terms and said, "There's a lot that can happen between conception and a baby being born; that's why folks argue about it. Some say it's a life all along, where I'd say it's a little more complicated than that. I'd say it can be hard to tell when a baby's life is worth more than a mother's, and it's true the other way around, too."

Her response shocked me. I wondered, from what she said, if she had ever had one. Then I shook my head frantically as if to dislodge the thought. Were people really allowed to do this? I asked.

"It's legal with certain constraints, yes," she told me. "But this is a delicate issue and people feel what they feel, so no running around town talking everyone's ear off about it. Mind your own business." It was probably the first and last time I ever heard my mother say *that*.

We never discussed it again. Over time, my views fell in line with her words that day: *It's a little more complicated than that.* I carried that with me. But I imagined that Marcia had explained her views to Michelle in the same way, stroking her hair and using her honeyed voice, the same one she used with me when I had a nightmare during a sleepover. I could see how Michelle would have heard that abortion was always wrong and left it at that.

I knew that most of her family's Methodist congregation agreed. The summer after our freshman year of college, they had led a fund-raiser for Choose Life Alabama. I told Michelle I was glad she seemed excited about volunteering and that I was proud of her, and then I politely made up an excuse for why I couldn't help. I volunteered elsewhere, finishing my National Honor Society hours at the local food bank. At the time, I had thought that polite deference—mind your own business—would be the only option. Now I thought about it differently, but I still found the idea of saying anything to Michelle or her family absolutely impossible.

It wasn't their business; that was part of it. I had the right to make my choice, and I would make it. But why the knot of fear tied down somewhere inside me that I couldn't access? Was I afraid that Michelle would judge me? I had spent so much of my life growing up trying to avoid that judgment, trying to wear the right things, to say the right things, to fit in with our—*her*—group of friends. That need for acceptance was not an easy habit to shake. But maybe I was also afraid she would try to convince me to change my mind.

Dreading the possibility of that conversation, I could feel myself already moving to form a mental defense. I had done this at work in the morning, on the subway home, and as I parsed the aisles at the bodega—phrases turned in my mind all day after my doctor's appointment. *You don't know what it was like with my mom trying to raise me on her own,* I would repeat in my head. *I can't go through that. I won't put someone* else *through that.* Or, *I'm not equipped. I don't have enough money, and I live in a walk-up, and I don't know when or if that will ever change.* Or, *I would need help. I don't want to go back to Alabama.* These were very valid reasons. They just weren't the real one. The truth was actually pretty simple.

I just don't want to have a baby. I never wanted to have a baby.

Still, something nagged at me. A feeling like I had told a lie or broken a confidence, but it was too late to take anything back. The only thing under my control was this decision.

CHAPTER 17

I felt relieved as soon as I scheduled the appointment at the clinic. The receptionist had spoken to me with pragmatic kindness, calling me "hon" before shifting back to efficient questioning about my work schedule and my healthcare coverage. She reminded me of Dr. Khanna. But the moment I got off the phone I realized it was the first irreversible decision I'd ever made. Suddenly, something like nausea was rising in the back of my throat.

I had faced a multitude of choices, so many they could not possibly be cataloged. The tiny ones: Crest or Colgate toothpaste? Wine or beer? Then there were the bigger ones, the ones that changed my life: to attend Cornell, to move to New York. But every decision I had ever made before could have been undone, could be altered or adjusted or peeled back just far enough that any avenue of life might still be open to me. Jobs can be quit, schools reenrolled in, purchases returned. I had never stared at a fork in the road where neither path came with a receipt.

As much as I knew I could not, did not, want to be a mother, I felt in my bones that this would be a different kind of decision. The kind where five, ten, fifty years in the future, I would not forget, and I would see as clearly as watching a film screen how my life could have been different. Does a presentiment of loss change you?

I had to trust that I really knew what I was willing to lose, I realized. But I also knew that this decision impacted someone else.

I had decided early on to wait to tell Mark the news in person as soon as he got back to New York after Christmas. Against every impulse I had, I ignored one of his calls the night of my visit to Dr. Khanna, feigning sleep. I couldn't tell him over the phone. Yet texting with him had been bad enough; talking to him when he was sober, actually hearing his voice, without acknowledging what had happened felt like a lie. It was true that Mark hadn't always been adept at picking up nuances via text, but he had clearly sensed something. He had asked if I was okay twice in the two days I had been back in New York. Both times I had lied and said yes.

I let myself into his apartment with the key he had given me, and then I spent an hour waiting for him to get home, standing up and pacing the whole time. I wasn't afraid of his reaction; it was more that the whole experience so far had been both intimate and surreal. Talking about it with Mark meant that it was *ours* instead of mine. My decision still, but two people forever changed by it.

As soon as he opened the door, I leapt up from the couch.

I didn't even wait for him to put his duffel bag down before I started talking.

"I have something to tell you and I'm just going to say it," I blurted. "I'm pregnant." In TV shows and movies, characters always stop talking right there. It's a test: They say "I'm pregnant," and then they dare the recipient of the news to display the correct reaction with no context clues. I didn't want to do that, so I kept going. "But don't worry, I have an appointment scheduled. I'm not going through with it. Obviously."

Mark dropped his bag as his face blanched. He crossed the room to me. "Seriously? This is for real? Oh my God, Jules." He sank to the couch and put his head in his hands, his shoulders slumped. I tried to read what he was feeling; perhaps it was the same sense of disbelief, a feeling of being separate from one's body, that I had experienced all the way back in the airport. I should have called him right then.

"I don't know how it happened; I've been on the pill," I continued uneasily. I still couldn't make myself look directly at him. "But I do know it's going to be fine."

Silence. I knew he was in shock, but I wanted him to be the one to tell *me* it would all be okay. To be the one offering reassurance. I looked at him, and he stared straight ahead at the wall, and I wondered if I should say something else.

Finally, he spoke. "I— Shit, I need some time to process this."

"Of course, I totally understand."

"Yeah." He paused. "Like, maybe it could be all right in a different way? I don't know."

"What?"

"What I mean, Jules, is that I love you. I know we're not really there yet, and I know that we weren't planning on something like this *at all*, but let's not . . . let's not do anything rash, huh?"

"Rash?" I turned away from him and fixed my gaze out the window. I hadn't thought beyond telling him my decision; I hadn't imagined he would be anything but relieved. It felt like we weren't even in the same room, a separation between us palpable even as my knee brushed against his. "Mark, I'm sorry. I know you're just finding out about this. I've had more time. But, trust me, my decision is anything but rash."

"And you never thought about how I'd feel about *your* decision?"

"I thought you'd be relieved! God, do you want to be a dad? At twenty-six? In a walk-up apartment? With some girl you're dating?"

"Some girl? I want to be with you!" He slammed a fist on the coffee table. "Don't make me sound like an asshole for that." I jerked away, visibly taken aback by the outburst, so out of character for him. He lowered his voice and took my hands, turning me toward him. "Sorry. I'm sorry. No, I don't want to have a kid right now. I travel all week, I have no time, I don't even want— Yeah, no. That would be insane. That's not what I'm saying. Obviously."

I sighed and half laughed at the same time. Fear turned to relief.

"But this doesn't mean I don't want some things to change."

Hesitantly, I asked what he meant.

"I'm taking the GMAT next month. I told you I could stay in New York, but if I got in somewhere else better, well"—he swallowed—"I want to know that you're serious about us. That you'd go with me."

"So you want me to say that I'd go anywhere for you? Right now?"

He didn't respond, but his unflinching stare said it for him.

Was this what we had been building toward, all this time? Through every moment of doubt, every disconnect? The first moment I knew I didn't want to follow him to business school—or anywhere—should I have told him with greater conviction? If I had recognized that as the breaking point, maybe I could have saved us both all this. Could have never gotten pregnant at all. Tears of frustration welled in the corners of my eyes, but I knew I couldn't stop now.

"I thought we were on the same page. When we met, you said you didn't want anything serious," I reminded him, trying to strengthen my wavering voice. "I told you I wanted to stay in New York. Forever. I wanted things . . . how they are." I threw up my hands, apropos of nothing. "I thought you were okay with that."

"Well, I am. Or I was. But I said all that when I was twenty-four, for God's sake. I don't know, people grow up, Jules." Then I heard his tone shift. It was subtle, indecipherable to anyone who didn't know him, but steeliness crept in. In the voice he used when negotiation was no longer an option, he said, "Forget the . . . pregnancy for a minute. Don't put this all on me. We both know you've been completely avoiding what I asked you at Thanksgiving. You shouldn't be in this if you don't see it going anywhere. Tell me where exactly you see this going."

"Why does it have to go somewhere? It's a relationship, not a train!"

"Oh, so you want to be together like this forever? Where we talk about maybe 'shacking up' but you always have one foot out the goddamn door? We've been together for almost two years!"

"You never even *hinted* that you wanted to move in together until you just sprung it on me at Thanksgiving. And, by the way, I do not have one foot out the door just because I don't want to move to Philadelphia or have a *kid* with you, and the fact that you even think that—"

"Look, I know you're all fucked-up about relationships from your mom, or whatever—"

"Don't you even dare—"

"And I've been patient with it, but it's enough! A relationship has two people in it. And, I don't know, if you can't stop being selfish about what you want now—"

"Oh, and it's *selfish* to not want to get more serious with someone who seems like he would rather drink bottle service with his 'bros' than *talk* to me? Who would yell at me like this when I just told him I'm having an abortion?" I jumped up from the couch and ran into the bedroom, slamming the door. All the noise, and our mutual anger, seemed to hang in the air for a moment, echoing until I heard Mark cross the apartment to the bedroom. He opened the door slowly and then came to sit beside me, finally quiet.

When had I known that I didn't want to stay with Mark long-term? The charitable explanation, the one I always allowed myself, was that I just preferred to live in the present, and so I hadn't thought seriously about it. But I had always planned for my future in some sense: I prepped for the SAT for almost a year before we took it. I looked for publishing jobs for more than six months before college graduation. When I knew what I wanted, I seemed more than capable of making things happen. It was evident that I had never acted with this kind of clarity with Mark. I didn't owe him a relationship, but I had, I realized, taken the path of least resistance instead of telling him how I really felt—about anything.

"I really didn't think that this would be . . . like this," I said at last, gentler now. "I knew we might want different things, and I should have told you when you first started talking about business schools. I didn't see it clearly."

Mark stared at the floor, his arms crossed in front of him. "I guess I just thought you would want to be with me more than you would want . . . what? Dana and Ritchie? Your job? I know you like your job, but aren't there other publishing jobs? I'm trying to understand, what is it that you even want, Jules?"

"So it's you versus the sum total of my life, huh?" He didn't respond, which told me that's exactly what he'd meant. Somehow, this made me feel lighter inside. It shored up my growing faith that I might, somehow, be doing the right thing. "Look, maybe we should talk about this more. I care about you. I love you," I said, even as the past tense—*loved*—trailed the words in my head, an uninvited ghost. "But I can't do it now. We can't work all of this out right now."

"When?"

"The appointment is on the twenty-first. And I can ask Ritchie or Dana to go with me."

"I can go with you."

"Think about it. You don't have to. I . . . I wouldn't make you, especially after . . . all of this."

"Well then." He shifted away from me. "I guess you really don't think of me as the most important person to you. The person you'd need with you. I'm nothing."

I opened my mouth to say, "That's not fair," but in a way, it was. He said it unfairly—to hurt me, to elicit pity—but that didn't change its truth. He wasn't the most important person to me. That was the part that made me feel low, heavy, laden with guilt. What a way to realize that something is over. *I should have known it sooner. This shouldn't have happened to us. To him.* Then I realized that he had continued to make my decision to have an abortion about only his feelings, and I got angry all over again.

"This can't really be it, can it?" He sighed audibly. "It's been almost two years. And you're pregnant."

My heart ached at the sound of that word. My whole body ached, suddenly. "But I think maybe it is."

"Well." He shook his head. "Thanks for making this all so clear for me, I guess. If you don't want to fight for it, I'm certainly not going to."

"If you're asking me to fight for it right now, to make everything okay for *you,* then I guess you're right. I'm not going to."

He stood and crossed back to the living room, slamming the bedroom door behind him. I pulled back the skin at the corners of my eyes and I pressed hard until I knew I wouldn't cry. And then I got up, opened the door, and walked past him out of his apartment, with no destination in mind.

CHAPTER 18

I left the building hugging myself, my arms crossed and wrapped tightly around my body as if I might be about to fall apart. I walked down Fifth Street like that for a while until I hit the dead end at Avenue A, and then I finally dropped my hands to my sides, knowing how crazy I must look. I tried Dana and Ritchie on the phone, but neither of them answered. Buzzing with adrenaline, I hadn't worn a coat, and a cold winter wind was blowing, whipping up off the East River or wherever the ephemeral Manhattan winds come from. I made myself stop at a coffee shop that I had passed before but never been in.

I wanted to text Dana, but my hands were shaking from the cold, so I just sat down at a table without ordering anything, willing my mind to go blank. As I tried not to think about anything at all, I found myself listening to a group of teenage girls sitting next to me. Their hushed conversation was punctuated with high-pitched giggles.

"So did you go, like, *all the way?*" I heard a girl with short black curls say to a girl with a slicked-back blond ponytail.

Michelle and I used to use that phrase, too, I remembered. *All the way.* It's one of those things that makes you feel so grown up as a teen—talking about sex!—but then it just disappears from your vocabulary completely. I imagined myself asking Dana if she had gone "all the way" after a date now. I could hear her response in my head: "All the way *where?*" she'd probably say. "Like, to Brooklyn?"

I missed the idea of sex as the final destination point. In reality, it was after that that things started to go wrong.

I checked my phone. One message, and it was from Alan, asking if I wanted to finish watching a documentary we had started a few weeks earlier.

"Can you come to Elsewhere, the coffee shop? Now?" I managed to type out.

Ten minutes later, Alan came in wearing his classic weekend outfit: brightly colored puffer coat, jeans, and messenger bag slung haphazardly over one shoulder. Seeing him look so normal made me feel like I could breathe again, like I had just come up from underwater.

"Jules, what's going on?" he asked, sitting down across from me and putting his hand over mine. "Your text freaked me out."

"How did you get here so fast?" I asked.

"I was already in the neighborhood. What is going on?"

"I think I'm going to have to avoid this neighborhood for a

while," I told him, because that was the first thing I could figure out how to say.

"What? What are you talking about?"

Tears welled in the corners of my eyes again, and I tried to force them back. I had never cried in public before. Or in front of any of my friends other than Michelle, come to think of it. "Mark lives here, and I think he and I just broke up, and it's all because I'm maybe a horrible person. And I don't know what to do."

Alan lowered his glasses, squinting at me with a look both confused and suspicious. "Babe, you are not a horrible person. What happened?"

Then my male coworker became the second person to find out that I was going to have an abortion.

Alan stayed silent for a minute. I kept crying, hiding my face in my hands. "Sorry if this is an inappropriate conversation," I finally choked out, laughing a little between sobs. "Don't tell HR."

He laughed dryly, shaking his head. "Jules. You know we're more to each other than that."

"I know."

"I don't know what to say," he admitted. "But I do know this: This is your decision. It is yours to make, and you are not a bad person for it. And I'm sorry if anybody has ever told you differently."

"But I don't even know if I want to have kids," I blurted out.

"So?"

"So I think that's why we really broke up. Because I'm supposed to want to have kids, or to 'move forward' and go to Philly, and apparently there's something wrong with me."

"What does Philly have to do with this?" He looked at me

quizzically, then waved a hand dismissively. "Never mind. Why are you *supposed* to want to?"

"Do you?" I asked.

"What, want to live in Philly? God no. Kids? Well, Marcus and I want to someday. Like, way in the future. But that just goes to show you: Not everything is a man and a woman and 1.8 offspring. Clearly." He snorted.

"Where is Marcus?"

"Honestly? Around the corner hiding awkwardly in the ninety-nine-cent pizza place trying to stay out of the way while I talk to you." He paused. "Good slices, though. Want one?"

And then I laughed hard enough that I cried for an entirely different reason.

"Let's go meet him," I told Alan. "I could use some pizza."

Alan and Marcus bought me two slices and a soda at the tiny pizza counter. They did their best to make me laugh until they were overdue to go home and walk their new puppy. I wanted to call Dana or Ritchie and explain what had just happened, but then I thought that maybe I wanted to tell them in person. Plus, telling Alan seemed like more than enough for the day. I decided that I would text our group thread and just make plans to see them later, maybe over the next weekend. I would keep moving forward. But for a moment, I found myself stuck in the past. I stared at the background of my lock screen, a black-and-white shot of the Cliffs of Moher. I had taken it on a trip to Ireland years ago that now felt like it belonged to a different person altogether.

I remembered my first year in New York, which I had spent pinching pennies and saving up for that trip. I hadn't had the time to study abroad in college or the money to travel right after graduation, but all I wanted to do was go overseas. Why Ireland? Because it was the distant, ancestral home of the O'Briens, I guess. Also the $500 round-trip tickets.

Anyway, I fell in love. The cliffs stark against the gray sky, the cobblestone streets in Dublin wet from a November rain. I even heard plenty of what Dana called my "hideous folk music." Mark and I had met right before I left for my trip, but I had stopped thinking about him when I arrived in Ireland. We had been seeing each other for a couple of months, but my feelings weren't set. I liked "having someone," and I also didn't really know what else I wanted from him.

That changed on the third day. I was checking into a hostel in Dublin, and I looked at my e-mail for the first time on the vacation. I didn't have cell service, so Mark had sent me a long note—the first and last love letter he would ever write me, as it turned out. He told me he missed me. He told me he was an idiot not to have "made his feelings known" sooner and that he thought we should give a real relationship a try. But the thing that really got me was the last thing he said. "I'm not trying to hold you down or hold you back," he wrote. "I just want to know you."

Now I knew it was so much more complicated than all that— that the best intentions for togetherness don't always add up to a life together. At the time, though, it made me feel brand-new. Like I wasn't the same person who had grown up so uncertain, shadowing Michelle, simultaneously desiring and fearing the attention of my mother. It felt like I had become a woman in my own right.

I told myself not to get distracted, to stay focused on the experience I was having alone. But as soon as I saw his note, I couldn't help it: A big part of me couldn't wait to get home. When I flew back the next weekend, Mark drove his parents' car in from Connecticut, picked me up from the airport, and took us to dinner at a restaurant. Our bartender snapped a photo for us as we were having a last whiskey at the bar—I fancied myself an expert after my trip—capturing us with our flushed cheeks pressed together and our glasses raised at the camera. In a gesture of sentimentality that surprised me, Mark had kept that photo in his bedroom. In it, I look happy in a distinctly twenty-three-year-old way, like I truly believed that, if I were lucky, nothing would ever have to change again. That the hardest part of everything was behind me. "I'm so glad you came back," I remembered Mark saying over and over.

I was angry with him, and I didn't care about him, and I cared about him more than I wanted to believe was possible, and I didn't want to be with him ever again. I remembered being the woman who loved him enough to want to come home from Dublin, but she felt so far away from me now.

CHAPTER 19

Dana and Ritchie came to meet me in Brooklyn the next day. With Demi at a yoga class that overlapped with Terry's day upstate visiting family, I decided it would be safe to invite them to the apartment. Dana suggested a party brunch; I countered by saying I would pick up bagels from Bagelsmith, her favorite, and get a spread ready at home, mimosas included.

A second after I buzzed the door open, I heard Dana yell up from the landing, "I'm not climbing four flights of stairs if there isn't an everything bagel up there. With lox."

"There is. And shut up, not all of us can have *Oliver* to push the button on an elevator for us." Oliver was the cute doorman in her building she not so discreetly liked to flirt with after a bottle of wine.

"Oh, I wish Oliver would push more than the button for the fifth floor for me when—"

"Okay, stop, we get it!" Ritchie shouted as they climbed toward me, and I laughed, one of those deep belly laughs, and it anchored me to myself somehow. I felt like I was back inside my body for the first time in a few days.

Ritchie pulled a gallon of orange juice out of her bag as Dana plunked a bottle of prosecco on the counter. "We have orange juice or prosecco or both—depending on what kind of day you feel like having."

"Oh man, guys, you have no idea."

Dana narrowed her eyes and cocked her head at me quizzically. I waved a hand to get them to follow me to the couch.

"Okay, what's going on?" Dana asked. "You're acting like my parents when they told me they were getting a divorce."

"What?"

"Remember, they had me over for that weirdly formal Shabbat dinner, and then it was like, 'Come sit on the couch, honey.'"

"Right! And then your dad said that there were books to help kids going through this . . ."

"And I was like, 'Dad, I'm not a *kid*, I'm twenty-one.' They're freaks; it was fine, I knew it wasn't, like, a passionate marriage anyway. Loved them both, still do."

"Rose and Ethan. The best."

We all laughed fondly, thinking about Dana's eccentric and lovingly loud family. I typically went to a Passover seder at their apartment every year, where the whole blended clan still celebrated together.

"Sorry, *so* not the point," Dana said. "But that's what you're being like. If something's up, just tell me. Are you okay?"

Yeah, never been better. "Well, remember the pregnancy test? It was positive."

Dana collapsed back into the couch. It rattled me to see how I was feeling reflected back in someone's expression: dumbfounded, defiant, and pitying at once. Then I looked at Ritchie, whose wide eyes watered with concern. She was always the less physically demonstrative of the two, in contrast to Dana's golden-retriever-like physical exuberance, but she leaned in to hug me first, burying her face in the crook of my neck.

"When you guys texted me about getting the test, I thought it was kind of a joke," she said quietly. "You know, like how I always used to freak out in college. Holy shit. I'm so sorry."

"Holy shit," Dana echoed. "You never said anything, so I thought everything was fine. You're serious?"

"Nah, just wanted to see if you'd freak out. *Yes,* I'm serious. But I'm okay now. I just wish it hadn't happened. Obviously."

"Well, no kidding."

"I'm glad you guys are here." I squeezed Ritchie tight and then sat up to compose myself. "I have an appointment scheduled next week. And I was wondering if, well, if one of you would pick me up."

"Of course," Ritchie said quickly.

I looked at Dana. She didn't say anything, but the way she raised her eyebrows asked, "Not Mark?" When she finally met my gaze, I answered her question, and I knew she knew. "Yeah, Mark and I are . . . taking some time. Or broken up. Or I don't know."

"Do you want to talk about it?" Ritchie asked. "Because we can, but you so don't have to."

"Yeah I . . . right now, I just really don't have that much to say. That's weird, right? The status of me and Mark is literally the last thing on my mind."

"No questions asked," Dana confirmed, getting up to pour a mimosa. "And I can pick you up. I'll be there."

"Thanks, D."

"Hey, we'll make a day of it! I'll take you back to my place, and we'll watch movies, and I'll paint your nails if you want. I know you can't do it yourself. And you hate pedicures."

"I really do. It's the—"

"Foot-pumice thing. I know. You weirdo."

"Dana," Ritchie scolded, but she was laughing. "This is serious."

Dana sat back down next to us and looked me in the eyes. "I know that. But this doesn't have to be, like, a big, terrifying thing. I don't want to make you feel that way."

"Thank you." I pulled them both in for one more hug. I didn't know what to add to my thank-you, because I just felt so much. *Thank you* for being there, certainly. For not acting shocked, for not asking questions that forced me to justify myself. I knew those questions would always be there—from the world at large, from a voice inside myself. The internal questions I would have to answer; that voice I would have to square with. But to not have to do so with my best friends felt like a blessing.

"So," I said. "Bagels?"

"Bagels," Ritchie said.

We walked into the kitchen, and I added, "Oh, and I haven't even told you guys the craziest part yet."

"That's not the craziest part?"

"My appointment is *next* week. And guess what's before that? Michelle's bachelorette party."

CHAPTER 20

The ritual of a bachelorette party seemed both archaic and uniquely of the Instagram era. The practice of celebrating the end of a woman's single days like the end of her individual freedom? Outdated. The $110 swimsuits printed with BRIDE and BRIDE TRIBE, to be worn only for a photo shoot at the hotel rooftop hot tub? Certainly our mothers hadn't contended with that. What would you have done with the nearly naked photos, put all fifty of the pictures in a coffee table album like your own personal *Sports Illustrated* swimsuit edition?

The details of the trip had been decided over an e-mail thread so long and so inefficient that we might as well have communicated by sending letters via USPS. Michelle had pushed for the swimsuits so that we could all wear them in the hotel hot tub;

Darcy had complained to the rest of us in a separate thread that she wasn't "bikini ready" after giving birth to Emma some months earlier and called Michelle "uptight and controlling." This all reached a climax as Ellen, in an attempt to smooth things over by confirming that the custom swimsuits would be one-pieces and Darcy could wear a sarong, accidentally forwarded the entire trash-talk thread back to Michelle. Michelle responded coolly with "order swimsuits via this link—matching shorts or sarongs are fine xo," but then e-mailed me alone with a command to "get control of this situation." As maid of honor, I was responsible for quashing the infighting. And so the final communication had been as follows:

> Hi, all,
>
> I know everyone has been so busy, so I wanted to consolidate all of the information into one e-mail so we're ready to go.
>
> Please order matching swimsuits via *this link* and bring your honky-tonk best for Friday night out in downtown Nashville. From Michelle: As long as you're in theme, no rules—other than no white! I've also made a reservation for Saturday bottomless brunch at Sinema.
>
> My flight gets in at 3 P.M. on Friday, and the rest of you can park at the hotel for $25 per night. Michelle and I will work out all other reservations and itineraries, so nothing for you to do there.
>
> Any other questions, let me know.
>
> Jules xo

It felt like a work e-mail aimed at the interns, if there existed a company whose sole business was issuing attire commands to white women in their twenties. I hated myself a little bit for the *xo,* but as of one week before the trip, no one had followed up with other questions, so I had to count it as a success. I called Michelle that night after work and got her voice mail; I felt a flash of disappointment and then thought it was probably for the best, because I didn't even know what I was calling her to say. I wouldn't—couldn't—have the conversation with her I had had with Dana and Ritchie, something I seemed to both long for and fear. Best to avoid it.

She called me back at three P.M. the next day, and I only saw the missed call after an hour-long edit meeting. Michelle always called in the afternoons now, and it took two or three attempts on both of our parts to actually connect. It didn't matter. I would see her face-to-face in six days. For better or for worse.

I slept for the entire flight to Nashville. As soon as we pushed back from the gate I put on my noise-canceling headphones and hit shuffle on a Zac Brown Band playlist Michelle had shared with us via text to "set the mood" for Nashville. But not even blaring country music could keep me up; the past few weeks had taken all my energy.

"You make loving you easy," the band sang. I caught myself thinking about Mark, even though I had never been the type to listen to songs and daydream about our relationship. I hit next, and "Chicken Fried" came on. *Better.* I drifted off and didn't wake up until the wheels hit the runway.

Once at the hotel, I struggled to haul my overstuffed suitcase down the hall, which was filled with the outfits designed to meet the aforementioned dress code, as well as bride-themed gifts for Michelle. The first night: coordinating "honky-tonk best," with Michelle all in white and a tank top proclaiming I'M THE BRIDE! plus of course one of her many pairs of custom cowboy boots.

I scanned my key to unlock the door of the suite Michelle and I would be sharing, but she heard me and swung the door open before I could even turn the handle. She grabbed me by the hand and pulled me into the room.

"I'm so glad you're here," she said, resting her forehead on my shoulder, and I pulled her into a hug without even thinking. It felt so good to let myself fall back into the past, into those moments when a hug from Michelle or Marcia seemed like it might have the power to fix everything.

"It's good to see you," I said.

"Well, good, because I really need you. Darcy and Jen's only job was to finalize today's itinerary for before you got here, but they didn't plan anything until tonight, so the afternoon is just open. And everyone is already on my nerves."

I realized as soon as she said this that I had been hoping her relief at seeing me was for a different reason. Embarrassed at how much I had wanted her to say something sentimental, I took a deep breath and tried to pull myself together. I wanted to pretend that the last several months hadn't happened, that things hadn't changed. But they had.

I took Michelle's hand and pulled her to sit down next to me on the edge of the bed. "Okay, well, we'll come up with something fun." I felt a sheen of sweat on my forehead and a weird, sickly feeling in the back of my throat. I wondered if it could be from the pregnancy, but I pushed the thought away. "Anyway, don't worry."

"Right, you're right."

I checked my phone. It was only three thirty. "I'll go put on makeup, and then we can get a drink on the roof before everything starts. Afternoon happy hour. My treat."

"I put toiletries and dry shampoo in the bathroom if you want to fix your hair. There's a comb, too."

A classic Michelle hint that my hair needed teasing, a suggestion she'd been making since high school to try to give me her preferred form of "volume." How could a comment be so annoying and comfortably reassuring at the same time?

I stood up, and she smiled at me. "We'll have fun tonight, right?"

"Of course," I told her. I still felt queasy, but I said nothing. I filled a glass of water in the bathroom and chugged it down.

Michelle's bachelorette party was my second. I had been invited to Dana's older sister Jane's party in Atlantic City the year before, but mostly as a favor to Dana; all the other bridesmaids were in their thirties. *That* party was almost sort of faux ironic, involving penis-shaped whistles and strippers that were *Jersey Shore* through and through—something Michelle would have loved after a few minutes of feigned embarrassment—but it definitely wasn't something that Jen and Sylvie would appreciate.

When we headed back down to the suite after a drink at the

upstairs restaurant to pregame a honky-tonk bar with the other bridesmaids, I realized that the two bachelorette parties had at least one tradition in common: the games.

"Okay," Darcy announced after we were all seated on the floor in a circle around the suite's glass coffee table. "Julie did what she could with the planning, but y'all know *she's* never had a bachelorette party—so I couldn't resist bringing some of my own games. Grab your drinks, ladies—we're going to see how well Michelle knows Jake!"

I remembered the concept from Jane's party. One bridesmaid had a list of questions about the groom—"What's his favorite beer?"—along with all his answers. If Michelle guessed his answer correctly, we drank. If she got it wrong, she did.

Everyone squealed in delight. "Let's see how well our bride really knows her groom, y'all!" Jen crowed.

Wherever Jake was for his bachelor party, I doubted that he was doing anything similar. I poured myself a glass of champagne and then topped off Michelle's, forcing a smile. "You've got this," I told her. *Today is not about you,* the voice in my head chided.

"Y'all are gonna be wasted by the end of this," she taunted.

"You're on," Sylvie said.

Michelle, as usual, was right. She flew through the first set of questions, to the point where I started taking fake sips out of my glass. She got stumped on only one question: What was Jake's favorite band growing up?

"Allman Brothers," Michelle replied confidently. "This is too easy."

"Got you at last!" Darcy laughed. "Tom Petty and the Heart-breakers."

"No way! I know he told me that before."

"Not what he said here—sorry, sweetie." Darcy shrugged while Jen started to chant, "Drink! Driiiink," sounding pretty drunk herself. *It's not a frat party, Jen.*

Michelle looked over at the answer sheet. "Well, I guess y'all were bound to fool me once." She smiled sweetly, made subtle but commanding eye contact with Darcy, and finally took a substantial gulp of Veuve.

"That's my girl." I clapped. Michelle had always been able to outdrink me in high school, and even when she was drunker than me, she had always been able to hide it better. Caught drinking once by her parents, I got red-faced and flushed, giving myself away by being too indignant. Michelle just smiled and kept her mouth shut, knowing, as always, how to avoid revealing too much.

"You're still killing us, Miche," I said. "But thanks. I need a break from drinking every turn." Already I felt tipsy and too hot. I put my glass down. I had promised myself I wouldn't go overboard—for a lot of reasons, not least of which was that I was afraid I might get too drunk and blow up Michelle's whole bachelorette weekend by telling her what was really going on with me.

"All right, y'all, we need to head to the bars in twenty minutes," Ellen said, using her schoolteacher voice as she started the final third of her pregame playlist. "Finish your champagne and get ready."

The next song was an old Jo Dee Messina track. I remembered it from high school, and a wave of nostalgia swept over me. I sank into the couch and glanced around the room. Everyone had jumped up from their seats, and it seemed like they were moving in fast-forward as they drank and applied lipstick and posed for Instagram story selfies. The champagne sat too heavily in my stomach as they swirled around me dizzyingly.

To my right, Michelle held up two skirts, one in each hand, looking for Jen to approve which one would replace her Lululemon leggings. Jen inspected them both seriously, while I focused on *seriously* not throwing up.

"I need to be casual because we're wearing the bride tanks, but still chic," she was saying. "You know?"

"The jean one," Jen said. "Or, I don't know, I like the ruffles on the other one."

Michelle contemplated them both for another full minute before settling on the jean skirt.

At least shoes had already been decided upon. Everyone had been told to wear cowboy boots in keeping with the honky-tonk theme. Of course, everyone other than me had multiple pairs, worn for weekends in the fall to SEC football tailgates. I hadn't been to one since I visited Michelle for an Auburn game early in our sophomore year of college. I had purchased a pair of ankle-height cowboy boots online for $30, the best sale price I could find.

"Jules, those aren't really cowboy boots, you know." Michelle turned her attention to me, her voice sounding like an eye roll. "They should be higher. Like, midcalf. Those are just an ankle boot."

"Northerners, right?" Darcy said, and I heard laughter from around the room. "No offense, Julie."

I looked to my left. Ellen sat in a club chair with Darcy standing behind her, quickly curling her hair. Ellen polished off the rest of her champagne.

"Darcy, you need a drink," Sylvie called from across the room. "If you can use a curling iron without burning anyone, you're too sober for the Stage."

Darcy raised her eyebrows and conspicuously filled her champagne glass with water from the carafe, and suddenly I knew what was about to happen. My queasiness amplified tenfold.

"It's a week early, so I wasn't going to say anything publicly." Darcy grinned, putting her hand on her stomach. "But I'm just drinking seltzer tonight. We're pregnant again!"

Ellen smiled happily, clearly having already known. Jen and Sylvie looked to Michelle for her reaction. And I closed my eyes, feeling like all the blood in my body had just rushed to my head.

A beat passed before I forced myself to open my eyes. No one moved at first, but then a grin spread across Michelle's face. "Oh, that's just the best news! Congratulations! I'm so excited!"

Apparently now free from worry that Michelle would be mad about Darcy stealing her thunder, Jen and Sylvie finally chorused, "Congratulations," in response. But they hadn't known Darcy for decades like Michelle, Ellen, Rebecca, and I had; I wanted to get up and say something, but my legs had turned into Jell-O. I felt trapped inside my own body.

Michelle broke her hug with Darcy and turned toward me. "Julie?" She narrowed her eyes. "What's going on?"

"Sorry, just feeling a little sick," I managed. "Darcy, congratulations."

Michelle sat down next to me and picked up the carafe from the coffee table. "Drink some water," she said. "I guess we can't all party like we used to!" Everyone laughed, and I downed two glasses while Darcy told the whole story: They hadn't been trying, Emma was just seven months old, but she and Warren were over the moon and hoping for a boy.

"Sometimes blessings just happen," she crowed. "But that's the last you'll hear of it tonight, I swear. Michelle, we're so excited for you."

Michelle beamed, and I croaked my agreement weakly.

"So," Darcy said. "Shots for the bride! I'll pour."

Michelle looked at me. "Julie? You going to be okay?"

I looked at Darcy, clearly blessed with whatever gene it is that makes pregnant women glow. Or maybe it was just genuine happiness; I could see it in her face, the joy shining out of her everywhere. Meanwhile, sweat was running down my arms and from the backs of my knees as I focused all my attention on trying not to throw up or cry. I wanted to climb out of my skin.

Jen herded Ellen and Sylvie into formation for a group selfie stick picture. "Everyone, over here after the shots! Smile and say 'Bride!'"

"I'll be fine," I told Michelle as she jumped up to join the group.

When we got to the first bar, Michelle started in on lecturing everyone about the scavenger hunt I had planned for her. Once again, it was Michelle all over—taking control of an activity that was supposed to be created for her so she could have fun. The scavenger hunt involved taking photos of a bunch of different actions: Michelle dancing with a member of the bar band, a member of the bridal party taking shots with a stranger, and so on. Michelle assigned us each a task. I got shots with a stranger, because Michelle decided I wasn't drunk enough. I had only had two glasses of champagne, but it was clearly two too many. My body felt alien to me.

"Michelle, please, something else," I said weakly. "I can't do shots right now."

"Come *on,* Julie. You're being so boring right now," she scolded. My stomach clenched again. Of course Michelle couldn't understand why I was so stressed. I hadn't told her anything. But it hurt that she seemed so eager to believe that I didn't want to participate in her night, so unaware of everything I had done in order to be there.

Then, perhaps sensing that she had been too harsh, she whispered in my ear, "You know Jen and Sylvie can't take more shots. I mean, look at them." We turned together and saw Jen trying to wrangle Sylvie with a pink feather boa, instead getting tangled up in it and tripping herself. Sylvie, oblivious, had her hand on the arm of a co-ed in a WHAT HAPPENS ON SPRING BREAK STAYS ON SPRING BREAK! muscle T-shirt who looked like he couldn't be older than twenty. Michelle and I winced in tandem as she squeezed his biceps.

"Yeah, we might need to intervene over there." I laughed. "Okay, I'll take one shot."

As I turned and pushed my way to the bar, the sweat of strangers slicked my exposed arms. The shrieks of other bachelorette parties, dressed in coordinated outfits almost exactly like ours, rang in my ears. Everyone in the bar was a carbon copy of everyone else.

Was this supposed to be fun? And if it was supposed to be fun, why did I feel so awful?

"One shot of whiskey for me and . . ." I spotted a woman in a BRIDE sash next to me and pulled her over. "And one for her."

"Wooooo!" the anonymous bride cried drunkenly, and I held a cool hand to my forehead. I didn't know if the sickness was from pregnancy or some strange sense of ennui or just plain guilt and fear from the secret I was keeping, but my stomach roiled. I picked up my shot and turned back toward Michelle, who was holding out her phone.

"Get ready to take that photo," I called out halfheartedly, and then I raised the shot to my lips.

It all happened at once. I squeezed my eyes shut and downed the shot, the camera flashed, my throat contracted, and I suddenly knew I was going to throw up. I dropped the shot glass on the bar and clapped a hand over my mouth, bolting away toward the bathroom as the bartender yelled, "Someone has to pay for those!" and Michelle called, "I hope that didn't blur the photo!"

I cut in front of the ten-deep bathroom line and I couldn't open my mouth to apologize. I made it to the stall and then I vomited. My insides clenched as I heaved.

When I finally made it back out to our table, I knew my eyeliner was wet and smudged, and if my face had been pale before, well—good thing it was dark in there. Michelle asked if I was okay, and I told her no.

"I'm so sorry," I said. "I have to go home. I'm sick."

"From one shot?" Darcy—totally sober Darcy—sneered.

"Oh no, babe." Michelle tipsily slung an arm around my shoulders. "Remember when this happened at Mickey's party junior year? Let's just get you some water . . ."

I thanked her, but I knew what she was getting at. I told her again that I was sorry, but water wouldn't be enough. I had to go home. I would buy them all a round of drinks, and I would try to be better tomorrow, I promised.

Michelle didn't argue, but she looked at me coldly and crossed her arms. "If this is because you're mad that I made you take that shot—"

"What? It's not."

She waited. Maybe for me to say I loved her, or to apologize again, but I couldn't. I felt the presence of everything she didn't know like it was right there in the bar, putting a wall between us. I didn't have the energy to reach through it.

She muttered something under her breath that I couldn't make out. "Well," she finally said. "Feel better, I guess."

"Have fun," I said weakly. "Y'all."

I walked out into the street, mobbed with costumed performers and teenagers and drunken partiers. I sank into a cab and closed my eyes, unable to even think or care about Michelle, maybe for the first time. By midnight, I was back at the hotel, alone in bed with only my supposed best friend's wrath for company.

CHAPTER 21

I woke up late the next morning to find myself alone in the room.

I peeled back the too-heavy white duvet and stood up slowly, feeling less nauseated than the night before, but still weak from throwing up. I checked the bathroom to see if Michelle was there and found it empty, the counter pristine, her multiple mysterious "night routine" products nowhere in sight. She must have slept in another room. My stomach flipped.

After pulling on my sweats and chugging a glass of water, I walked down the hall and knocked hesitantly on the door of Room 314. Darcy's.

I was afraid I'd find Darcy alone and have to hold an awkward pre-coffee conversation, but what I saw might have been worse. She swung open the door to reveal a party already in progress: A picked-over room service cart bisected the room, displaying wedding-diet approved foods like nonfat Greek yogurt and brûléed grapefruit. A cacophony of sound drowned out Darcy's "Oh, hi" as Jen turned up the volume on a Carly Rae Jepsen song and Michelle popped a champagne cork for mimosas. Everyone was there. Other than me. I felt like the unpopular kid no one had bothered to wake at a sleepover.

"Wait, let me open the champagne bottle again," Michelle said, not registering my arrival. "I need someone to get an Insta story of it."

I drew in a breath and walked farther into the room. The exclusion stung, but what I felt more deeply surprised me: I realized that maybe I didn't really *want* to be there. In high school, I would have run over to Michelle right away and whispered something funny in her ear. She would have grabbed my arm and laughed, not telling anyone else the joke, and I would have glowed at the proof that our unspoken bond remained intact. But now, even as I registered a flash of disappointment at what had happened, I had no desire to prove, as I usually did, that I was a closer friend to Michelle than Darcy was.

Maybe I wasn't.

"Hey, y'all," I offered. "Sorry I slept so late, but I'll make up for it at brunch."

"Feeling better?" Michelle asked without looking up from the champagne bottle.

"For the most part. Here, give me your phone. I'll take the Insta story of you guys." I didn't care about being in it.

I filmed as Michelle mimed popping the cork off the bottle of Perrier-Jouët, and the other girls crowded around her, clapping and laughing. They dropped the pose as soon as I finished, and Darcy instructed everyone to grab their phones and "reshare it with the hashtag." Ellen kindly offered me a mimosa.

"I think I'll hold off until brunch," I said, laying a hand on my stomach. "But, Michelle, I brought something for you." I reached into my pocket and pulled out a curly straw that spelled out BRIDE.

"Ooooh, cute." She finally gave me a half smile. "Thanks, Julie." A pause.

"Now, can you go get dressed and then call the Uber? We should leave in like thirty minutes."

After a mimosa and an order of eggs Benedict, I almost felt like myself again.

Sure, Rebecca, Jen, and Sylvie had taken "bottomless brunch" a little too literally, asking for multiple mimosa refills before their glasses were empty and forcing all of us into a series of blurry selfies. Yes, the music was loud and clublike, inspiring Michelle to stand up and dance in our booth, looking around to see who might be watching her. But something about the predictable routine of sliding into inebriation with the women I had been drinking with since I was a teenager was surprisingly pleasant. Some things never changed, for better or worse. Maybe the previous night would be forgotten.

"Julie, you've got this, and we can all Venmo you, right?" Ellen asked when the waitress finally dropped our check.

I said a silent prayer that everyone would reimburse me quickly, but I knew it was my responsibility as maid of honor to coordinate the group payments. "Yeah, of course. So . . . forty-five dollars per person, and then can you all add in an extra five or six for the Uber?" The UberXL to the south side of the city had cost me $40.

"Well, I paid for the room service for Michelle this morning," Darcy said. "There are a lot of things like that. I don't know about y'all, but I think it's silly to be calculating for all the little expenses. Like, who owes who a dollar fifty."

"Well, I'm not going to charge Michelle for a coffee or something, but . . . the Uber was more expensive," I said, looking across the horseshoe booth to try to catch Michelle's eye. After our conversation about my side jobs over the shower weekend, I hoped she understood why I couldn't afford to take on the bulk of the group's expenses.

She typed something on her phone, not looking at me.

"I can pay whatever?" Ellen asked hesitantly. She was the quietest of the group, so I didn't expect her to side with me strongly, but I knew she could read the tension and wanted to diffuse it. I flashed her a smile.

"Oh, also I don't have Venmo," Darcy said. "Sorry, forgot to say. But don't worry, I brought forty dollars to cover my cost of the brunch."

"What the fuck," I almost snapped. I caught myself. "Okay, that's fine. Maybe we can stop by an ATM later?"

Michelle finally set her phone down on the table, and I looked at her expectantly. "Look, I'm sure the little things like Ubers will just all even themselves out. Let's stop worrying about it. Plus, some people were out later and paying for more things for me last night," she said pointedly. "Come on, let's go. I'm ready for a tipsy walking tour."

"OMG, let's stop at Acme on the way. Cute guys!" Jen said loudly.

"Jen, you're married."

"I don't know, for, like, Julie, then!"

"Or me!" Rebecca chimed in.

I felt myself fade away, receding inside my head as the loud, drunken conversation crashed over me like a wave. My ears buzzed, and I felt dizzy. *Could I afford this weekend? Why didn't Michelle care? Didn't she understand? Had I really done something* that *wrong?*

Screw that, the other voice in my head retorted.

My phone dinged. I pulled it out of my purse, grateful for some form of distraction. I had one text. From Michelle.

"We'll figure this out later. Stop making such a big deal of this rn," it read.

I dropped my phone back into my purse. Wordlessly, I turned to follow the group out of the restaurant, weaving around tables of women laughing hysterically, hugging, having the time of their lives.

I resolved to talk to Michelle as little as possible for the rest of the day.

CHAPTER 22

Michelle called three days after I got home. I hadn't spoken to her since our chilly good-bye in the lobby of the hotel on Sunday, the taxi loitering outside while I tried to decide if I should apologize again for Friday night, or if what she had said at the brunch meant that she owed *me* an apology instead. Ultimately, I just hugged her stiffly and said, "Get home safe." She didn't avoid my embrace or confront me, but she didn't tell me she loved me like she usually did when we said good-bye, either. I got in the taxi and didn't look out the window until we pulled away.

I had been foolishly telling myself that it would be easier to work everything out after my procedure was done two days later. Pregnant—it was still hard to admit that that word applied to me— and still dealing with the fallout from Mark, I was not exactly feeling like my best self. But I answered her call. If there was any hope for us working things out, I had to stop turning away from her.

"Hi. Look," she said as soon as I said hello. "If I was a little uptight at the bachelorette party, that's on me. There was so much going on. You saw how Jen and Sylvie treat every weekend away from their husbands like they're on senior spring break in Cabo." She laughed conspiratorially, and I snickered in spite of myself. "And I just didn't want there to be drama over bills and stuff during the weekend."

I owned up, too. "I *am* sorry I got sick and copped out—awful timing. Mostly, I feel shitty that I let some personal stuff get in the way of your weekend. Anyway, everything's okay now. Is your Nashville hangover gone yet?"

"Personal stuff?"

So she had picked *this* moment to be perceptive. Great. "It's nothing," I said quickly. "I just mean I was stressed."

"Something was going on."

I sat down on my bed and sighed. "If I tell you not to worry about it, will you leave it for now? I'm fine, I swear."

"I guess," she said, but then her voice changed. "But I think I deserve to know what's going on. First off, I'm your best friend—"

"You are, but just trust me that—"

"And *second,* you were being lame the whole trip, Julie. You were sick at night, okay, but even before that. You were distracted, you were acting like you didn't even care, acting like you were 'too good' for matching tank tops, and parties, and weddings—*my* wedding—and it's not fair. Then the whole time out, you were sulking that you didn't feel well—"

"I wasn't sulking. I was sick because I'm fucking pregnant!"

And then time stood still. That was an expression I had never truly understood before. I knew what it meant, but I had never felt the whole vast expanse of my life held up in one frozen moment. I sat there in my pocket of silence, feeling wholly apart from my room, my bed, my life. Did I really say it by mistake? To punish her? Or to punish myself? *Say something, say something.*

"Julie, oh my God," she whispered, and Michelle never said "oh my God." "Why didn't you tell me?"

"A lot of reasons?" I said lamely.

"I'm sorry, I'm sure you're still in shock, but it will be okay. I think it'll be perfect. But forget me, what does Mark think? What do *you* think?"

I thought a lot of things, actually. I thought about Lily and Brooks, the names Michelle had picked out for her future children and had clung to, unchanged, since she was a child herself. I thought about how happy she had been for Darcy when she announced her pregnancy at the party. I thought about how she sounded more excited, more interested in my being pregnant than she had been about anything in my life for months. I thought about how I was about to change everything between us, probably forever. And I couldn't handle another good-bye right now.

"I think that I'm not . . ." I trailed off, and shut my eyes. I gathered myself. "Michelle, I'm not having it. That's why I didn't say anything. Because it's really hard, and really personal, and . . ."

The silence buzzed loudly in my ears until she spoke up. "Julie, you can't mean that . . . no. I'll help you, my mama will help you; come home if you want. But you have to think about this. I know you're scared about your future, and you're scared that you're on your own, but—"

"I'm actually *not* scared of my future, Michelle. That's not what this is about. Not anymore." This wasn't completely true, but I wanted it to be. I needed to believe it, finally.

"I can fly up there." Her steely voice, resolved. Marcia. "I will come get you."

"Please don't. Or do, or I don't know." I sighed, already exhausted. "But this is decided. I can't have a baby. And more than that, what matters is that I don't *want* to. I know you don't understand, but please." Please what? Tears started to form and I blinked furiously. I had cried more in the past month than in the past three years, and I was sick of it. Sick of everything.

"What do you want me to say?" she hissed. "Julie, you *know* how I feel about this. How I thought *you* felt about this. It's wrong! You're being hasty, and you're just throwing a *life* away, and for what? So you can read books all day?"

And there it was, the question I feared the most. In all my introspective walks around the city, where I made up arguments in my head to support my decision, I had never been able to face that one. It made sense to point to the way my mom had struggled, how parts of her life had crumbled under the strain of trying to raise me alone. It was also easy to say that I couldn't afford a child in New York, not even if Mark helped; that was plainly true. It followed, then, that a "right to life" did not promise that a child would have a good one. The pregnancy was making me sick and exhausted, and making it through nine months of that already seemed like too much to bear. What Michelle had asked, though, was the big question: For what? Like I had to have a full justification for what I would offer up to society as a payment for shirking motherhood. As though it wasn't enough just to be a woman. To be myself.

My head felt hot, as if the fast-mounting anger and hurt might burn me up from the inside. I wanted, for the first time, to truly hurt her back. "Well, I guess some of us do want more than a husband or a baby out of our lives, yes."

"Oh, that's what you think?" She made an exasperated sound caught somewhere between a shriek and a snarl. "You want to make me say it? Fine, I'll say it. You act like you're above needing a guy, like *I'm* so needy, but then why are you dating Mark? You don't seem like you love him; you don't do things for him—"

"I don't 'do things' for him? What are you even—"

"Not even that, it's that you're all, 'I'd be so happy alone,' but then why are you with a guy that you can't even decide if you're excited about?"

"Well, Mark and I broke up, so . . ." I paused, both stung and surprised. I lay down and sank into the bed. "And anyway, you knew I felt like that?"

"I see more than you give me credit for."

"Well, maybe I'd give you credit if you'd talk about something other than yourself. Than your wedding."

"Hey, at least I love Jake! Heaven forbid I talk about that or get excited about that. And sorry that I haven't made a mess of my life, is that hard for you?"

"Oh, I have no doubt you love Jake. He's the perfect 'happy ending,'" I spat. "But you want me to be just like you, just because it makes *you* feel better. It validates you, it always has, and don't try to tell me that's not true. I know you, too. You fucking forget it, but I do."

She stayed silent then. I heard her drawing a breath, composing herself so that she could call me the hysterical one, perhaps. When she still hadn't said anything a minute later, I thought she might have hung up. And suddenly everything seemed real again, horrifyingly real, and I was embarrassed at what I had said. Shame spread through me slowly, like the feeling of waking up after a night of heavy drinking.

"I don't want to fight with you about this," I finally said. "I literally do not have the energy to fight about this anymore."

"That's not what I called to do. But if you're not going to listen to reason, or think about what you're really doing, then—"

And then I did something I had never done before. I cut Michelle off completely. A time of firsts in my life indeed, I thought, as I said, "Michelle, that's it. Stop it. I made my decision."

"Then I just don't know what else to say," she said in a way that made it sound like there was a period after every word. "Except that you should be ashamed. You lost yourself."

"No," I told her quietly. "I think this is who I've always been." I bit my tongue to resist the urge to say "I'm sorry."

"Well, then I guess I'm the sorry one here, Julie." Her voice wobbled, and it sounded like she was about to cry but didn't want me to know. "I can't believe you."

It had finally happened, I realized. We had drifted too far apart. I tried to figure out when it had started and couldn't. Perhaps the day almost a year ago, when she had called me to ask about using Jake's monogram, but it also might have been far longer ago.

"So, now you're finally concerned about me again? About what I do with my life?" I replied. "Like I said, when was the last time you talked about something or someone other than yourself? And you *still* wonder why I didn't come running to you when I had a problem?"

"Well, we can't all be you, Julie!" she shrieked, hysterical all over again. "You found a life that made you happy. And then I find someone that makes *me* happy, and I talk about it, and all you can do is spit all over it and make fun of me—I know you do, don't lie—like nothing and no one back home is good enough for you! Well, I think I've had enough."

By the time I went to say something back, the line had gone dead.

I kept the phone in my hand as I turned over on my side, curling my knees up toward my chest. It was ironic: Michelle had always thought of friendship as something you could never lose, and relationships with men as something you could—therefore making relationships the more precious resource. For me it was always the opposite. I saw true friendship as more rare, more purely special. It was like being in love without the fragility, the only thing that it made any sense to invest in. Now it looked like we were both wrong. I pulled a blanket up over me, all the way to my chin, and stared at the ceiling in silence.

When Dana got off work at ten, I told her what had happened. Her matter-of-fact response? "Insensitive bitch. I'm sorry, but it's true." We didn't have long to dwell on it. She had to go to work early the next day, but she promised that she would still be there to pick me up from the clinic.

"I'm sorry if I've totally taken over your life talking about this," I told her before we hung up the phone. "I hope I get the chance to pay you back soon."

"I actually hope a situation like this never comes up," she said lightheartedly, trying to make me laugh. "But thank you. And don't apologize."

For a moment, I thought about how I wished I could have known Dana when we were growing up. I imagined her telling off girls like Darcy, imagined us applying together to all the same colleges. But who knew how that might have worked out, or what it would have meant for us as adults? History had a strange power over friendships. Maybe it was simply the process of watching someone change slowly, almost imperceptibly, until one day when you finally noticed how different they'd become. The friendships that could survive that transformation were unbreakable. But how many relationships withstood such evolution? I couldn't know how Dana and I might have felt about each other if we had grown up together. I decided that it was enough that I had her now.

"You're the best."

"Call me if you can't sleep," she said, and I said, "You, too," but after hearing her say it, I knew that I would fall asleep just fine.

CHAPTER 23

That night before the procedure, I did fall asleep quickly, but odd dreams plagued me all night, in the predictable way they always did in times of stress. In the clearest, I was stuck in Birmingham, trying to make a flight back to New York. Every time I looked up, my gate had changed. As I ran through the terminal, the hallways mutated and changed shape, twisting in that kaleidoscope way that dreams do. I knew I was trapped. I started to scream, but everyone just sat there at their gates, flicking through magazines, playing *Candy Crush*. No one even looked up.

I woke up gasping. I looked around at the room, growing light in the early morning sun, and recognition settled over me slowly. I was safe in New York, in the middle of my very own confusing life after all. At nine thirty, I took an Uber to the clinic on Thirty-Fourth Street by myself.

The lobby of the office was clean and workmanlike. It had the same plastic chairs and water-stained magazines as just about any doctor's office, but the staff was unusually helpful and kind, all offering pens and smiles when I said I needed something to use to fill out the paperwork. As I wrote on the clipboard, I said a silent thank-you for the fact that I lived in a place where I could do this at all—and without having to walk by dozens of protestors at the door. I felt sick enough already without having to deal with all that.

They warned me at check-in that I might need to wait for a bit, but I couldn't get my eyes to focus on any of the "10 Tips for Amazing Abs!" magazine articles that were on offer. My mind wandered, and I found myself remembering a night from a long time ago. The first time I had ever thought about what it might mean for someone to have an abortion.

It was a summer night right before my senior year, and I had gone over to Michelle's while her parents were out at a charity benefit. I didn't even bother to leave a note for my mom on the kitchen table. A year had passed since Michelle and I had pulled into the driveway after the trip to my father's house. That day, I had felt like my relationship with my mom might really have been about to change, that I might walk into the house and find her waiting for me, and I could tell her that I understood why she had lied, what she had tried to protect me from. That hope glowed inside me for only a moment, but when I walked inside and she wasn't there, it was like a firefly released as soon as I had caught it in my hand. When she finally came home late the next day, I didn't tell her where I had been. Without her knowing why, we took another step back from each other and fell back into the rhythm of coexistence, she with her boyfriends and me with Michelle, silently counting down the days before I left for college.

The evening of the benefit was warm, late August, with a breeze blowing just hard enough to cut the humid air and make it bearable to be outside. Michelle grabbed us a bottle out of her parents' liquor cabinet, making a big show of sneaking it by her brother, even though he was too busy with a video game to notice and wouldn't care if he had. We took the bottle and one of those battery-powered lanterns out into the backyard, and we went to sit on the hillside under a willow tree that we had climbed as kids. Michelle sprawled out on the grass, one hand propping up her head and the other raising the bottle to her lips. She handed it to me after a couple of swallows, and I followed suit.

"Okay, now I can tell you the big secret. But promise not to say anything," she said, keeping her voice hushed even though we were the only people around, maybe for miles. When she spoke quietly and lightly like that, it reminded me of wind chimes. It didn't seem possible that an actual human voice could sound like that, but hers did. She knew it, too; she always asked boys at school to lean in so she could talk right into their ear, even if only to ask what teacher they had for homeroom.

"Promise." I took a long swallow—we had stolen rum, apparently—and grimaced.

"DeeDee's pregnant."

"Shit."

"Language," Michelle mocked in a singsong voice, imitating Marcia.

DeeDee Morrow wasn't a close friend of ours, but she was a cheerleader and she was on student council, so everyone knew her. She had been dating Jack Grable for all of junior year, and most of our high school knew him as an athlete with scholarship potential.

"So it's Jack's? How do you know this, anyway?"

"Of course it's Jack's. Oh my gosh, what if it weren't?" Michelle snorted. "Anyway, Darcy helped her get the pregnancy test and was there when she took it. So Darcy told me, but Darcy knows I tell you everything anyway. So now *you* can't tell anyone."

I had no one to tell, and Michelle knew it. She was the vessel through which all gossip flowed.

"Isn't it just awful? Can you imagine? Poor DeeDee."

I couldn't imagine. I imagined that being pregnant would be hard no matter what, but there was a whole other kind of shame in the whole town talking about it. In having no choices.

"What is she going to do about it?" I asked, even though I knew. If Darcy had already found out, everyone would know soon. Parents, teachers, pastors, *everyone.* And we all knew that this was not a place where these kinds of things just quietly "went away," to use one of Marcia's euphemisms.

"What are you asking? Of course she'll have the baby." Michelle sounded genuinely shocked. "But since we're graduating next year, the only question is whether she'll get engaged to Jack after graduation or not. And that's not much of a question. She kind of has to, right?"

"I guess," I said, thinking of DeeDee's professed plan to bulk up her extracurriculars in order to get into Tulane, like her sister. I wondered if it would matter now.

"It's just sad," Michelle concluded. "But that's why you use birth control."

"Miche," I scolded. "Shut up, you're a virgin, too." We both were, though I knew Michelle had been wavering about whether she would finally sleep with her long-term boyfriend, Jared, after homecoming next month. Maybe I'd do the same with my date. He wasn't a long-term boyfriend, but unlike Michelle, I wasn't so convinced about the point of waiting for true love.

"Not for long." She giggled, drinking more and dribbling a little bit down her chin. I reached out and wiped it off her face, getting my hand sticky. "But when we do it, we'll do it right," she added. "Can you imagine getting stuck here married at eighteen?"

"No way," I agreed. "That's why I'm applying to Cornell."

Michelle made a face. "Can't you go to Auburn or something? There are plenty of good schools we could both go to." She planned to apply to Auburn, U of A, and a handful of other schools that had solid academics but were closer to home and fully Marcia approved.

"I don't want to get stuck here at eighteen," I joked. "We'll be *best* best friends no matter what, though," I swore. "After all, I know all your secrets."

"Oh yeah? Prove it."

I closed my eyes and thought about the things that Michelle had told me were her biggest secrets. A random assortment of stories came to mind, but nothing particularly meaningful: her ninth-grade crush on Liam Teale, the universally agreed upon "nerd"; the fact that she hadn't gotten the joke in *Clueless* where Tai says, "No shit—you guys got coke here?" Then I remembered the big one. The one from last summer. It was the summer right after Michelle and I had found my father.

It happened like this: One normal night, Michelle had wanted to use the home phone. She thought Jonah was on the line in the basement, talking to his friends about how to beat some video game. Her mom was out with friends and not around to scold her, so she picked up the extension in the living room to yell at Jonah to get off the line.

But it wasn't Jonah. It was her dad, talking in a hushed tone, saying, "I need to be with you again," to a woman whose voice Michelle had never heard. She hung up the phone quickly, but in the intimate whispers she had heard enough—or so she told me. She sat frozen on the sofa until her dad finally came upstairs, not noticing her, and then she took the phone to her room and called me to tell me what had happened.

I felt so sad for her then. My dad's absence was an old wound, and even if our road trip had reopened it a little, it was something that rarely flared up and hurt anymore. But Michelle adored Rich and had looked up to him every day of her life. "What are you going to do?" I asked unhelpfully.

"I don't know," she had said, and Michelle never said she didn't know.

So I came to school the next day armed with her favorite candies and ready to support her if she wanted to cry in the bathroom or go on the warpath and tell her mom what she had overheard. I wanted to be there for her like she had been for me. But she didn't do either of those things. She came in bright and smiling, with just a little bit more makeup on than usual—Marcia usually insisted on keeping it "subtle." Today, Michelle was dressed to impress.

"Are you okay?" I whispered.

"Why wouldn't I be?" she said. The look that passed between us might have been invisible to everyone around, but it told me everything I needed to know. She strode over to her boyfriend's locker to flirt, and that was the end of that conversation. She never brought it up again.

And so, for all I knew on the night under the willow a year later, the "secret affair" could have been nothing. Or it could have still been going on. Marcia and Rich had become slightly more demonstratively affectionate to each other over the past year, in a way that would have been imperceptible if I hadn't spent almost all my time around them. Earlier that summer Michelle and I had watched as Rich had sat behind Marcia and wrapped his arms around her while we all stretched out on a flannel blanket watching the Fourth of July fireworks. She leaned her head back into the crook of his shoulder and closed her eyes. Michelle said, "See, *that's* exactly the part I want someday," and I had known precisely what she meant. But it was hard to tell how genuine the moment was, considering what we knew. I understood then that you could never truly know what passes between two people. How they change each other.

"Earth to Julie," Michelle said, grounding me back in the moment beside her, under the tree, the rum bottle nestled against my side. "So," she continued, her tone slightly changed. "What's my biggest secret?"

I thought for a minute. "I'm not going to say."

I thought she might challenge me, but she just raised the bottle in her hands to her lips for one last sip.

"I knew I could trust you," she said.

I had thought back to that night over the years, but usually as a sign of how close Michelle and I had been, about all the intimacies we had both known but that had lain silent between us, never needing to be said. Later, I plumbed it for what that history might tell me about why Michelle had chosen Jake. Jake had fallen for her first and pursued her hard. I understood why she found his steadfastness, his apparent loyalty, so attractive.

Now I thought more about DeeDee, who, I had heard, was still married to Jack, now with three kids. I wondered if she was happy. I thought about Michelle's incredulous reply: *"What are you asking? Of course she'll have the baby."* I thought about what it would mean not to have any choices.

"Jules O'Brien?" A small brunette woman holding a clipboard stood across the room. I snapped to attention. She smiled at me kindly. "You can come back this way."

CHAPTER 24

I t ended before I really even knew it had begun.

The staff briefed me on this beforehand, but knowing that the aspiration procedure would take only ten minutes didn't mean those ten minutes would *feel* like ten minutes. But they did.

The light sedative they gave me left me technically awake, but I still felt hazy once it was over. Uncomfortable due to a few cramps—which I had been told might last the day—and a little bit different, but somehow it felt like a good kind of different. Relieved. That surprised me, too.

The clinic recommended that patients leave with someone, and I found Dana in the waiting room like she had promised. She jumped up and crossed the room to hug me as soon as she saw me. "Are you okay?"

"Okay," I said, nodding sleepily.

She called us an Uber back to her apartment, and we rode in reverent silence for a few blocks before Dana was back to being, well, Dana.

"Getting this day off was a fucking nightmare, but I did it," she said. "Now I'm completely at your service. We can watch Netflix, or even chill and listen to your awful folk music." When I didn't say anything, she said, "Am I talking too much?"

"You're not. Netflix is good," I assured her. I placed my hand on my stomach as I felt a subtle cramp. It subsided quickly. I looked up and saw Dana watching me nervously.

"And I'll order you food. Whatever you want. And by that I mean whatever you want as long as it's sushi or Chinese. Ritchie can stop by later, too, if you want."

I put my head on her shoulder. "Thanks for being so, I don't know—normal about this."

"Why wouldn't I be?"

"What, did people just talk about abortions when you were growing up? Did you get a manual on how to deal with them sensitively?" I was kidding, but part of me wondered.

Dana shrugged. "Well, it's not like anyone *wanted* to have to have one. But you're not the first person I know who has or anything."

"I don't want to tell anyone about it," I told her, repeating what I had said to her a million times before the procedure. "But I think I just mean not *yet*. I actually might want to be open about it. Someday soon. Does that make sense?"

"Yes," she said, as we pulled up in front of her building. Oliver the doorman came out to open the car door for us. "Oliver, you're such a *gentleman*," she flirted.

"You have the best building. You're, like, a real grown-up." I gave her a playful shove as we walked up to the door.

"Nah," she said, throwing her arm around me and pulling me close for a brief hug. "You are."

Alan called at eight that night. I was already asleep, curled up under piles of blankets on the left side of Dana's bed, but even groggily seeing his name on my caller ID made me happy.

"Are you okay?" he asked without saying hello.

"Everyone keeps asking that like I'm going to die or something. It's a completely routine procedure." I didn't want to say that it wasn't a big deal, because it was a big deal—for some people, in some circumstances. Somehow, though, the truth was that the fact of it actually hadn't been a big deal for me. Or, at least, not for the reasons anyone would suspect.

"So . . . ?"

"Yes, I'm okay. Dana's taking care of me. It's amazing, actually— I've never seen her so maternal. Ironic, right?" Dana threw a pillow at me.

"She used one of her precious vacation days on you?" Alan snorted. "Kidding. I'm glad you're okay. I'm glad Dana's there with you."

He filled me in on the day's office drama, and we had a normal conversation that was boring in the good way. How *did* I feel?

I wondered. Dazed, happy, confused, exhausted. All those things. Most of all, I kept experiencing this profound sense of relief.

A small part of me wanted Michelle to call, too. Just because I wanted the chance to hang up on her—though, at the same time, I wanted her to take care of me like she had done once when I had a horrible stomach flu while visiting her at college. I had been a complete mess in front of her, and she had loved me anyway. I wanted to ask her where that love had gone.

"Do you care if I go back to sleep?" I finally mumbled to Dana. The luxury of a whole Saturday stretching ahead of us made sleep sound even more enticing.

"Do you care if I keep rewatching *Parks and Rec*?"

"Nope," I said. "I can sleep through anything."

It did take me a while to relax, though. I had a mental loop going, in which I replayed every major decision I had ever made that had led me to this exact moment, tossing and turning in someone else's bed on the strangest day of my life. It occurred to me that I had been wandering through the past few years like they were a maze; I knew there was an exit somewhere, but in some unknown location. Meanwhile, it seemed like everyone I had grown up with had built some kind of traditional adult life. Houses, marriage, children. Retirement accounts. Graduate degrees. Which of them had found everything they really wanted, I wondered, and which of them had been content to just settle down and stop looking? Or maybe they didn't see it that way. The whole mess of life is just simpler to some people, I decided. I envied that.

But I couldn't shake the feeling that if I didn't make a move for what I really wanted—finally moving into my own apartment, working on something that really mattered to me—I never would. It was time to start over, one more time.

I spent all Saturday scribbling notes. If I wanted to write for real, and I was pretty sure that I did, I had to start somewhere. I also needed to figure out a lot of things. Crashing with Dana and avoiding both my roommates and the process of finding a new apartment was not exactly a life plan.

So I sat on the living room floor making lists, and Dana sat in the club chair across the room, ostensibly working on her laptop but secretly just watching me—checking to make sure I wasn't having an emotional breakdown, probably. I could see her blue eyes peeking above the screen about every five minutes. It reminded me of my mom. When I was a kid, she sometimes used to pretend to read in the park, but she would always be watching me from behind the pages of her latest Danielle Steel to make sure I didn't do anything too reckless. It had annoyed the hell out of me back then. I never recognized it as a gesture of love until now.

Before we went to bed that night, I told Dana that I had something important to say.

"Are you going to tell me what you've been frantically writing all day?" she asked, sitting next to me on my disheveled couch bed.

"Well, first, I've decided I definitely want to live by myself when I move out. I've been looking at studios and I think I can afford it. If I live in, like, deep Brooklyn, anyway."

Dana smiled. "That's amazing, if you're sure you're ready. But, I'm buying a place up here," she said, meaning the Upper West Side.

"We're going to have to be in an even longer-distance relationship." I took her hand mock seriously.

"Everyone keeps moving to fucking Brooklyn."

"It's even worse than that, actually. I'm going to be *writing* in Brooklyn."

I told her the thought I had been having for a long time. The bit about how the only time my mind ever relaxed completely was when I was reading a true account of someone else's life. How that made me realize I wanted to write, too.

"I'm keeping my job at Thomas Miller, though, obviously. I still love it," I told her. "But maybe I can do this as some kind of extra freelance work. Solo apartments in New York don't exactly pay for themselves."

"So does this mean I'll be getting my apartment back soon, and I'll never have to go to Bushwick again?" She leaned over to hug me. "I'm kidding. I'm happy for you."

"Me, too."

Dana got up and left the room, but I stayed put.

I thought about a lot of things then, sitting there in the quiet. I thought about what I could possibly create, how I could plant something in the world that wasn't a person. Maybe writing could be that for me. Or maybe it could just be love. I stared out the window and watched the leaves blow, illuminated under the streetlamps. From Dana's fifth-floor window, only the highest leaves of the trees were visible. Viewed cropped from my angle, they looked as if they were frozen in midair, borne of nothing, magically suspended as the gleam from the streetlight buoyed them and streamed through them.

This—this day—would be part of my story. It would be part of where I came from, even if it wasn't visible from every angle.

But I knew then, too, that it wouldn't be everything. Not even close.

CHAPTER 25

I walked into the office on Monday with nothing but an intense resolve to get back to work. Between beginning my search for a studio apartment in earnest and diving into a new young adult novel Imani had just acquired, there was plenty to keep me busy. As I scrolled, I saw one message in my inbox that shocked me: an e-mail from Michelle. It had been almost a week since our fight and I hadn't been expecting to hear from her.

It had been impossible to keep our conversation out of my mind, of course. In almost twenty years, Michelle and I had never spoken to each other like that. We squabbled like sisters when we were young, but even then she always "won," and we'd make up within the hour anyway. I could never stay mad at her for long.

I thought about what it would have been like to call her from Dana's the night after the abortion, in some alternate reality where she might have spoken to me with love and concern rather than shock or condescension. But because I had seen the movie *Bridesmaids,* I thought that all prewedding bridal-party fights ended in a "Don't even bother coming to my wedding!" I didn't do anything, waiting instead to be dismissed as maid of honor. Hell, after everything, a part of me *wanted* to be uninvited. But public spectacles— at least, the bad kind of public spectacles—weren't really Michelle's style. I should have known that. When I opened the e-mail, it was simply a group message to all the bridesmaids specifying footwear and jewelry restrictions for the ceremony.

Maybe I had been included by mistake? But no: A follow-up e-mail then came to me separately, suggesting that my gold block heels would look particularly good with the peach-hued bridesmaid dresses. "I know what happened between us," she concluded. "And this doesn't change it. But everything is already set for the bridal party and for the reception, and the dresses, and I do hope we can put it aside for this one weekend and that you'll still be there."

And I do hope you'll remove the stick from your ass, I thought at first. The anger didn't hold. I could e-mail back and tell her I wouldn't come and end everything just like that, certainly. But the plane ticket had been purchased, the dress altered. The first weekend of our friendship, we had dressed up for a fake wedding. Faking a friendship at her real wedding made a fine bookend to the last two decades. Even more than that, though, if Michelle and I never spoke again in our lives after the wedding, I knew our friendship couldn't end without ever seeing each other again.

So, it was decided. I sent a conciliatory e-mail, confirming that

I would attend. In six weeks, I would be back in Langham. And maybe I could finally say good-bye for the last time.

Later that afternoon, Imani called me into her office for our weekly meeting.

I sat down across from her at her desk, noticing her gold earrings. Three inches wide, triangular, and knifepoint sharp at the bottom, they were the sort of thing I wished I had the confidence to wear. Marcia had once told Michelle and me that oversize gold jewelry was "tacky." When I was younger, Marcia had represented the pinnacle of femininity to me, and I had readily taken her word as law. I wondered about that, and the coded language behind it— it was obvious now that Marcia's distaste was never for the jewelry but for the wearer. Now I wondered why I had ever listened. I decided I would look for a similar pair that weekend.

"Feeling better?" she asked, not looking up from the stack of papers in front of her.

"I—" I almost forgot that I had called in sick on the day of the procedure with "food poisoning." "Yes, much better. Thanks."

We started to compare notes on a manuscript—young adult contemporary, we both loved it—and I thought about how much I admired Imani's insight. She never said "um," never punctuated her opinions with a question mark at the end. I had told her this before, once or twice over the years, and she had thanked me sincerely. But for some reason, I was still afraid of gushing too much, of being too effusive. Imani never seemed like someone who had a lot of time for personal declarations at work. Which was why her next question surprised me.

"You're out of the office for your friend's wedding this month, right?"

"In March. But yes, soon."

She eyed me levelly. "How is the planning going? You don't get to be my age without being a bridesmaid quite a few times and . . . whew. Sometimes it's better than others." Imani was thirty-seven, one of the many personal facts I'd learned from being her assistant. It can be a strangely intimate job.

"Well, let's just say it's been . . . expensive," I ventured, and we both laughed harder than I expected, Imani flashing both rows of perfectly white teeth.

"I hear that." A beat. "Well, anything else for today that's on your mind?"

My abortion? A friendship falling apart? Was this an entry point to talking candidly about Michelle, or would Imani have more respect for discretion? Then I remembered a safer topic: the salary letter.

"Well, actually," I said. "I'm applying for apartments on my own for the first time, and I need a salary letter with my updated compensation. Can I get that from you, or Howard?" I had been stunned at how easily I'd gotten my raise, which, while not hugely impressive, was still more money than I'd thought it would be. It made me a little mad that I hadn't stood up for myself sooner.

"I'll have it for you tomorrow. You're moving to live by yourself, then?"

"I am." I shifted in my chair. "I'm excited, but a little . . . nervous."

Imani smiled and shook her head, in an affectionate kind of disbelief. "Well, I'm just impressed. It's difficult in publishing, especially when you're on your own. I would know. It took me almost ten years."

Imani lived in Park Slope, a Brooklyn enclave full of families and successful writers, far out of my budget. But it made me feel better to know that it hadn't happened for her right away. As silly as it seemed, I always imagined Imani springing forth from Wellesley at age twenty-two in a jewel-toned sheath dress with an editor title and keys to a brownstone.

"Well, I've done some freelance editing work on the side," I admitted, hoping that was okay with the company. "Editing for a professor at Columbia, fixing résumés, that kind of stuff. Boring, mostly. But it helps."

Imani nodded approvingly. "You're a hustler. But that's why I hired you. Takes one to know one."

"I know you started at a literary agency," I said. Feeling emboldened by her compliment, I went on. I glanced at her bare ring finger. "But how did you really do it? I see . . . I see a lot of people who aren't sure they can make it in this industry, not by themselves."

I had said nothing about marriage and nothing about family, but she seemed to intuit my meaning. She leaned toward me just a little, placing an elbow on her desk and resting her chin on her palm. "Well, to be honest, I did it by working three nights a week as a bartender for the first three years of my career. Roommates, ramen noodles, you've heard it." She shrugged. "This push for acquiring diverse books, for diversity in publishing—and the effort is still halfhearted sometimes, but, you know—that just didn't really exist fifteen years ago. Sometimes I wondered why I even wanted it so much. But I did. I read so much as a teenager, and I just knew I wanted to help bring stories into the world."

I knew the broad-strokes outline of Imani's career trajectory, but she had never shared the personal aspects behind it. I stayed still, hoping she would continue.

"My parents would call all the time back then, panicked, especially my mom. The industry was so foreign to her, but mostly it was just that they were more traditional. She asked for a long time if I would move back in at home, if they could introduce me to someone 'suitable.'" I knew Imani's parents were Nigerian, though she had been raised in New Jersey. "My matrimonial status continues to be . . . somewhat of a talking point across the extended family. The world I live in now is very different from the one I grew up in." She raised her eyebrows. "I imagine you might know a little something about that."

A warm feeling bubbled up inside me, and I couldn't describe it exactly except to say that it felt like recognition. Like hearing a familiar voice at a crowded party where you thought you didn't know anyone. I couldn't imagine exactly what the particular struggles of Imani's life had been like, and how different they had been from mine, but I knew that, in a way, she had stood very near to where I was now standing.

"I do." I smiled. "Most of the women I went to high school with are married, actually. Having kids, too."

"Something I always assumed I would have done by now." She had turned her head slightly, and she stared past me out the window. "But life . . . unfolded differently. And to be honest, I am glad it did." She smiled and shook her head. "Anyway, all this is to say that I'm proud of where I am now. Proud to say that I kept at it in this industry, and that I took the unglamorous opportunities, the side hustles, dealt with the disparaging comments. But here's the thing: The 'big cost' isn't the grunt work. It's the thought of all the lives you could have lived instead. All the things that were expected of you, all the paths that might have been harder, or easier, but certainly would have been safer." She paused. "But the less afraid you become of those ghosts, the more the rest of your life comes alive. That's what I've found to be true, anyway."

I stared at her, awed. I was afraid to do anything to disturb the pocket of quiet intimacy that had wrapped itself around us. But then Imani shook her head quickly, as if to shake off the moment of vulnerability, and she arranged her features into their usual expression of steely confidence.

"So that's how you got here."

"The much-abridged version." Then Imani stood up, and I followed suit. She smoothed the front of her emerald dress and checked her watch. "Anyway, well, that's time. I'll have the salary letter on your desk tomorrow."

"Thank you, Imani," I said, for far more than just the salary letter, and as I met her eyes one more time I knew that she knew what I meant.

CHAPTER 26

The sun came up at 6:42 on the day before Michelle's wedding. I knew because I had been up since four, lying motionless on the futon in the living room of the house I grew up in. From the moment I stepped off the plane, I had been rethinking my decision to fly all the way to Alabama for "closure." How could I still stand up in front of Michelle's entire family and give a toast? How would Michelle look at me when I finally saw her? It felt like her anger might really have the power to turn me to stone.

I spent the morning reading for work, avoiding my phone and my mom as much as possible. When it was finally time to get ready for the rehearsal dinner, I took my turn in the bathroom, and then my mom helped me zip up the black dress I had selected for the occasion. She chattered the whole time I got dressed, wondering why I hadn't spent the previous night after my arrival with

Michelle. I told her that I didn't want to intrude on her and Marcia's prewedding time together. A few of the other bridesmaids had stayed at the house with the two of them, but I left that detail out. I wanted not to care that I hadn't been invited, to respond to this the same way I would to not being asked to a game night at Darcy's house—with a shrug and a sense of relief. But I couldn't. This was still Michelle. Even if the past few months had made us seem like strangers to each other, we weren't. I had known her for my entire life. *Forget it,* my mind insisted. *I'm here to say good-bye.*

That evening, I walked into the front door of Jacques' Bistro quietly, barely breathing. I had sent a simple text to Michelle to tell her I was on schedule, and I would be at the restaurant at six P.M. as planned. She liked the message to acknowledge its receipt, but we had still only communicated in tense wedding-related e-mails since the fight. I winced as my heels clicked on the tile floor, announcing my presence. The act of arriving alone instead of with Michelle or with the other bridesmaids felt conspicuous in itself.

Fortunately, Michelle had rejected a traditional rehearsal with an intimate group in favor of a large welcome dinner, inviting not just her bridal party but also everyone coming in from out of town. *Out of town* simply designated "not within thirty minutes of Birmingham" and thus comprised almost half of the wedding's two hundred planned guests.

I scanned the room apprehensively as I approached the two long tables. Everything was bathed in candlelight, with dozens of votives adorning the bistro bar and long candlesticks dripping wax onto white tablecloths. The room hummed with indistinct conversation as guests milled around sipping predinner glasses of champagne, but then I heard Michelle's laugh over the din as clearly as if she were the only person in the room. The *clink*s of glasses, the snippets of conversation, were all white noise, but I knew the jingling laughter belonged to her even though I couldn't see her. It's funny, the human ability to pick out one voice in a crowd. Why was Michelle that person for me? It reminded me of something I'd read, that the cry of a baby sounds wholly distinct to its mother, but that thought flipped my stomach, so I pushed it away and headed into the throng.

I didn't know how to approach Michelle. I thought about simply greeting her quickly and then falling into small talk with whoever was nearby, busying myself until dinner. I thought about walking straight up to her and making a barbed remark, raising an eyebrow and daring her to make a scene at me in front of all her guests. As anger and anxiety coursed through me, strong enough to make the hairs on my arms stand up, I felt a hand on my shoulder.

I spun around so fast I nearly collided with her. I thought about the moment we met, when I crashed into her on the first day of third grade. How far we'd both come since that day.

"Julie," she said, and the cool tone of her voice denoted both an icy remove and, somehow, a greater note of respect than I had predicted.

"Hi," I breathed, looking her up and down. She wore a white lace knee-length dress, sleeveless, which I had found browsing Revolve several months earlier and sent to her, eager to stop looking for outfits for her and get back to work. I hadn't realized she had actually chosen it. I felt a wave of guilt in realizing that I hadn't known. Maybe I hadn't been paying attention as closely as I'd thought. She tucked her hair behind her left ear, revealing one of her large diamond studs.

"New earrings from Jake." She gestured. "My 'something new.' Do you like them?"

My mouth fell open. *That's it?* She didn't have a snide comment planned, or a passive-aggressive remark? I almost sighed in relief, but then I felt a little sick at having assumed the worst. For every time Michelle had been judgmental or dismissive, there was a moment in our history that showed me how much she could be just the opposite. But that didn't matter, I told myself. I was done weighing our respective strengths and faults. I had tired of arguing my own side, even just to myself. I stayed quiet.

She narrowed her eyes, and her expression seemed to contain a hint of genuine curiosity. For once, it seemed like Michelle wasn't sure what I would do next.

"Well. They're beautiful," I said. This wasn't the time, wasn't the place. Maybe there would never be a time or a place for us to have a real conversation ever again, I realized. But I would let that be up to her.

"Julie, I—I am glad you're here," she said, squeezing my elbow, and I didn't know if the words came from the woman who had once been my best friend or the woman who needed to telegraph to the room that everything was okay. Was it love, or was it self-preservation? But of course those two things could run together, braided so no one knew where the threads originated. She leaned closer to me, and I wondered if she might be about to say something more.

Then Jake walked up behind her and wrapped his arm around

her waist, pulling her close to kiss her on the ear. He gave me a lopsided grin. *Did he not know?*

"Hiya, Jule," he said excitedly. "Sorry for the PDA. Just can't wait to marry this girl."

He didn't. This shocked me. I couldn't imagine Michelle not telling everyone she knew what I had done, couldn't imagine her not wanting to spin the story or be the first to break the news of our falling-out. I had seen her do that for all our lives, from the gossip about DeeDee Morrow to spinning the Divinyls tale about my father. But this time she had not.

"I'm so excited for you two," I said, giving a tight-lipped smile. This wasn't entirely truthful, but I realized that it wasn't quite a lie, either. Seeing them look happy, so clearly excited for whatever lay ahead for the two of them, did make something flicker inside me. If I had stereotyped him as a little bit too much of an old-fashioned, oblivious fraternity type, well—he was also a guy who seemed to really love Michelle. I knew she loved him in return.

"We're excited, too. Mind if I steal her for a minute?"

"I'll round up the rest of the bridesmaids," I told them. "It's almost time to sit down for dinner."

I knew then that I could make it through the rest of the night—the endive salad, the toast from Rich, the forced mingling—and probably even through the wedding. What I didn't know was what would be left of us after it was all over.

Michelle and I didn't get a chance to talk alone for the rest of the night. When I told Dana the week before how nervous I felt about the wedding weekend, she had assured me that this would be the case: "Oh, no one *really* gets to talk to the bride at a wedding," she said. "Big weddings are about making everyone feel included, which means that no one *actually* is. She'll be mobbed by her extended family the whole time, and then they'll all turn around and complain that they didn't get enough time with her anyway. Which is why I'm eloping, but that's another story." We had both laughed.

Her counsel had reassured me at the time, but I found myself strangely disappointed as I stepped into an Uber, alone, after dinner. At first I had thought I would want to fight with Michelle, to finally call out all the things that had changed between us and all the ways I'd been hurt. Then I had thought I'd be grateful for a lack of attention, for the ability to say a wordless good-bye and slink away. Now I felt something I hadn't expected: I just missed her. I wanted to be at the Davises' house, which had once been the closest thing I'd ever had to a home. On the eve of her wedding, I wanted us to talk about marriage, about how she felt about it and how I did, opening up to each other in the real and genuine way we'd seemed incapable of ever since she had gotten engaged. I wanted my best friend. I knew I might be missing a person who only existed in the past. It seemed like there was no way to go back and get her, at least not without reverting to a version of myself I couldn't be anymore.

She told me I had lost myself, a voice reminded me.

Maybe something would happen at the wedding, I thought. But more likely not. I would get through the weekend, and it would all be over. That was what I wanted.

I walked into the house to find it completely dark, my mom

already asleep. I stepped out of my dress and left it pooled on the floor, lying down without the energy to even brush my teeth.

The next morning, I arrived at the country club four hours before the wedding for hair and makeup. I also had photos to take with the bridesmaids as we helped Michelle get dressed—not to mention a level of normalcy to try to achieve before the ceremony.

I told myself it was fine to feel hesitant as I entered the main hall. *Hesitant* was the word I was using in my mind in place of the much more accurate "still utterly consumed with dread." As soon as I opened the heavy oak door to the parlor, I found the other bridesmaids and some of Michelle's family sitting on antique couches in front of hair stylists, waiting for Michelle as the photographer clicked away. Marcia stood up and crossed the room to approach me first, her beaded floor-length dress swishing audibly and her heels clicking severely on the wooden floor. But although she gave me a quizzical look—probably because I hadn't stayed with Michelle the night before—she hugged me warmly, draping her tanned arms around me and holding me close for several seconds. I knew then that Michelle still hadn't told her everything. Just like with Jake the night before, I felt myself more than a little bit moved by her discretion, but it also made the hug feel like a lie. I breathed in Marcia's signature Hermès perfume and pretended that the embrace was meant as a sign of forgiveness. That she was saying she loved me anyway.

"You look beautiful," I told her.

Of course, she still wasn't as striking as Michelle, who came out of the dressing room a minute later clad in her strapless mermaid gown, covered in Chantilly lace and adorned with silk buttons all the way down the back. I had seen all the pictures of the dress, of course, but none of them had done it justice.

I bristled when I first saw her without meaning to, the same as I had the night before at the restaurant. Then my stomach churned nervously, and, just as suddenly, a stranger emotion filled me: I had to stifle an impulse to run and give her a hug. I hadn't expected seeing her in her dress to flood me with such feeling, like a dam breaking inside me, but it did. Every scene from our life seemed to flash before me involuntarily, from the day I first saw her play dress-up for a wedding to the day she told me she thought she would marry Jake. I wanted to freeze time.

I wished it could be like when we were young. She stole the cooler Spice Girls lunch box and we argued about whose turn it was to pick a movie at a sleepover, but we always forgot what we were fighting about and made up before the sun went down. Everything had been simple, immaterial. I wanted to be able to forget this fight just as easily, but how could we when it was about so much more?

"So, do I look okay?" she asked the room. Her voice wobbled a little, weakened by nerves. It wasn't the voice she used when she already knew she looked amazing and just wanted everyone else to confirm it. All the bridesmaids started to coo and exclaim, their praises indistinguishable, and so I took a deep breath and stepped closer. That's when I saw it: a flash of green on her right wrist. The jade bracelet I had given her the week we met. I paused for a minute and just stared.

"My something old," she said.

"You look perfect," I told her quietly, getting hold of myself. "Almost as good as when you married Ashton."

She didn't laugh, but I swore I saw a smile playing around the corners of her mouth.

"Let me get the back of your dress," I said, pivoting behind her to fiddle with the silk-covered buttons.

Enough, I reminded myself. *Just get through the day and forget it.*

After a makeup artist caked my face with foundation a shade darker than would have been flattering, the staged group photos followed. They were a blur of posed smiles and aching cheeks. Jen and Sylvie fought to stand so that their "good sides" were showing, and we obliged the photographer with a "silly shot," tongues out and bouquets cocked at odd angles. I stretched my mouth into an approximation of a genuine smile, but it threatened to slip off at any moment, as if held up precariously by a piece of Scotch tape.

"All right, y'all," Darcy called, stepping in as acting maid of honor, a title she had clearly been assigned in my absence. She cradled her pregnant belly. "It's almost four o'clock. Let's get our girl married!"

We walked out onto the lawn, where the guests sat on white wooden folding chairs. One by one, we made our way down the grassy aisle to the altar, followed finally by Michelle on her father's arm. The string quartet played the processional, but I didn't watch them—or Michelle, really. I looked at Jake and studied him as he grinned at her unabashedly. Guilelessly. In a strange way, it both thrilled me and gave me a feeling of relief.

At the altar, I fixed Michelle's train dutifully and then stood stoically still, holding my flowers. "Dearly beloved . . . ," the pastor began, but the words floated over me. I suddenly felt like an imposter being there.

Maybe she really should have just cut me out of the wedding. Why do this?

I started listening again at the vows. "For better, for worse," Michelle said. "In sickness and in health."

Whom did I love that much? I wondered. Could there ever be anyone? And without even meaning to think it, I knew that the answer was Michelle.

"'Til death do us part," she finished. She smiled at Jake, and then, just before he started to echo the vows for his turn, she glanced back at me. Maybe she was looking at the other bridesmaids, or maybe it had been unintentional. But something in my gut said she was looking for me.

I knew I should stay at the reception long enough that leaving wouldn't attract too much notice—in the form of a direct confrontation, anyway. There would be whispers about my lack of participation no matter what, but I no longer cared.

Jen's husband, Mitch, was nice enough to ask me to dance for one song, even though Darcy shot daggers at us with her eyes the whole time. Michelle had clearly briefed her on my diminished role in her life. Mostly, I just sat at the head table and listened while Ellen, mercifully unaware of any tension between Michelle and me, chattered on about her new position as a kindergarten teacher in a neighboring district. I helped myself to a lot of champagne in anticipation of having to give my toast.

When the moment came, I stood up from my chair and took the microphone from Jake's best man, Darren. I looked out at the sea of guests looking up at me expectantly, at the perfect peony floral arrangements at the center of dozens of identical round tables filling the country club ballroom, at the candles twinkling on the windowsills. I had the power to disrupt the entire scene, and while I had never done anything so bold in my life, there was a temptation about it, the same way there is about jumping off a high building. The call of the void. I could do anything, I realized. I could tell the truth about my friendship with Michelle in dramatic movie fashion, or I could put the microphone down and simply walk out, never to see any of these people again. I could do the opposite and give a glowing, fake toast, sucking up to the entire audience of the Davises' family and friends the way I might have once in my youth, pretending that nothing was wrong. Or I could do something else entirely. I could do what the best version of myself, somewhere deep inside me, knew to be right. I could simply say what I felt. What I had known in my heart as I watched Michelle say her vows to someone she truly loved, and who loved her in return. *Loving someone without the hope of changing them is the only way you can love them.*

Even from afar.

I smoothed the sides of my $395 bridesmaid dress and took a deep breath.

"I've known Michelle for almost my entire life. Tonight, she's embarking on a new chapter in her life, and I have to say: I can't

believe the eight-year-old girls we once were are *here*." I looked at
Marcia, dabbing at the corners of her eyes, and I willed myself not
to tear up, either, though for entirely different reasons. For everything about who we had grown up to become that I wasn't putting
into words. "The truth is, I can't think about growing up—I can't
think about my *life*, really, without thinking about Michelle. She
taught me to tie a high ponytail, she basically taught me to drive,
she taught me so many things. From high school cliques"—I resisted a pointed glance at Darcy—"to a certain secret road trip I
won't reveal details about, we had . . . we went through everything
together. And so I couldn't be happier that she's found a partner
who wants to share her life in that way, too. All the ups and downs.
Because that's love." I swallowed. "Real love, and . . . anyone who
knows Michelle knows the kind of boundless love she's capable of."
I glanced around the room again. Ellen nodded and dabbed a tear
out of the corner of her eye. Marcia squeezed Rich's arm. Was this
really the last time I would ever see any of them? If it was, then this
was my good-bye—not just to Michelle, but to everyone. What
could I possibly say? I suddenly felt that I owed them a greater debt
than I had ever realized, even if my life had taken me somewhere
far away.

"And there are so many people in this room who have loved
Michelle so well in return. I've been the recipient of that love, too.
Jake, you're lucky to be joining this family, but I know you know
that." Light laughter echoed from around the room. "I'll wrap this
up. But I want you to know I see the love you two have found with
each other, and I hope it will always shine as brightly for you as it

does tonight. Through everything that's to come. Michelle, Jake, congratulations. Cheers."

I caught Michelle's eye just for an instant as I sat down. She mouthed, "Thank you," at me, and I closed my eyes and nodded, tears welling in my eyes, but I didn't go to her. I turned back to Ellen, plastered the smile back on my face, and waited for it to be time to go home.

When it was finally late enough that the lights dimmed and everyone in the ballroom seemed whiskey-drunk, I grabbed my mom from the back corner table and asked if she was ready to leave.

"Baby, I was ready two hours ago," she told me. "Actually, I was ready to go back when I first found out I wasn't getting a plus-one."

"Thank God." I linked my arm with hers tipsily. "Me, too."

"Leaving already?" Darcy hissed, catching me by the elbow just before we made it to the door. "My goodness, you must be exhausted with everything you did putting the wedding together. And you were so quiet, we barely even noticed you helping at all!"

"Actually," I said in a syrupy tone to match hers. "The only thing I'm tired of is spending time with you. Which, now that this wedding is over, I just realized I never have to do again. Have a great night!"

I walked away quickly, hauling my mom behind me by the elbow as she tried and failed to contain her sputtering laughter. I snuck one glance back at Darcy, and she was still standing there in the hallway with her mouth open.

The country roads lay quiet and dark ahead of us as we started for home. Michelle and I never got lost on our drives back in high school, not even on the darkest, unmarked dirt roads when we drove for miles late at night. Now I had no idea where we were.

"Can't believe I have to be our eyes on the road tonight." My mom sighed, shaking her head. "If only Marcia had just let me bring Jeff, because I had to talk to Daryl and Renée Palmer while I was *sober*, and believe me, that is a tall order for anyone. As I'm guessing you know based on what you said to Darcy Palmer on our way out."

I cocked my head and looked at her. "It's funny. Every once in a while, you sound exactly like me."

She laughed. "No, baby, sometimes you sound exactly like *me*."

"Wait, Jeff's still in the picture?"

"Well now, that's a long story. I hope so. I think that if I just—"

"Mom, wait. I have to tell you something."

She raised an eyebrow at me, just visible in the dark. "Is it about why you wanted to leave the wedding so early? I know something's not right."

"Michelle and I had . . . a fight," I admitted, halfway impressed that she had actually noticed. "But it's not that. I thought you should know that Mark and I broke up. That's why he didn't come with me to the wedding."

I heard her sigh, and then she was silent. The car bumped and lurched over the grooves of the potholed road. She reached an arm awkwardly across the car cup holders to squeeze my hand. "Oh, Julie. That's terrible. Are you okay?"

"I am. I mean, I sort of broke up with him."

Silence again. This was a cardinal sin in her rulebook, breaking up with an acceptable man, at least so far as I could ever tell.

"It just wasn't working, for a lot of reasons I don't want to go into," I continued. "But you seemed so interested in him, so, you know, sorry."

"Julia," she said sternly. My given name, all three syllables strongly pronounced, which she hadn't used since I didn't know when. "You know I want you to find someone to be happy with, and God knows I want you to do better at it than I've done, but if you really don't love Mark, then the hell with him, and that's how I feel. In fact—"

"Seriously?"

"Of course," she said, like it was silly that I was surprised. "It's what you want that matters."

"I'm going to remind you that you said that when you start asking me if I've found a boyfriend again. You used to ask me every time I came home from Cornell."

She swatted at me. "Oh, stop it. Now we can share dating stories! I'm allowed to ask."

"You are. I just want you to understand that I might be happier on my own. For a long time. What would you say to that?"

We hit a stoplight, but she kept staring ahead at the road with a faraway look in her eyes. "I'd say I don't really understand anything about that," she said finally. "But then you don't know what it was like trying to find someone to help take care of us. Of you. You don't know the half of what it was like to try to raise you without your dad—I know you think I made a lot of mistakes—or what it's been like to be here without you, alone, so I'd say fair play to both of us. I'd say I guess I want you to be happy."

I almost challenged this. I almost asked, "With the time you spent looking for someone to take care of us, couldn't *you* have taken care of us?" But I didn't. There were so many pieces of her life I could never know. Not everything made sense to me, but suddenly I understood, in a new way at last, how much different the world she had been raised in was from mine. It could be my choice to live differently. To be the person who comes to save myself.

"I want you to be happy, too," I said. "I do."

We drove on for about thirty seconds in silent contemplation of the understanding that had just passed between us. And then we were back to normal.

"Now, anyway, let me tell you about what Mindy and I did for Eleanor's fiftieth birthday last week," my mom began. "Really, get ready, you've never heard anything like it."

CHAPTER 27

The fun part of arriving back in New York after the wedding was secretly looking up apartment rentals on StreetEasy while I was at work. The less fun part was the need to retrieve the last of the belongings I'd left at Mark's apartment over the last two years.

We kept in touch via curt texts over the month that included the anxious days of the procedure and the even more awkward days around the wedding. I had wanted to keep him up-to-date, at least. It felt strange that he wasn't there. I had spent most of Michelle's engagement thinking that he would be, imagining us dancing at the reception or locking eyes over one of Darcy's more ridiculous comments. We had remained mostly civil, but every time I looked at my phone and saw his name I felt my heart folding in on itself, like something in collapse. It wasn't a feeling of regret, but I couldn't remember a type of sadness that had felt so simply deflated.

I went over to see him after work on a Wednesday, making the long walk from Astor Place down East Sixth Street because I knew I'd have to spring for a cab on the way back. I knew I could move a couple boxes of my clothes and books in a car, but the emotional weight was something else.

Mark opened the door on my first knock, and apart from being unshaven he looked the same. It had been only weeks since I'd seen him, but I had wondered if our breakup would somehow transform him into a stranger. It surprised me how glad I felt to see him. Intimacy rubs strange grooves into you; the roads of connection are smoothed and worn by gestures and intonations repeated over and over—erosion by force of habit. Seeing Mark's sad smile, knowing the particular blend of pain and disappointment and resentment behind it, awoke our very particular connection in me. Long after I had ceased to miss him, I would miss the specific way in which we had known each other. No one else would ever traverse the exact same path to my heart.

"Thanks for making the time to be here," I said in the awkward, slightly formal parlance that was now the language we used to talk to each other.

"Yeah, well. I have most of your stuff in that box there. Look around for anything else."

I walked into the apartment, observing the gleaming countertops, the spotless floors, the lack of plants or flowers or anything living. It was Mark stripped down to who he would be alone. Somehow it made things easier.

I did a quick sweep of the bedroom and grabbed the one photo of the two of us I had ever framed, the one taken by the bartender the night I came home from Dublin. I tucked it away furtively. I wasn't sure either of us deserved to have it, but from a place beyond logic, I wanted it. I didn't want to forget him. Us.

Mark appeared in the doorway behind me then, leaning against the frame. "Do you remember when we took that trip to Vermont for the weekend?" he asked quietly, mournfully. "That first time we went away together?"

A wave of sadness rose in me momentarily and then subsided. The thing about memories: How you remember them and how they actually happened are usually different. And so the way you remember *becomes* the memory itself, taking on a life that the truth of it never could.

"I do," I told him. "That was a great trip." That was only half of the truth, though, from my side. The hiking was great, but Mark had invited along two of his high school friends to camp with us, and after the first night he spent far more time talking to them than to me, comparing consulting with finance and Wharton with Harvard.

Mark wasn't a bad person, not at all. That didn't mean it hadn't been just a little wrong all along.

I moved past him, closing the box in the living room and picking it up with a significant effort. "Before I leave," I said with a hesitant, sad smile, "is it too cliché to say that I'm sorry? And that I know you're going to meet someone way better for you?"

"Yes," he answered. "Too cliché and way too soon." He kept his mouth in a straight line at first, but right before I turned to leave, I saw a slight crinkle around the eyes, the hint of a smirk at the side of his mouth.

He shook his head and sighed. "I hope you find whatever it is you're really looking for, Jules."

"You, too," I said.

It wasn't happiness, exactly, but I could only hope that it would make a start.

The next day at work, Alan popped into my cubicle to hear about how the final move out had gone. He held up two Diet Cokes from the break-room vending machine in a celebratory way, like they were bottles of champagne.

"We're celebrating, bitch," he announced as he sat down next to me at my desk.

"That . . . my ex-boyfriend didn't burn all of my stuff after we broke up and I had an abortion?"

"Dark. No, that you're getting a new apartment. And, more importantly than all *that,* that I'm working on editing something I love. *Gossip Girl* meets murder mystery—think *Elite* in novel form. Finally something that's up my alley."

"But your work on the *Fresh Blood* series was—what did Howard say, 'Truly inspired'?"

Alan groaned. "Am I never to live that down? Anyway, shut up and dish with me. And drink some soda. We are also celebrating that I finally figured out how to tip the vending machine and get these babies for free."

I watched Alan as he took a sip. He had ditched the hipster horn-rimmed glasses, switching to a more subdued pair of black frames, acquired on his most recent Warby Parker trip. Underneath,

I saw the lines crinkle at the corners of his eyes as he flashed me a smile; he looked older, but in a good way. It was hard to believe we had been working side by side for almost four years.

"You know, maybe you really should quit and work in tech and start an app instead of talking about it," I teased him. "I hear they even give you *meals* for free. No vending-machine tipping necessary."

"Maybe I'll start looking for something," he said, a far-off look in his eyes that was more serious than any expression I'd ever seen him make at work. "But we'll see. I do love publishing, too. I'd better; nobody goes into it for the money."

"Ha. Yeah, I love it, too, but I probably should've stuck with the business degree. Or the—"

"We get it, you had a lot of majors," he teased. "Now, tell me about the new apartment."

It wasn't definite yet, but I had finally decided that morning to put in an application on an apartment in Kensington, deep in South Brooklyn. The place wasn't much. To fit my budget, I was looking at walk-up studios with barely serviceable "kitchenettes." But I had never had a place of my own, and every apartment that didn't come with more Craigslist roommates looked like a palace, I told Alan.

And then he asked me about Michelle.

"The wedding is over," he said. "You survived."

"I did. Barely, at points, but yes."

"So, does that mean that's it? Are you guys really just never going to see each other again?"

I shot him a pointed look. "Would *you* be friends with her after what happened?"

Alan sipped his Coke. "I'm not saying what she said wasn't horrible," he said in a measured tone. "You have every right to tell her to fuck off from now until eternity. Believe me, I've had some pretty unforgiveable stuff said to me under the pretext of 'values.'" He shrugged. "But when you first started working here, all I ever heard was Michelle this, Michelle that. All those inside jokes and stories I never got. I guess I'm just trying to say, I wish I had a friend that had known me my whole life."

"I know what you mean," I told him, but it was so much more complicated than just the day of the fight on the phone. Michelle and I had existed in relation to each other in a certain way for almost our entire lives. If she was the sun, then I was the planet, my whole path determined by her gravity. As two separate entities, could we have anything in common ever again?

And still, in spite of all that, I knew exactly what Alan was saying; I had been thinking about it, too. I thought about it when I lay awake next to Dana at night after the procedure, at home with a friend who was so much like me—someone I wanted in my life forever—and yet a part of me still missed Michelle. The history, the way she had felt more like family than most of my real family. As the heat of my anger subtly died down, I caught myself trying to figure out if maybe we could be worth fixing. As different as we were.

"Look, I know you and Michelle are different. Like, uh, *really* different. And she was awful about what you went through. But I'm willing to bet that you said some not-great things, too. And it's just whether or not you can accept the flaws in her. I would know," he added, alluding to his decision to try to mend his relationship with his grandparents after what had happened between them a year and a half ago: They had uninvited him from family Christmas when he made his relationship with Marcus public. It had broken my heart, so I could only imagine how he felt.

"Yeah, I . . . said some things, too," I admitted. Then I looked him in the eyes and smiled. "To love someone without the hope of changing them is the only way you can love them."

"What?"

"Nothing," I said. Just that I finally knew what I wanted to write.

Two weeks later, I submitted my first essay to the *Times* Modern Love section from the very café where I had broken down and told Alan I was pregnant. It made for a good kind of poetic symmetry, I decided. Also, the café made great lattes.

I sent the e-mail off to the editor—essay text in the body, no attachments—and waited to feel like I had accomplished something big. I checked Facebook and scrolled through my news feed as I finished off my coffee. Darcy had entered her third trimester, posting that pregnancy was "exhausting but so totally worth it!" A college acquaintance announced that she had been accepted to Harvard Business School.

I imagined hypothetical status updates that I could post. "*So excited to tell you all that I finished an essay about my former best friend who I don't know if I even want to talk to anymore!*" Or "I'm turning twenty-six in a month, and is that still your midtwenties or am I now in my late twenties? Please help." Or "I'm signing a lease on an apartment that even my mom—who once lived in a van following the Grateful Dead for six months—thinks is too small."

I clicked out of the page. As usual, social media silence was probably the best strategy.

I walked out onto the street without any real destination in mind. It was a quiet Sunday, but in the good way. Two years before, I probably would've been heading to a boozy brunch with Dana and Ritchie. We still went to brunch, but more like once every few months than once a week. Honestly, it was kind of a relief. Sunday evenings were a little bit less depressing without a mimosa hangover coming on.

I thought about Alan and Marcus, who were probably walking their dog down the picturesque Brooklyn Heights waterfront. I thought about Ritchie, spending the weekend with her parents at their New Jersey shore house. And I thought about Michelle, recently returned from her honeymoon with Jake in Turks and Caicos. After seeing the Instagram pictures, which both made me angry and hurt my heart a little bit too much, I had hidden her from my feed.

Instead of trying to text any of them, though, I changed direction and started walking a little bit faster, heading toward the Strand Book Store. The early spring sun shone warmly on my face, and it felt like a luxury that I didn't have anywhere in the world that I had to be. As I walked, I pulled out my phone and opened my e-mail to read what I had written one more time.

When Your Greatest Romance Is a Friendship

I was the one who said "I love you" first.
Here's how it happened: We had gone to get soft-serve

cones—twists, like always—at the Tastee-Freez in our home-
town on a sweltering Alabama afternoon, in the kind of hu-
midity that feels like you're wearing it like a scarf. We took the
first freezing-cold bites of our cones at the same time. I watched
Michelle close her eyes as she swallowed. When she opened
them again, she shot me her trademark mischievous grin.

"If you promise not to tell my mama, I'll go buy us two more
of these right now," she said, handing me her cone. "You eat
these two. We are going to sit here and eat ice cream until
we're sick."

"Wow, I love you," I blurted, and we both giggled.

"I love you, too," she said, and I knew it was more than just
a joke over ice cream. She meant it. We meant it.

We were eight years old, but I can remember that moment
better than I remember some entire romantic relationships.
This may begin to give you some idea of how I felt about my
best friend.

In some ways, my friendship with Michelle has all the hall-
marks of the nonplatonic love story our society is much fonder
of telling. We had a meet-cute (I tripped and bumped right
into her on my first day at a new school). I remember that first
"I love you." We even had the moment where she met my
parents—and Michelle is the only person still in my life who
has actually met both of them.

The next part of the essay recounted the day Michelle drove me
to see my father. I scrolled past those lines, feeling choked up in
spite of myself. My heart beat a little bit harder as I thought about

how much it had meant to me that day when Michelle said, "I'm staying." She was the only person who had ever said that to me.

I scrolled down to the final paragraphs.

But my story with Michelle has one more thing in common with a romantic relationship: a breakup. It happened the way breakups always do: over the one big, "unforgivable" thing that is really the cumulative breaking point of a thousand other tiny moments.

Why? Well, suffice it to say that I am a chronic overthinker, quick to doubt myself, and yet still somehow too convinced that I'm always right. Michelle's flaws I will not detail here, except to say that she once forced me to buy a $395 bridesmaid dress. We are just two people bumbling through a mess of life. We're okay without each other, I think.

Or maybe we aren't. I still do not know if I made the right decision about us. It feels like it sometimes, and other times it does not.

People are fond of saying that you never forget your first love. Maybe Michelle, in a way, was mine. But when I think about that day she drove with me to Tennessee, when I think about the way she looked at me when she promised me, "I'm staying," I know something else, too: I know that you cannot change who taught you how to love, a subtle but critical distinction. And I can see her sitting next to me in my mind, with all her sugar-dipped snark and her Alabama drawl, the same way I can see my face when I look in the mirror.

CHAPTER 28

Moving in New York is an experience that can cause even the most devout residents to wonder what the hell they're doing living in the city.

Once my lease application had been approved, I promptly spent all my savings on the assorted deposits and broker fees for the new apartment. That meant hiring movers for the big day was a no-go. I ordered a new bed from Sleepy's that wouldn't be delivered until the afternoon and didn't own any of the other furniture from my old apartment, so all I had were garment bags of clothes and boxes. I still couldn't fit all of it in an Uber, so I rented one of those $19.95-per-hour U-Hauls and said a silent prayer that I still remembered how to drive.

"Don't kill us," Dana warned as she climbed up into the

passenger seat next to me. "I'll be so pissed if I die in a U-Haul in Brooklyn."

"Thanks for coming to help. And . . . I'll try not to?"

"Encouraging." She slid on her sunglasses. "Okay, let's get this over with. I have to work tonight. Again."

"Hold on." I held up a hand. "Just got an e-mail."

"Oh good, yeah, check your e-mail while we hold up all the traffic on Flushing Avenue."

The message came from modernlove@nytimes.com. Just two lines: "Thank you for sending your writing to Modern Love. Although I don't find your essay right for our needs, I'm grateful for the opportunity to consider it."

"What?" Dana asked.

"My essay got rejected." I stared straight ahead, convincing myself I did not feel anything about this. It was always a long shot. "But, to be expected."

I felt awkward for a minute, because I didn't want to be the subject of consolations. But this was Dana, so of course she knew exactly what to say.

"This is amazing!" She grabbed my hand.

"It is?"

"You can't be a *real* writer until you've been rejected by the *Times*. It's a huge deal! Lots of writers have—you're in great company. I bet even, like, Faulkner got rejected."

"Right, William Faulkner, noted writer of *New York Times* personal essays."

"Whatever, you get it. You're on your way. You'll get the next one."

For whatever reason, I actually believed her more than I doubted myself. The rejection still stung, but I smiled, turned the key in the ignition, and pulled away from the curb.

We made it to the new place in one piece. Dana took off to go squeeze in some Saturday hours at work as soon as we'd dumped everything I owned on the parquet-wood floor of my new eleven-by-fifteen-foot fourth-floor box on Cortelyou Road. "But I'm super excited for you, I swear." She kissed me on the cheek. "We'll have dinner or something soon."

"Good luck at work." I hugged her good-bye. "Just wish me luck returning the U-Haul. I'll need it."

As soon as she left, I sat down on the floor, because there was nowhere else to sit, and I waited for the deliverymen to drop off my bed. Killing time, I started scrolling through my recent messages. I stopped on Alan's name, and I texted him that I had moved in, and I'd have him and Marcus over for drinks soon. I sent Ritchie a picture of the bare-bones living space of the apartment, and I knew she'd write back soon with a list of design suggestions, and probably links to her favorite "midcentury modern" inspiration on Pinterest. I thought I might even send my mom a message, too, but as I scrolled down in search of the last text from my mom, I got stuck on another contact name instead: "Michelle—your BFF."

I wanted to call her. The desire wasn't from my conscious mind but rather from somewhere deep within me, as much as I told myself that the urge didn't make sense at all. Maybe I wanted to call the Michelle who now existed for me only in the past: the one who had read my only *actually* published essay, a piece about our failed road trip to my father's house that I had submitted to a niche literary magazine at Cornell. She had pored over every sentence of the first draft, and she even sent flowers to my dorm the day the issue came out. I tried to reconcile that Michelle with the one who told me I had lost myself.

I couldn't condone hating another woman for her choices; I wanted, more than anything, to be resolute in that. But I thought then of the little things, all the smaller irritations. For every time I complained about an offhand comment or a #wifeymaterial Instagram post from one of Michelle's friends, had they rolled their eyes at all of us in New York, with our stories of artfully staged cold-brew coffee and our refusal to eat lunch away from our desks? Somewhere—everywhere, actually—someone thinks you're doing it wrong.

I knew then what I would do: I would send the essay to her. I wanted her to know. She might not even respond, but I knew somewhere deep inside me that I had only written it because I hoped, somehow, that she would see it. I drafted an e-mail before I could change my mind, reading only "I submitted this essay to the *Times,* but it didn't get published. Decided I still wanted you to read it. Jules."

Then my phone buzzed with a notification. It was a comment, from Dana, on a photo I had posted on Instagram of the two of us grinning in the cab of my U-Haul: She had written "us vs everybody" with the heart emoji. It was stupid, but I caught myself smiling, and I thought, *To hell with all of it,* and just let myself feel glad about it, the tiniest thing, because sometimes in life it is very nice to just be happy and, for once, not interrogate yourself as to the reasons why.

CHAPTER 29

On Saturday, Ritchie and I had lunch in my new neighborhood. Mostly still a residential area with lots of families, it wasn't chock-full of painfully hip spots like East Williamsburg—not yet, at least—but that made me like it even more. Each place we walked by looked homey and lived-in, like they were just waiting to become my regular spots. I hoped it wouldn't change too quickly, even as I knew that I, somewhat guiltily, belonged to the wave of gentrification sweeping over Brooklyn.

"You know, I grew up coming here, near Eighth Avenue in Sunset Park. My great-aunt and -uncle lived in the neighborhood when they moved to the US," Ritchie told me as we walked down Cortelyou. "My parents wanted me to have the 'suburban life' in Jersey, or whatever, but I always loved it in Sunset Park."

"Let's go there next weekend," I told her as we stopped in front of her subway stop. "Unless you're sick of coming all the way out here already."

"Never." She hugged me tight, and we laughed when her glasses got caught in my hair, forcing us to stand cheek to cheek as we untangled them. "See? I'm literally trying to get stuck to you."

We eventually said good-bye, and I turned to walk the three blocks home. I clutched my keys in my right hand the whole way, enjoying a tangible reminder of the fact that this place was mine. My own apartment. My home.

I climbed the four flights of lopsided stairs, excited to go inside and spend the rest of the day reading, undisturbed. But when I rounded the turn of the final staircase, there was someone standing there blocking my door.

"Um . . . excuse me?" I said, but then I saw the short pastel skirt, the blond hair cascading down her back, and by the time I registered that it was *her,* she had spun around, her eyes locking with mine.

"Miche—"

"Julie," she blurted at the same time.

"Hi?" I asked, unable to ask even the obvious "What are you doing here?" question.

"I read your essay." Her voice sounded breathless. I glanced around, taking in her monogrammed LV suitcase, trying to figure out what this all meant. "I couldn't believe that you wrote about me. Us."

"And?"

"Well, I can't believe that you did. After everything we said."

"So, what, you just . . . flew up here?" I asked, incredulous, even though of course that made perfect sense for Michelle, her particular brand of impulsiveness mixed with generosity.

"I didn't think; I just did it."

"Well, wow," I said. I didn't want to offer anything else until I knew why she was here, even though the part of me that had known her for so long wanted to pull her in for a hug, let this fight go the way so many of our fights had in the past. I couldn't remember a time when Michelle had been the first to apologize about anything. She stayed quiet for a minute. I crossed my arms and leaned against the stair railing, waiting her out.

She reached into her Michael Kors tote and started fishing around for something. "Anyway, I have something to show you, and it couldn't wait." She pulled out her phone, thrusting it into my hands. "Look."

I stared at her screen. It was an e-mail of some sort, sent from someone with an address at Bustle.com. "What is this?"

"You told me the essay didn't get published in the *Times* . . . but I submitted it to *Bustle* as a personal essay. And they're going to publish it. Read the e-mail."

I dropped my arms to my sides, stunned. "Literally, how did you—how?"

"Okay, I had a little help from Alan." She grinned. "I remembered you talking about him, and I thought he might have some connections and be able to help on the publishing side."

"You remembered?"

"Anyway, I messaged him on Facebook after I read the essay. His friend—I don't know, this Meghan woman—is an editor at *Bustle*, and he made an introduction for me. It's good, Julie. It's really good. Oh, and he also gave me your new address. I'm not a stalker, I swear."

"Holy shit." I clapped a hand over my mouth. "Sorry, this is— I can't believe this. Thank you. But . . . I mean, why?"

"I'm obviously trying to say that I'm sorry, damn it. I'm trying to say I'm sorry for how I acted." She sighed, staring down at the floor. "A few times over these months, I guess. And especially at the bachelorette party. Maybe I went a little crazy."

Without me even making a conscious decision to forgive her, I felt the walls inside me crumble and turn to dust. I lunged forward and hugged her. "Hi," I said into her shoulder, laughing, and she said, "Hi," too, and then I pulled away from her, trying to figure out what we were supposed to do next.

"Look, there were . . . plenty of times I wasn't totally honest with you, and I think I should've been," I said. "I'm sorry for that, too."

"But I have to say this, Julie," she said, a note of stress in her voice. "This doesn't change how I feel about what you decided to do. I don't agree, and I'd probably tell you the same thing again." A pause. "But, I don't know, it's *you*. I shouldn't have said it like I did, like it wasn't . . . your decision to make. I should have loved you through it anyway."

"Thank you," I said. I thought of Marcia again then: To love someone without the hope of changing them is the only way you can love them. But this time, one small thing really had changed. Michelle and I were both finally ready to admit being wrong. This didn't mean I was any more at ease with her views, or she with mine. Parts of us would always live in disharmony, and we would have to think about what that meant. Still, her apology, our understanding—it had to mean something. Forgiveness is how things begin.

"And what I said about you thinking you were too good for us," she added. "I don't really mean that."

I laughed. "I actually think maybe you did." Before she could protest, I added, "But it's okay. Maybe I did think that for a while, trying to put Langham behind me. I don't know why that was so important to me for so long, but I swear, I'm over it. And I'm sorry I made you feel that way. Just admit that you always thought you were better than me in high school and we're square."

"I did not—"

"Admit it."

"Fine." She chuckled. "I was a bit of a brat back then. Sometimes."

"Back then?"

"Excuse me, are we makin' up or not?"

"Sorry, I'm sorry. Yes. I just can't believe you finally admitted it."

"And I never will again," she said huffily, but I could tell she wasn't angry anymore. "But I'll tell you a little secret: You'd be amazed what marriage teaches you when it comes to compromise."

"So you're a marriage expert already?"

"So sassy. But then, that's the Julie I always loved."

I took a deep breath. "This feels very seventh-grade us to ask, then, but does this mean we're, I don't know . . . us again?"

Michelle pulled back, looking me in the eyes. "I decided I can't imagine a life that doesn't have you in it."

"There are always going to be things we don't agree on, though," I warned her. "I see that now. I mean, we should talk about it, but that's not going to be easy. Maybe it means our friendship is going to be different."

"Maybe," she said, her voice lower. "I still want to know you, though."

"I do, too." And I did, even though I knew it might take some work. Even if it would never again be the easy, everyday kind of friendship that I had with Dana or Ritchie or Alan. It made me think of how people say you can never divorce your family: Even if you don't speak to them, your mother is always your mother and your sister is always your sister. This felt the same to me. Like family, and no family has ever been perfect. If anyone knew that, I did.

"So, like, do you want to come inside?" I laughed, realizing that we were still standing awkwardly in the hallway.

"I did fly three hours from Birmingham, so, uh, yes."

I fiddled with the lock. "Just a warning—I have, like, no furniture yet. Definitely not Marcia approved. But I do have a bottle of wine in the fridge."

"Well then, perfect."

I heard her draw in a sharp breath as we walked into the room, the one and only room of the apartment, which contained the kitchen and the bed and the Ikea dresser I had yet to try to assemble. I realized that it was entirely possible Michelle had never seen a studio apartment.

"It's . . . very cozy," she said.

I elbowed her. "You don't have to lie."

She laughed. "But your own place! That's something. I just

realized I'll never live alone again." I couldn't tell if she sounded relieved or wistful.

I opened the fridge to take out its sole contents, a bottle of sauvignon blanc and a tiny wedge of Brie cheese. "Not too early for a glass, right?"

"Definitely not," she said, sitting down on my bed. There was a moment of awkward silence, like maybe neither of us had thought much past the moment of reconciliation, but then she was back to being, well, Michelle.

"So, does that mean I can finally tell you about the honeymoon?" she asked.

"Yes. I'm even ready to scroll through a hundred photos of the beach from slightly different angles."

"Okay, but really, Turks was so gorgeous I couldn't help it."

I laughed gamely. "Kidding. I can't wait to see."

"I do want to hear what's going on in your life, too. I haven't exactly been great about that lately, have I?"

"Well, there's a lot to catch you up on." I smiled, popping the cork out of the bottle. I realized how excited I was to finally tell her about my job, my apartment search, my conversations with Imani. About everything. "But you can start."

"No, no," Michelle protested. "You start."

CHAPTER 30

I wanted the visit to fix everything, but I still felt a little uneasy as I watched Michelle pull away in her Uber the next morning. Of course, it would take a while, I told myself. We would need more than one night to recover from the last year. What it felt like, maybe, was stepping onto a boat and pushing back from the dock. We were setting off on a new journey, one I felt sure I wanted to take, but I just didn't have my sea legs yet.

I didn't know what my life would look like in a year, and so I couldn't know what Michelle's would, either. Would she have a baby? Would her blog become popular like she hoped it might, letting her launch her own boutique? Would I be there for the ribbon cutting, or would I miss it because I was finally traveling through Europe, like I had always wanted to? Would these next months, years, take hold of our tenuous strings of peace and knit us back together? Or would we grow apart completely after all—just in a kinder fashion this time? I suspected that in moments of quiet I might be angry with her again, and that my anger might take me by surprise—in the same way it shocked me that I still felt some kind of love toward her at her wedding when I was supposed to be furious. My feelings would ebb and flow, and I couldn't predict them. I had no divine wisdom, but at least for one moment I could maybe convince myself not to pretend I did.

Not long after that, I watched, from far away, as Alabama furthered an attempt to pass legislation that would criminalize abortion for all women in all contexts.

"The ACLU will sue," Dana kept promising me. "It's going to be okay. Women who don't want abortions don't have to get them; women who do, will."

I tried to believe her. I tried to think about women like Darcy, holding their babies in their arms, and then women like me, free to choose to hold the full breadth of other possibilities instead. I thought about all the women who didn't have the choices—the finances, the freedom—the two of us did. I was lucky, actually. Luckier than I had ever realized. I wondered if Michelle knew how lucky she was, what power and privilege she truly held, and how she would wield it.

Then I waited for something to happen next, something definitive, but it seemed like nothing did.

The unadulterated excitement of having my own place only lasted until the end of the second weekend. Specifically, it lasted until I tried to cook a full meal for myself.

As I cleaned up from dinner for one, I realized something: The tiny sink in my studio apartment "kitchen"—an unfair description, since *kitchen* seemed to imply a separate room—was too small to wash my frying pan in. Like, I couldn't fit the whole pan in my stupid single-person sink. It was official: This was *still* not the happily ever after that I had been looking forward to for my whole life. Real life springs up like a weed among even the best of fantasies.

Then my phone buzzed with a text. It was Dana, and she had just closed on her purchase of a one-bedroom apartment on the Upper West Side. I congratulated her happily because I knew how much she had wanted it, but it was still a little bit hard. *Don't compare your life to anyone else's,* I reminded myself. *It never comes out in your favor.* I promised to take her out for a glass of champagne that weekend.

Somehow, though, life is often at its best and worst at the same time. I sprawled out on my bed that night, boxes still piled haphazardly around me, and I started smiling for no reason. My chest felt so warm and full it almost hummed. Finally, I recognized the feeling—which was similar to happiness, but somehow both quieter and more unexpected—as bliss. I had heard that word thousands of times but never innately understood it until that moment. I stopped moving in fear of scaring it off. I stayed there for what might have been an hour, and I didn't even have the urge to look at my phone or watch TV—just the desire to stay still and laugh, tingling with the knowledge that hundreds of terrible and wonderful things hadn't even happened to me yet.

I dedicated all of the next day to finishing the unpacking process. I sat on the bare wood floor in a small patch of sunshine in the morning, wearing nothing but a bra and underwear, contentment settling over me slowly. I was examining a collection of old T-shirts I had forgotten about in a box my mom had sent (I had *really* been obsessed with Sum 41 in seventh grade) when the phone rang.

"What would actually be worse: Dying young or living forever?" Michelle asked by way of hello.

"Living forever, obviously."

"No way," she countered. "Dying. I'd love to live forever."

"You so *would* think that."

"Same to you," she mocked, and her voice sounded heavy with affection.

We settled into the familiar routine of conversation, though the intermittent pauses showed me that things were still a bit formal between us. I talked about the apartment decorating process as animatedly as I could, and she told me about her and Jake's struggles with reupholstering a sofa, but I found my mind miles—and years—away. With her question, I remembered a night I had forgotten for almost a decade.

When we were eighteen, right before we left for college, Michelle and I used to drive out to this hill that overlooked the interstate.

The street hit a dead end there, and there weren't any houses, so kids used to use it to hook up or drink or do whatever they couldn't do at home. Sometimes Michelle and I would go out there with friends and take a water bottle full of vodka, but this one time we went there just to talk. We sat on the hood of her car, the darkness closing in around us, and all we could see were occasional headlights flashing by on the highway below and then disappearing. Our shoulders were touching, but if I had turned my head to look at her it would've been too dark to see her face.

I was upset about something that I can't recall. Maybe a guy; more likely my mom. We were playing the random question game to try to take my mind off it.

"What are you the most afraid of?" I asked her a few rounds in. It had been lighthearted until that moment.

She was quiet, breathing in and out slowly. Then: "Maybe losing things. Well, not things. You, my parents, my brother." She paused. "And having people judge me, I guess. I don't know; I always want to seem like I know what I'm doing, like I have it together. I know you probably think that's silly."

She was being honest with me. I could feel it. She was defenseless, a rarity for her.

"No. No, I don't."

The wind blew in her hair, and it flew up against my cheek. I couldn't see it, but I knew it looked perfect. Wind gave her a mysterious, ethereal quality where it gave me only pink cheeks and cowlicks.

Then she surprised me.

"What's the *worst* thing you've ever done?" she asked. "Not like cheating on a spelling test or telling a white lie. The absolute worst."

The question terrified me. I flipped through my mental back-logs of shame: I could finally tell her about the anger I sometimes felt toward my mom, so visceral at moments that it kept me up at night—and the time it had led me to blame her out loud for my dad leaving and never looking back. Or I could tell her about the brace-lets I had shoplifted from a mall kiosk. I could even tell her about the times I had been jealous of her and the way that jealousy some-times inspired me to change myself in order to fit in like she did, twisting and bending my real identity in ways I was starting to real-ize I hated.

I didn't yet know I would live to see a day when these things felt small. Right then, they bubbled and twisted up inside me, roiling so strongly that I thought I would be sick with it. How could I tell anyone about any of it?

Then all of a sudden, that fell away. I can't explain what ac-counted for the change, but when I took a deep breath and laced my fingers with hers, it was like shedding my skin. I had never trusted anyone before, not really. Maybe it was finally time.

I squeezed her hand, and in her familiar grip I felt something new growing. I could start to own those parts of myself, I realized. The parts I was afraid of. Looking back, that might have been the true birth of my conviction, which would grow and grow and ulti-mately take me far away from the place we sat that night. But at the time, it just felt like something good; holding her hand, I knew I was safe. Safe, and yet wholly alive, and close to the beating heart of everything real.

"Seriously," she whispered. "You can tell me."

And then I did.

ACKNOWLEDGMENTS

To become an author is to finally understand why acknowledgments list the publishing team first. I'm beyond thankful for my brilliant editor, Cassidy Sachs, who believed in Jules's story—and in me—all along. Cassidy, you made this book sharper and better in every possible way. Special thanks to Rebecca Odell and Katie Taylor, as well as to the entire team at Dutton and Penguin Random House at large. Working with you is an author's dream, and I couldn't be in better hands.

A huge thank-you to Allison Hunter, my fabulous agent and all-around life inspiration, without whom quite literally none of this would ever have happened. Allison, your passion and energy know no bounds. You are the keeper of my sanity (and the keeper of the good rosé), and I would be lost without you. Thanks to everyone at Janklow & Nesbit.

It is truly no exaggeration to say that this novel wouldn't exist without Arvin Ahmadi, who supported me when I started writing it, forced me to continue, and stopped me from trashing the draft no fewer than three times. Arvin, you are my absolute champion, my first reader, and my 14/12 best friend. Thank you—I owe you more than I can ever express (and also probably like twenty dollars' worth of ninety-nine-cent pizza slices).

The same can be said of Ashley Balcerzak, a first reader of just about anything I've ever written and an invaluable support throughout the six (!) years I've worked on some version of this book. Thank you. This is a story about a best friendship, and I couldn't have written it without your years of advice, our inside jokes, daily e-mails, and more. Thanks, too, to Alberto Pettinato, who is the exact husband you'd want your best friend to have (and a true friend of mine in his own right).

I have the greatest friends in the world. I wish I had the space to write each of you a paragraph but, in any case, massive thanks to: Meredith McGowan, Anna Steward, Holly Baron, Emma Stein, Bruno Mendes, Stanley Kay, Rebecca Nelson, Danny Parisi, Kelsey Sutton, Alex Hampl, Sallie Lotz, Isabelle Fisher, Ben Fisher, Joey Yagoda, Nicole Bleuel, Alex White, Julie Jiganti, Phil Ross, Dylan Glendenning, Christine Lobo, and Jennifer Hung—and even more of you than I have the space to name. It truly takes a village, and my gratitude knows no bounds. Special thanks as well to Jess Reimers (another very early reader and supporter), Olivia Banks, Brandt Rosentreter, and Amanda Grimm, who are *my* friends from home, and for life. I wouldn't be me without you.

Thank you to my writer family, including but not limited to Patrice Caldwell, Adam Silvera, Cristina Arreola, Laura Sebastian, Sarah Gerton, Jeremy West, and Jeffrey West. You've taught me so much about the writing world, and just as much about life.

Thank you to my colleagues at Yext (past and present), and especially to my content dream team. You supported me while I wrote, sold, and edited this book, and I'm so thrilled that many of you who started as "just colleagues" have turned into lifelong friends.

David Kaplan and Catherine Weaver deserve their own section. Thank you for believing in my writing and my voice even before I did. Thank you for the many literary discussions accompanied by even more oysters. David, I'd call you the greatest colleague I've ever worked with, but you know that doesn't cover it—rather, you are (both!) simply the greatest friends, and I could not count myself luckier to know you.

A million thanks to my family, and especially to my mom, who inspired and nurtured my love for reading and writing in the first place. All of my parents (Todd, Deb, and Bert), to whom this book is dedicated, deserve endless appreciation for their steadfast love and unwavering support of my writing from the moment I claimed to be "working on the great American novel" at age six. In every sense, I would not be here without them.

Thank you to my grandma, Marge, who has been such a force in my life since the day I was born. (She also let me read her a twenty-five-page short story *over the phone* when I was nine, and then she told me that I should be an author. Thanks, Grams!)

Thank you to the entire Chamberlain family—especially Hanna Wetters, a trusted early reader—and to all of the Sterioffs. All of you have shown me such love, support, and enthusiasm, and I couldn't be more grateful. Thanks, too, to my *new* families, Otis and Greene. It's a delight to have you in my life (and to have a sister at last—hi, Caroline!).

And, finally, to James Otis: What can I even say? If I had a muse, it would be you. Thank you doesn't even begin to cover it. Everything I know about love is because of you.